# THE SEASON OF
# REBELS AND ROSES

## VIRGINIA SÁNCHEZ-KORROL

PIÑATA BOOKS
ARTE PÚBLICO PRESS
HOUSTON, TEXAS

*The Season of Rebels and Roses* is made possible through a grant from the City of Houston through the Houston Arts Alliance. We are grateful for their support.

*Piñata Books are full of surprises!*

Piñata Books
An imprint of
Arte Público Press
University of Houston
4902 Gulf Fwy, Bldg 19, Rm 100
Houston, Texas 77204-2004

Cover design by Victoria Castillo

Names: Sánchez Korrol, Virginia, author.
Title: The season of rebels and roses / by Virgina Sanchez-Korrol.
Description: Houston, TX : Piñata Books, an imprint of Arte Público Press, [2018] | Summary: In 1887, Inocencia, eighteen, horrifies her parents when they learn she wants to marry and work with Sotero Figueroa, a mulatto journalist and independence movement activist in Puerto Rico.
Identifiers: LCCN 2017061348 (print) | LCCN 2018008027 (ebook) | ISBN 9781518505027 (epub) | ISBN 9781518505034 (kindle) | ISBN 9781518505041 (pdf) | ISBN 9781558858657 (alk. paper)
Subjects: LCSH: Puerto Rico—History—To 1898--Juvenile fiction. | Figueroa, Sotero—Juvenile fiction. | CYAC: Puerto Rico—History—To 1898—Fiction. | Figueroa, Sotero—Fiction. | Political activists—Fiction. | Journalists—Fiction. | Clubs—Fiction. | Racially mixed people—Fiction. | Social classes—Fiction.
Classification: LCC PZ7.S1949 (ebook) | LCC PZ7.S1949 Se 2018 (print) | DDC [Fic]—dc23
LC record available at https://lccn.loc.gov/2017061348

♾ The paper used in this publication meets the requirements of the American National Standard for Information Sciences—Permanence of Paper for Printed Library Materials, ANSI Z39.48-1984.

Printed in the United States of America
Cushing-Malloy, Inc., Ann Arbor, MI
May 2018–June 2018
5 4 3 2 1

For **Aura**
who loves Inocencia
and
**Ramón**
who has her courage.

This is a work of fiction based on historical facts, referred to in the Timeline of Events, 1815–1899 in this book. Historical figures, characters, dialogues, places and incidents are either the product of the author's imagination or are used fictitiously.

# ACKNOWLEDGEMENTS

My interpretation of Inocencia Martínez Figueroa's life in New York City and her friendship with the esteemed poet, Lola Rodriguéz de Tió, has many godparents. Without their support this book could not have been written. I am forever in their debt.

Aura Garfunkel, Asunción Lavrin, Olga Wagenheim, Juan González, Lauren Korrol and Anelisa Garfunkel generously offered critical insights. Their expertise helped me flesh out the characters within their historical moments. Alberto Hernández shared his research from Cuba, including the issues of the newspaper, *Patria*, New York City directories and the vast resources of the Library and Archives of the Center for Puerto Rican Studies at Hunter College. Edna Acosta-Belen and the team of researchers at the Center produced the Puerto Rican Heritage Poster Series and the Study Guides. These materials formed the framework on which I crafted my story.

My colleagues at Brooklyn College, Karel Rose, Antonio Nadal and Carlos A. Cruz broadened my understanding of literary styles, as did Elena Dodd's comments of a first draft. The Piermont writers, Carole Weaver-Linser, Lisa Coughlin, Beryl Myers, AnnE Miller, and Edith Knoblick, led by novelist, Jeanine Cummins, challenged my narrative until all their questions were answered.

I owe a debt of gratitude to Gabriela Baeza Ventura, Marina Tristán and the team at Arte Público Press for their continuous support in producing the finished product. And to Nicolás Kanellos, scholar and meticulous editor, I hope this book stands as testimony to your stalwart dedication to recover and tell our stories.

My personal support team are the loves of my life. Chuck, Lauren and Pam suffered endless conversations about this book and other projects, but still continued to support me to the finish. Without them, nothing in my life is possible.

# CONTENTS

# THE SEASON OF
# REBELS AND ROSES

**PART I**

# 1

# PONCE, 1873

Not one of them had fallen to the ground—not even one. The child gawked at the branches of the trees, her skinny legs folded beneath her on the hot prickly ground. *Quenepas*, the tree's olive-size fruit growing in bunches like grapes, stubbornly clung to their branches in the same place she'd seen them that morning. Not one round fruit was on the ground.

"*Mira*, Inocencia, it's time to harvest the *quenepas*," Papá had said to her the day before. "They're more abundant this year than last." Instantly, the seven-year-old's mouth had watered. She could hardly wait to taste the sweet slick pulp she knew lay hidden inside the leathery shell.

"Hmmmm," she now waited, growing tired of wishing the fruit would fall. She studied the tree's solid trunk, off-shoots and jagged bark mentally separating sturdy branches from shaky limbs. *What if . . .* In a flash, her eyes lit up. She kicked off her shoes and rolled off her long stockings, crumpling them into balls. Taking a sudden leap, Inocencia rushed towards the tree. She gripped the craggy footholds with bare toes, thrusting her arms up to catch a low branch, then swung her leg right over it. Her fingertips could barely brush the fruit. She grasped the branch tightly between her

3

thighs and shimmied up the limb, extending her arms way up as high as she could reach.

Suddenly, she landed flat on the ground, a scrunching sound coming from her left ankle.

"Ouch, ouch, ouch," she cried, cradling the ankle with both hands.

Hearing the girl's yelps, Don Pedro, the stablekeeper, rushed to her side. *"Ay, ay, nenita,"* he murmured, showing the soft heart he'd always had for the plain, unruly girl. As she was helped to her feet, Inocencia spied a bunch of *quenepas* lying on the ground beside her. *I did that! I brought them down,* she told herself between sobs. That day, Inocencia learned that if you wanted something badly enough, you had to go for it with all your might.

She was eighteen when she attended her first public lecture. The topic was the 1868 Lares revolt for independence from Spain, and one fiery speaker, in particular, caught her complete attention. His words boomed with a passion for justice that inspired the impressionable girl. Her pulse began to race so fast that she found it difficult to remain still, not to jump to her feet and voice her approval.

The charismatic speaker was the mulatto journalist, Sotero Figueroa. His rousing calls for freedom from colonial repression, for an independent Puerto Rico, enthralled the audience. Inocencia's mind soared, taking intellectual leaps she'd never known before. She was excited to join in the movement, to bring about this liberation he spoke of. All of those things she wanted with an urgency she didn't quite understand. And she wanted this man, too, in ways she hadn't expected.

For a second she thought of her family. Like others in Ponce's white society, they believed that even a hint of

African blood polluted family trees. *But I'll get around that.* That's when she realized she'd crossed a forbidden social boundary. *I'm destined for an exciting, challenging future,* she promised herself, jutting her square chin forward in mock defiance.

Shortly thereafter, Inocencia joined Doña Lola's women's group.

"An educated mother knows enough to educate her children," Lola would say, going against the grain of popular belief that women would use book learning to write love letters to their lovers instead of improving their minds.

Like Inocencia, the others in the group were daughters of small landowners or bureaucrats. Each one yearned to expand her own horizon. They spoke of women's rights, read essays—some written by Doña Lola, herself—and devised strategies for social change. They signed petitions and joined protests. That's how Inocencia began to believe in women's rights and freeing her people and crossing society's color line.

# 2
## MAYAGÜEZ, 1887

Doña Lola held the spectacles up to her eyes. She pushed aside the lace panels on the veranda's French doors with her index finger and peeked out from her safe spot in the parlor. *What is it about this one,* she wondered unable to pry her eyes away from the figure slouching against the lamp post, not more than a stone's throw from her front door. Swiftly, she pivoted to the other side of her hiding place for a better view, then returned to her original position, all the while observing the man's every move.

*I've seen that sullen face before.*

She thought of 1877, the last time she'd been forced into exile. *That was . . . ten years ago! Just after my poetry collection was published—probably too many poems about liberty and love of country to please the Spaniards. My daughter Patria was only ten, not much older than Laura is now. Ay, how she cried, inconsolable. I thought she'd never stop. She so missed her primos and abuelos!*

Doña Lola peeked out again. He hadn't changed his position. Watching and waiting, he stood in the morning sun. *Just like the last time. Is he the one? If he dares to enter my home asking for passports, I'll scream bloody murder.*

Despite the slovenly condition of his uniform, she could tell he was a soldier even before she'd put her glasses on.

6

Narrowing curious eyes into brown slits, Lola adjusted the spectacles, perching them on the tip of her snub nose. She thought they offered a sharper view of the morning's intruder who'd already wormed his way into her day.

*Oh, my goodness! Anyone would think that creature is ordinary and take him for just another low-ranking soldier in that drab, broad-brimmed hat and pinstriped uniform. That fancy touch of red around the collar—hmmpf! Probably thinks he's somebody. Well, no. He isn't special.*

*I'll bet he's hanging about for the fun of it—a Civil Guard, nothing to do, looking for law-breakers, protecting citizens? Uh-uh. Not this one. He isn't protecting anybody.*

*He's here to intimidate me.*

She'd seen him before, of that she was sure, as certain as she was that she'd sensed the man's dead-eyed stare boring holes into the back of her head. That was a feeling she couldn't shake.

Suddenly, Lola dropped hold of the curtain's edge! He'd shifted position. Rapidly jerking his head, he looked up in her direction, as if she had called out his name. Like a pistol shot finding its mark, the man's low-browed, dark-eyed squint pierced the door she hid behind. In a flash, Lola whirled aside, keeping her short, plump figure out of sight.

*I'll call for Bonocio! Wait. How silly of me! That soldier can't possibly see inside the house from where he's standing, half-bathed in sunlight.*

Doña Lola stuck her nose out the side of the curtain. Just then, he lifted his hand to his face as if he were going to shield his eyes for a better view. Instead, he began to caress the fat, greasy walrus mustache he wore.

"Ugh," Lola uttered, "plotting his next move." She imagined a colony of lice slowly crawling out of his facial hair, into his nose and ears. Still, it was the act of stroking facial hair that caused the memories to come to her in waves.

"Of course! Now I know who he is. He was *there!*"

*He was there in the general's office the day I was brought in for questioning. The general tried to get me to confess, to admit my literary salons were for plotting a revolution. That man stood guard by the door. How could I forget him?*

*Is there evidence? Something I forgot to destroy?* She took a deep, shaky breath and tiptoed cautiously away from the veranda and into the parlor. Walls of familiar books, paintings, the piano, armoires and displays surrounded her, giving her confidence. She glanced at family keepsakes in a glass-enclosed display case: pictures of a honeymoon in Europe, her children, aging parents, sisters and brothers. Quickly, she raised her cold fingers to her lips and realized she never wanted to leave her home again.

Catching a glimpse of herself in the gilded wall mirror above the secretaire, Lola saw a thinned-lipped, chalky white face as she eased herself into the desk chair. She let her *lorgnette* hang loosely from her neck on a black ribbon and ran her fingers through her nut-brown hair, surprised to find perspiration.

*I'm acting like an old fool. This whole thing has unnerved me, a mature woman used to confrontation, to speaking my mind. Is this what happens when one grows old? I'm suddenly . . . afraid?*

*Don't say or write anything incriminating.* She sat still, her jaw suddenly clenched. Feeling the tension steal across her shoulders she felt chilled and began to tremble. *Just what I needed,* she thought. *Cold sweat in spite of the warmth of the room.*

Lola opened the bottom desk drawer and began to shuffle aside the stack of letters she'd yet to answer. She reached deep into the back for her diary. Quickly, she turned to December, looking to see if she had written anything that could incriminate her. She flipped through the entries past January, past Bonocio's trips, past Patria's lessons, past the women's group meeting, past schedules and meetings and personal incidents, until she came to March. And there it was.

"A most disagreeable day!" she'd written.

"The new governor, Romualdo Palacios, had summoned me to the city hall. It was a bright day, nothing more than a hint of humidity in the air. Foolishly, I dressed in black, felt overheated. Then had to wait for the carriage wheel to be fixed."

*I was so distraught having to wait inside. Annoyed that my parasol wouldn't open. I remember catching my finger, trying to open it. There was a drop of blood on my glove and I couldn't wipe it off. Didn't have time to change.*

"The general's office was pleasant, cool. One of the guards escorted me to a seat in front of the general's desk. He was late, but I'm sure he is a very busy man," Doña Lola had written.

*He was late! Never even apologized. Treated me in a curt, disrespectful manner.*

"As he is concerned with all the citizens under his authority, the general wanted to know about my literary salons. I informed him that we discuss literature, music and the latest philosophies, and if he would like to attend, I was issuing an open invitation to him."

*The nerve of that scoundrel! He actually accused me of conspiracy.* "Your little gatherings, señora, where you and your friends plot against the government, is conspiracy, Madame! Reason enough to charge you and your rebel friends with treason."

"We spoke of some cultural meetings where people actually gathered to plot against Spain. I told him I knew nothing about such plots."

*Seething with anger, I sprang from my chair. The parasol crashed to the marble floor, making such a bang. Everyone must have heard it outside the room. But the two guards did not react, just stood rigidly by the door. When I looked at the general, I saw the reflection of sunlight on his bald head. I remember thinking how strange, to actually have a spot of sunlight on your skin shining like a mirror, like he was some sort of saint.*

"The general offered me sound words of advice. He asked me to be on the lookout for anything suspicious. He mentioned that his people would be watching over us for our welfare."

*That's when I knew that he knew. It was me who wrote to the ministry about his abuses, about how he rounds up liberals like common criminals, about his heavy-handed rule. And he hasn't even been in office that long that he should dare to question my loyalty.*

"You should know, general, that I never even think of Spain! Not even when I raise a toast to Spain's famous writers!" (My exact words!) "You, Madame, are to think only of Spain as fatherland!" (His exact words!)

"As the general found no reason to detain me, he allowed me to take my leave."

*The whole experience was harrowing! I was shaking with anger.*

"As I prepared to leave, I bent down to pick up my parasol. A gentleman might have done that for me out of courtesy, but there were none in the room."

*I remember the two soldiers. They were right there in the room standing guard on each side of the door. One looked straight ahead, but the other, ay, that fetid-smelling little toad, never took his eyes off me. He witnessed my humiliation.*

※※ ※※ ※※

"Yes. He's the one!" She mumbled under her breath as she closed the diary. "The spy sent to watch me, sent to gather evidence to exile me and my family again." Lola heaved a deep sigh, recalling his sneer, visible under that detestable fat mustache.

Lola lowered her head. *I hated living in exile before . . . not just because it drove us from our homeland, or because it disrupted our efforts to bring down the colonial government. It was simply, I don't know . . . the feeling of constant waiting, the day to day endurance of a disconnected life, away from family and community! Wrenched from our native soil, from everyone and everything we loved, it was lonely, it seemed unending . . . unbearable.* Those lost years, she knew she could never recover them.

Lifting the edge of the lace curtain between thumb and index finger one more time, Doña Lola squinted toward the street.

"Ahhh!" she gasped, her cold hand shooting up to cover her mouth. The soldier was not there. *He must be in the house! I've got to warn Bonocio.*

"*Madre mía,*" she hissed. In exasperation, Lola darted furiously about the parlor. "This oppression *will* come to an end. Right now . . . and I'm not so old I'll give up without a fight."

She ran to the kitchen and grabbed the bread knife from the cutting board, then made for the broom hanging on a hook on the wall. Lifting the hem of her skirt with one fist, Doña Lola dashed down the stairs to her husband's bookstore, both knife and broom clutched tightly in the other.

# 3

# MAYAGÜEZ, 1887

From his bookstore, Bonocio heard Lola's determined footsteps running down the wooden staircase. He held his breath. *That nosy soldier! She must have seen him from the balcony!* Instantly, he pushed himself away from the desk, covering the editorial he was writing with a yellow folder to keep it from prying eyes. He got up and rushed to intercept her.

"Bonocio!" Lola called, checking the two large work tables near the printing press towards the back. No one was there. She shifted her vision towards the front of the bookstore, thinking perhaps Bonocio was outside. He wasn't there either.

The store's clerk, Ulises Sanabria, turned towards the sound of her brisk, clickity-clack heels on the tiled floor. Lola ran past the bookcases, carelessly catching her broom in one of the shelves. She tripped and bruised her shoulder against a cabinet.

"Doña Lola! Is there anything . . . "

"No, no, Ulises. Don't bother yourself," she answered, frowning at her clumsiness. She almost stabbed herself.

About to call his name again, Doña Lola saw Bonocio's graying head peer out from his back office. He was dressed in his usual white suit with a flouncy cravat.

"I know! I know, Lola," Bonocio tried to calm her down, holding up both hands. "He was right here ... nosing around among the newspapers for what seemed like an eternity. But everything is all right now."

More than a head taller than his worried wife, Bonocio reached out to embrace her.

"The soldier! You're talking about the soldier, aren't you?" she said, taking a step back.

"Yes, Lola. I'm talking about the soldier. And I'm keeping my voice down because . . . "

"Because he is still here?" she whispered, her brow lifted in astonishment. "Oh, no, Bonocio. Where is he?!"

"Lola, listen! *Shhh!* . . . There are customers in the store."

Clasping Lola's broom, he pried his wife's fingers from its pole and stood it upright against the wall. Then, he carefully took the bread knife and placed it on the desk. He took both her hands between his own, all the while, looking into her eyes.

"Now, what were you going to do with that knife and broom?"

"Oh," Lola grinned. "I'd forgotten. I planned to smack that guard's rear end with it, then sweep him out of our house! The knife? I think that was probably just in case . . . "

"He is *not* here." Bonocio smiled, letting go of her hands. He pulled out the desk chair for her and lightly tapped her shoulder for her to sit down.

"I don't know why I became so unsettled. It isn't at all like me to get so upset. But, Bonocio, he was the one . . . the one who was there. Remember? I told you about the day I was called in for questioning? He was there."

"I do, Lola, I do remember. My dear, this sort of thing happens to me all the time. What can you expect from a government that wants to stifle our words, even our thoughts . . . "

"This *doesn't* happen to me all the time." Lola's eyes flashed in anger. "I'm always in command of situations, but this man just gets under my skin. He's pure evil."

"Well, every time a stranger enters the store, I wonder, Is he friend or foe? Who sent him, and why is he here? And it's usually nothing at all." Bonocio leaned his tall frame against the edge of the desk and tried to comfort his wife. "Look Lola, I've known you since we were children. You've always had more courage in your little finger than anyone I know."

"Always had . . . until now."

"Nonsense. You'll continue to write outrageous essays, give your memorable piano recitals and meet your women's group. No one can silence you, my love."

"We. *We*, Bonocio, will never be silenced." She arched her eyebrows to confirm their unity, then took hold of his hand. "We are joined together, now and forever.

"It's the girls, Bonocio. It's Patria and little Laura I fear for. If we're forced to live in exile again . . . "

"Lola, Lola, Lola . . . Those are bridges yet to be crossed. For now, we keep close contacts with our allies. Let the women in your group know your concerns. I hope they realize our independence movement is not a game."

"Okay, my love." Lola smiled wanly. Rising from the desk chair, she lingered for a moment at her husband's side, catching comfort from the scent of his tobacco, holding on to the musky warmth of his body before moving towards the stairs.

"And, Lola," Bonocio pronounced grim-faced. "It might be temporary, but we should make plans to leave Mayagüez as soon as we can . . . and move to the house in San Juan."

# 4

## PONCE, 1887

"*¡Ay, gracias a la Virgen!*" Inocencia exclaimed, catching sight of Sotero Figueroa among a crowd of men and women entering the La Perla Theater to attend an assembly of liberals. She tossed her head back and wetted her lips in anticipation of his noticing her.

"Inocencia! Be patient. You can't just run up to him!" warned Kirina. Sensing an afternoon full of indiscretion, young Doly gaped shamelessly at her two older sisters.

Inocencia nevertheless thrust ahead into the crowd, well ahead of her sisters. "Hurry up, girls," she called. "There are hundreds and hundreds of people here today. I don't want to have to explain to Mamá that I lost both of you at the assembly."

So intent was Inocencia on keeping Sotero within sight that when he stopped to speak to his friends, she almost crashed into him.

"Oh!" gasped Inocencia, her cheeks flushing. "I'm so sorry, Don Sotero. Please, pardon me."

Composing herself, Inocencia said, "Uh . . . well, I'm here because maybe . . . maybe I could help the conference organizers in some way?"

"Buenos días, Señorita Inocencia. May I introduce Doña Lola and Don Bonocio Tió?"

An amused expression flashed on Doña Lola's face as she pretended not to have noticed the undercurrents she caught between Sotero and Inocencia. "Inocencia! My dear," she bellowed, "this is going to be one wonderful convention. Just look at all the women here today. I'm sure we'll find our entire discussion group among them."

Then turning to Sotero, she confided, "Inocencia and I have already met. She belongs to a group of young women interested in educational reforms." Doña Lola glanced warmly at Inocencia and said, "Young women are the future of this movement, Don Sotero. Don't forget that. And this gentleman, my dear, is my husband, Don Bonocio. I don't think you had the pleasure to meet him at our last group session."

"I'm charmed, young lady," said Don Bonocio, lightly kissing her hand.

A slight grin dimpled the corners of Sotero's lips. He observed Inocencia with renewed interest. *I was right about this girl. There is something about her.*

By the time the sisters caught up with Inocencia, she was standing beside Sotero distributing leaflets from the steps of the majestically columned La Perla. Her radiant, infectious smile dazzled the entering delegates.

Finding a niche against the nape of her neck, her straw hat had slipped from her head revealing her dark chestnut curls.

🐾 🐾 🐾

Once inside the theater, Inocencia herded her sisters into a side aisle, four rows away from the stage. "*Shush*," she gestured toward the girls, trying to catch the snippets of conversations swirling around her.

"Now, remember, behave like properly educated young ladies," she whispered loudly. "Or the next time something exciting happens, I won't bring you with me."

"Oh, Miss Bossy," Kirina chided her sister, "You know Mamá wouldn't have let you come here today without us to chaperone you."

"*Ay*, Kirina! Don't be ridiculous."

The liberal leader, Ramón Baldorioty de Castro, took command of the stage to thunderous applause. "Victory!" he shouted, raising both arms up high before the wildly cheering audience. Inocencia joined in the ovation. Like Baldorioty, she supported a plan that gave Puerto Ricans a voice in Spain's government. While she applauded, she looked around, searching for Sotero among the clusters of delegates taking their seats in the front rows.

When she spotted him, her eyes lit up like fireflies. "Look, girls! There he is," she whispered excitedly.

"Why do you care so much about that *black* man, Inocencia? He looks obnoxious to me," Doly spat out.

"*Shush!* Kirina never acted as rudely as you when she was your age! Besides, I'm *not* interested in that man. I'm interested in *politics*! There's a big difference. And he is not obnoxious!"

Inocencia glanced at Kirina, suddenly appreciating her maturity. Then she took stock. "Oh no, the party is *split*, Kirina. Some of those delegates are pushing for local reforms only. Imagine that—they want us to stay a colony and not have a voice in Spain where laws are made!" Inocencia scrunched up her face in disgust.

A studious girl, Kirina had no idea of why her sister was complaining. She narrowed inquisitive eyes trying to make sense of the two factions. "So then, Puerto Rico would separate from Spain, right?"

Inocencia caught the edge of concern spilling from her sister's tone. "No! Oh, no, no, no. Listen to Don Sotero and

Don Ramón. You really should take notes if you want to educate yourself. Their plan still needs Spain's approval. It's really the best, I'd say. It would keep Puerto Rico associated with Spain, the way Canada is to England."

She nudged Kirina and giggled. "Certainly Papá and others who come from Spain wouldn't want separation.

"Oh look, Kirina!" Inocencia said, shifting her attention to a handsome, young black man. "That's the doctor I mentioned to you, Dr. Celso Barbosa."

As the Martínez girls gawked, Dr. Barbosa looked in their direction. He smiled and tipped his hat to them, catching the sisters by surprise. The girls quickly covered their faces with the fancy hand fans they carried. But Inocencia didn't bat an eye and shamelessly stared in his direction, remembering the gossip she'd heard about him: his radical American education caused conservative delegates to distrust him. Inocencia found him interesting.

"He isn't at all pleased with the party platform. Actually, he came out for total independence," Inocencia murmured. "They say Dr. Barbosa belongs to a secret liberation society, but that's probably a rumor."

"I know all about that Dr. Barbosa," piped Doly, distractedly pushing a sweaty, dark curl away from her face. "Isn't he fighting with the governor? The governor . . . or somebody else, an official . . . because they won't let him become a real doctor?"

"Yes, I've heard that too," Inocencia confirmed. " . . . Because he studied medicine in the United States, and not in a European university.

"And here I thought you were only interested in your hair and pretty dresses," Inocencia said, smiling at her little sister. She still hoped to interest her in issues other than how she looked.

❧❧  ❧❧  ❧❧

During the heady days of the assembly, there wasn't a moment when Inocencia did not burst with pride! *It's a wonderful thing to be a liberal,* she reasoned on more than one occasion. Goosebumps covered the back of her neck when she mentioned Doña Lola or Don Sotero's name in casual conversation. Those names alone were enough to make her feel special.

She wanted so much to be counted among the young liberals whose voices were beginning to be heard. She was so proud to be playing a role in liberal efforts that she'd daydream for hours about Sotero, her flawless, fiery revolutionary. She also dreamed of convincing her parents that she was old enough to make her way in that world of ideas and politics, just like Doña Lola had.

Some two weeks after the days of endless debate in framing the party's mission, Inocencia's euphoria began to wither. Aghast, she learned that the liberals had chosen the most benign option of self-rule. When Sotero unleashed a series of scathing articles aimed at changing hearts and opinions among party members, she brooded that the liberals had lost more than they won. And with the gnawing realization that there really was *nothing* she could do to help the situation, she mourned the demise of her dreams. She could not even hand out leaflets.

Inocencia took to sitting on the veranda for days on end, an unopened book in her lap. She watched the townspeople go about their daily business, street peddlers hawking their wares, groups of chattering girls, their chaperones not far behind. She pined for a glimpse of Sotero, praying this would be the day he chose to ride his horse along her street. Afraid he'd found someone more interesting, more beautiful, more eager to engage in stolen conversations, she began to despair.

All she wanted was to see the tall, handsome mulatto with the laughing eyes.

"*I* know what you are doing, Inocencia."

Inocencia pursed her pale lips tightly, and frowned. She stiffened in her rocker, wondering how she could bash those words into oblivion.

"*You're* waiting for that *black* man you were with at the meeting," Doly's voice grated on her nerves.

Icily, she turned and glared at her younger sister until the impish girl curled her finger around the hem of her smock and began to shift nervously from one foot to the other.

"Doly, please, go away. Can't you see I'm reading a book? Besides, it is almost time for Papá to come home for the midday meal. Don't you think you should get ready?"

On the second Monday in June, less than two months after the Ponce meeting, Inocencia met Sotero in the Plaza de las Delicias. Intermittent rain showers had abated, leaving shimmering puddles in the plaza. Sotero sat on one corner of a stone bench in front of the Cathedral of Our Lady of Guadalupe. Out of respect for her reputation, he conspicuously maintained a discrete distance from Inocencia, who sat on the opposite corner of the bench.

They pretended they were solitary strangers enjoying a pleasant afternoon in the plaza, but the nervous looks on their worn faces would have alerted anyone that this was not the case. Now and then, Sotero played at reading his newspaper. Inocencia held a prayer book in her hands, but rather than feigning meditation, she watched some barefoot little boys competing to see who could jump the farthest into and out of the puddles.

"I'm leaving!"

Stunned, Inocencia turned to face Sotero. Her disbeliev-
ing heart thumped wildly in her slender chest.

"You're going to do what?"

"Inocencia, I *must* go. It's useless to try to convince me
otherwise. My newspaper has been targeted. Do you understand that we are fighting for our political future? And frankly,
the more incompetence I see among the cowards in our own
party, the more I'm inclined towards total independence."

Inocencia was shocked at his rushed words. *He's discussing treason against the government of Spain right out loud
in a public place!* Frightened that he may have been over-
heard, she rose from the bench and glared at him, her eyes
wide as saucers slicing right through him. And then, he
shocked her even further when he continued speaking in
slow, measured tones.

"You must listen to me very carefully. I will not see you
again . . . at least not for a long, long while."

Inocencia inhaled a ragged breath of air, bringing the tips
of her fingers up to her lips.

"Listen to me," Sotero continued. "This governor, Palacio,
is moving rapidly to silence our party's leaders. His pretext is
that we're supposedly boycotting Spanish businesses. . . .
Don't move," he warned as a passerby sauntered by.

Once the disinterested man was gone, he said, "They've
been jailing our people . . . —many of them. My contacts tell
me Baldorioty and I are on the list. I've got to leave . . . hide
before they find me. And no, I don't want you to know where
I'll be . . . until it is safe for me to return to Ponce."

With that, Sotero stood up and calmly placed his straw
hat on his head. He smoothed out the lapels of his white
jacket, placed the folded copy of his newspaper under his
arm and retraced his steps out of the plaza.

As if time stood still, Inocencia watched him. She stared
at the languid rhythm of his muscled back until he became

lost in the afternoon congestion of market-bound wagons and pedestrians. Until she could see him no longer, she didn't move her head, her glazed eyes or her slumped shoulders. Her face, like the pale statues on niches in the cathedral behind her, revealed deep sorrow.

# 5

## PONCE, 1887

*"Shhh . . .* listen!" whispered Inocencia, catching Lucita's eye. She pressed her finger against her pursed lips and gestured for her not to move or make a sound. The girl quickly squeezed her eyes shut! She held her sweat-soaked body taut, like a bow about to shoot an arrow, wishing she could disappear into the overgrown bushes.

Holding the hem of her white muslin skirt so it would not snare on the thick brush along the side of the dirt path, Inocencia eased her slender body into a protective stance not far from where Lucita stood, and again whispered, *"Shhh!"*

Inocencia stood very still. The scent of damp earth and fresh foliage in the mountain clearing filled her nostrils. Alert to every movement, every aspect of her very being, she consciously tried to slow the pounding in her chest. Fine golden hairs began to rise on her bronzed bare arms, where she had pushed up her cotton sleeves. Her palms were suddenly moist with perspiration as she tightened her grip on the basket she carried.

"Be very still, Lucita. Listen. . . . "

Inocencia strained to catch distant sounds in the surrounding countryside. *Hoof beats. Galloping horses! But where?* Instant panic drove cold fear into her heart. She held her breath. Sounds easily bounced off the mountain passes. *Is my imagination playing tricks on me?*

Then, silence. In the tree above their heads they heard the unmistakable buzzing of a nest of wasps. Inocencia gestured to Lucita that they should move along. Perspired and exhausted from their unpleasant ordeal, the two young women continued their half mile trek in the searing heat, the silence broken only by the long moo of a stray milk cow and the occasional crow of a rooster.

Finally, they were not more than sixty feet from their destination: almost hidden by overgrown brush, there was a small palm-thatched hut on stilts. Suddenly, she heard a grunt and someone or something shuffling. A tethered bay horse near the shack caught their scent. She noticed a group of red hens pecking at scraps under the house. There was nothing unusual, nothing to attract undue attention. She and Lucita, on the other hand, stood out like scarecrows, clearly visible to any passerby or search party.

Inocencia placed the basket on the ground and looked around for places where armed guards could hide. The sweltering sun burned her exposed arms, so she pulled down the sleeves of her dress. Once she decided it was safe, she and Lucita continued toward the hut.

The shack's front door was a makeshift plank latched unevenly to the frame. As they approached, it began to open slowly. And in a second, there stood the handsome Sotero Figueroa. At first, he had worried his hiding place had been discovered, but then was relieved to see his unexpected visitors. Sotero quickly ushered the women into the house. Before closing the door behind them, he surveyed the surrounding terrain, keen brown eyes searching for any sign that they might have been followed.

"What in heaven's name are you doing here?" He laughed, turning to face Inocencia. "How did you find me?

Don't you know they've been searching for me high and low since Baldorioty and the others were thrown into prison?"

Inocencia pushed a dangling, curl behind her ear. Suddenly, she found herself at a loss for words. Lips sealed, she simply handed the food basket to Lucita, not sure of what to do next, and folded her hands in front of her. *Do I at least make a pleasing appearance in spite of all I've gone through to get here?* She wondered. Gradually, her vision adjusted to the dim interior. She smiled shyly, looking down at the floor and, for the first time, became aware of the crudeness of her surroundings.

Sotero was not at all prepared for the company of ladies. At first, he stood tall and confident in the center of the room. Then he realized he was clad in the garb of a *campesino*. The peasant's loose fitting, coarse, cotton top and calf length pants were held in place by a cord tied around his waist. He felt uncomfortable being seen like that by Inocencia.

"How *did* you find me?" he asked, somewhat embarrassed.

"I knew where you were because for months I've begged your servant to tell me," she confessed. "But no one else knows we're here . . . I promise.

"The horse and cart are with Don Pedro. He brought us here. . . . Oh, the cart's well hidden . . . behind a shed a little bit away from the main road. You'll be proud of us. We walked the rest of the way." She grinned, her words trailing off as she tried to avoid direct eye contact with him.

"It wasn't easy to find this place," she said acting lighthearted. "But, you understand, we can't stay very long." She found herself rushing her words. "I can already see afternoon shadows. We can't get caught in the mountains . . . on the roads, I mean . . . after dark."

She breathed in deeply, as if the conversation had been too much to bear. "Soon, the women will start kindling cooking fires." She wished she could hide her flushed face under the shade of her hat, but she had forgotten to take it from the wagon.

Sotero gazed at the lovely woman standing before him and said, " It was too dangerous for you to come here . . . even if you were not followed. Although . . . I am so happy to see you. . . . "

Inocencia looked up into his eyes, losing herself in a sea of deep mahogany. "Ohhh," she whispered and lowered her gaze.

"Doña Lola," she murmured just above a whisper. "She is the only soul in the entire world who knows where I am. She promised to say I spent today helping her prepare for her poetry salon."

"I understand, Señorita Inocencia." He lifted an arm as if to gather her in an embrace, but changed his mind, heeding an unexpected sense of restraint. He found himself sympathizing with her predicament. Surprised to learn he cared deeply about her, Sotero was determined to protect her from scandal were it to surface from the day's encounter.

⚜ ⚜ ⚜

For her part, Lucita felt like an intruder. She saw the glances and soft exchanges between Inocencia and Sotero. *I would have kissed him already,* she thought. In spite of the harrowing time Inocencia had just put her through, Lucita decided she would keep her mistress' secret. *Even if her parents torture me, I'll never tell where my mistress was today.*

Lucita scrambled to unload the contents of the basket while looking around at the possibilities in the rude hut. A desk angled to catch the light from the one window in the room was covered with books and pamphlets, sheets of written paper, an inkwell and pens of varying sizes. On one corner of the desk a kerosene lamp sat precariously, barely lighting anything through a crystal font covered with soot. Certainly, the desk offered no solution.

The stocky girl stepped over piles of folders on the floor. Two tiny green iguanas scooted out of her way. Sotero's clothes hung from pegs on a windowless wall. A crude shelf held some soap, a razor and five candles. The only other furniture in the room was a board on which lumpy bedding was covered with a soiled sheet. The bed was out of the question.

Lucita was not discouraged. She twisted her long black braid away from her face, wiped the top of a stool she found under the desk with her bare hand and laid a white cloth napkin across it. Using the picnic basket as a makeshift surface, she deposited tin containers of yellow rice, red beans and pieces of fried cod fish. She had pilfered the food from the Martínez kitchen that morning. Another tin she had carried in her apron pocket for safe keeping gave off the intoxicating aroma of ground coffee beans. *Now where am I supposed to find water for brewing coffee* she huffed, and decided to leave that problem to Don Sotero.

With the food delivered and set out, Inocencia and Lucita moved towards the door. They were ready for the return trip.

"A moment, please. Before you leave, Señorita Inocencia," Sotero said. "Might you be so kind as to take some letters I've written for Dr. Betances and Doña Lola?" As he handed her the letters, Sotero briefly held her hand between his own.

A surprised, "Oh," escaped from deep within Inocencia's throat. She gazed at her pale hand trapped between his dark, protective palms.

Mistaking her emotion as a plea for caution, Sotero added, "Please forgive me, señorita. I understand perfectly if you don't wish to take the letters. It was insensitive of me to ask you."

But Inocencia already held the letters in her hand and had every intention of complying with his request. At that moment, she could not have been in any more danger than she already was, for she had fallen insanely in love with this dark, exotic man of political controversies and lofty ideals.

"Of course, Don Sotero, I am honored to help the cause," she whispered and turned to leave.

Seeing Inocencia and Lucita retreat, Sotero called after them, "Please do not risk coming here again. I fear for your safety more than mine."

"¡Señorita Inocencia, *darse prisa! ¡Se acercan soldados!*"

Suddenly, Don Pedro was shouting at the top of his lungs. He raced the frenzied horse and cart towards the shack. "Come quickly!" He yelled, "There's a cavalry regiment on its way!"

Inocencia and Sotero both jumped to commotion at the same time and sprang into action! Sotero lunged for the pistol that hung sheathed in its leather holder on a peg near the door.

"Run!" he shouted at Inocencia and Lucita, forcefully pushing the women towards the door. "Hurry to Don Pedro . . . before . . . "

Don Pedro lengthened the reins so that his frightened animal could gallop faster. When he was close enough to Sotero's shack for the women to scurry on board, he called out again!

"¡Señorita! The cavalry is on its way!"

Once the women secured a foothold in the cart and Don Pedro gave his horse rein, Sotero felt the women were safe and bolted towards his tethered mare and mounted. Within seconds, he had galloped into the dense brush, the sure-footed bay quickly finding her way to the dirt road and into the mountains. Sotero raced towards a hidden cave he had prepared. Inocencia had climbed onto the front plank next to Don Pedro. To her great surprise, he thrust the reins into her hands and scrambled towards the back, where he and Lucita uncovered the loaded rifle he kept for protection.

"Look towards the road in front, señorita!" he pleaded. "And trust Huracán! He knows the way. We'll handle things in the back until we're on the main road and no one will think to stop us."

*Was Don Pedro intending to fire at the guards!* Inocencia suddenly felt sick, as if she were trapped in some horrid nightmare! Gripping the horse's reins tightly with both hands, her fingers felt about to break. *Sotero is safe, Sotero is safe. . . . Please, God, let Sotero be safe.* She repeated the phrase over and over in her mind until the moment Don Pedro assured her that they were no longer in danger.

It was then that she began to unravel and lose her composure. Her rigid fingers were bloody where the leather had cut into her skin and for the first time she thought about her predicament.

*¡Dios mío! How could I have faced my parents if I'd been caught?*

# 6
# MAYAGÜEZ, 1887

"You must *help* me, Lucita," Inocencia pleaded, about a week after their adventure in the country "Doña Lola doesn't expect me until next week for the women's group. But I'm going to deliver the letters today. I need to make a good impression, and you've got to help me to do that."

"Sí, señorita, I'll do whatever you need. But don't ask me to go with you."

Inocencia knew the girl was tired of playing a pawn in her deceptions, but she put that thought out of her mind.

"Besides, señorita, your mother wants me . . . "

"First! Boil rainwater so I can wash. Quickly, go! No, wait. Don't forget to bring the juice of a lemon so you can rinse my hair. And, Lucita, don't make a sound. I don't want to wake a soul in the entire household.

"Oh, and another thing. Where in the world did you leave the large tub?"

"I'm not sure, señorita. I think Señorita Kirina used it last." The girl was busily searching for drying sheets in the cedar storage chest at the foot of Inocencia's bed.

"Find it. Bring it into the bedroom. *Quietly.* When we're done, you can ditch the water right into the courtyard before anyone knows what I'm doing."

When Lucita finished carting pails of warm water, bathing, hair washing and drying, she dragged the metal tub to the edge of the patio and spilled out the dirty water. Next, she gave Inocencia's thick, straight hair one hundred brush strokes, massaging coconut oil into it until the smooth brown strands shone from bronze to deepest burgundy.

🎔 🎔 🎔

Trailing a scent of rose water and lemons in her wake, Inocencia went in search of her sisters. She found the girls at their morning lessons, gave each a slight hug followed by a breezy "Good morning, girls." Then, she settled herself in the cane seat rocker near the terra-cotta pots of golden oleander.

"I see you're both very busy. I won't disturb you."

Lazily, Inocencia began to flip through the pages of a ladies' illustrated magazine published in New York City. A solitary housefly buzzed in circles around the oleander. And while Inocencia pretended complete absorption in the magazine, her half-closed eyes kept watch over the sisters' every move.

"Looks like we're in for another hot, sticky, boring day . . . just like yesterday," she mumbled loud enough to distract the girls. "If we're lucky, we'll have showers this afternoon. *That'll* be exciting." The rocker's runners creaked monotonously against the marble tile floor.

Kirina shot her sister an exasperated glance, then glanced at Doly, who strained to make sense of Inocencia's strange behavior.

"*Ho hum*," Inocencia sighed. "Nothing to do . . . no one to talk to. Just lessons and chores."

After a moment of creaky rocking, Inocencia stopped and broke the silence.

"Papá sure is lucky. He is going to Mayagüez this morning . . . going to the stores for merchandise. At least, that is
what Mamá said."

Both Kirina and Doly snapped to attention. The plot was
hatched. The sisters were on their way to adventure. Floating visions of social butterflies in pastel dresses, and matching parasols, Kirina and Doly dreamed of shopping. Inocencia pictured herself on Doña Lola's doorstep, handing her
calling card to the maid.

While Inocencia waited in the foyer, Doña Lola appeared
at the top of the stairs of her home wearing a summery
marigold day dress. Out of habit, she held her spectacles
close to her eyes to peer over the railing. Surprised to find
her visitor was Inocencia, she smiled and said, "What a
pleasant surprise!" Doña Lola came down the stairs at a fast
clip to welcome the young woman.

"Oh, Doña Lola. I didn't mean to barge in on you today,
but I have an important letter from Don Sotero. He asked me
to deliver it as soon as I could."

Lola gave the envelope a cursory glance. "Another pleasant surprise," she said, despite having expected the communication from Sotero. She knew Sotero was writing a history
and had questions about the roles she and Don Bonocio had
played in the Lares revolt.

"I didn't think I should wait until the next meeting of the
women's group on . . . "

"Inocencia, please," Doña Lola interrupted. "It's wonderful to see you now, today and next week as well. Rosa is just
about to bring down some refreshments. Come, join me?
Don't be shy. Let me show you my lovely garden."

Doña Lola tucked her arm into Inocencia's and led her
into a tiny pocket of a garden surrounded by brick walls on

three sides. Hesitant at first, Inocencia felt warm pleasure coursing throughout her body. She was about to have refreshments with the patriot she most admired.

Easily slipping into conversation, Inocencia hung onto Doña Lola's every word. And Lola, wise in the ways of mentoring, encouraged the young woman's admiration. She respected Inocencia's passion. "That girl," she'd often told Bonocio, "may be impetuous, but she isn't frivolous. She's curious . . . wants to know about everything." As Lola reflected on Inocencia's qualities, she patted the young woman's hand as if she were one of her own daughters.

The women sat at a small, wrought-iron patio table, getting to know each other over tall glasses of *horchata de ajonjolí*, the sweetened juice of sesame seeds.

Inocencia loved the pungent sweetness of the sesame drink. She liked the smoothness of the milky liquid on her tongue, and how the taste complemented the cheese-filled puff pastries Doña Lola had served. She slurped the drink much too fast, her attention never leaving Doña Lola's expressive face.

"Living in a colony is like living in a house, you see," Doña Lola mused in polite conversation. "You know the good and the bad about it. But everything about that house is owned by an outsider who lives across the ocean and doesn't know the first thing about the place."

Listening to her mentor, Inocencia felt excited to be treated like an equal. *I could never have this conversation at home. Doña Lola is like a friend who's also a wonderful teacher.*

"Now, we who live in the house want to make changes," Doña Lola continued. "Let's get rid of foreign control. We'll make all our own decisions. But, here's the problem. The house people are split. Some want complete control; others want partial. Because of all the infighting, nothing changes. The foreigner wins in the end!"

"Why can't people cooperate if they all want the same thing? Has it always been like that?" Inocencia took a quick gulp of her *horchata*. "I don't remember such strife when I was growing up. I'd hear stories, yes. People were fighting against slavery, and I was afraid our house would burn down during a slave uprising. But, our lives weren't falling apart like today."

Doña Lola's apple-red cheeks rounded as she smiled at her guest's innocent remarks. *This girl was probably schooled in the basics: manners, the domestic arts and a succession of romance novels.* An image of her own extensive education in science and literature came to mind. *My young friend lacks a sense of history . . . enough knowledge to fend for herself in the circles that Sotero Figueroa frequents.*

"My dear Inocencia," Doña Lola breezily picked up the conversation, "your generation hasn't been tested. Today, our society is more progressive, I'll grant you that, but at the same time, remains backward in its politics. And, in its educational system."

"Oh, Doña Lola! I agree with you. I see how backward my own parents are. They've raised us as if we were preparing to live in the last century."

Lola raised a bold eyebrow, wondering if she should say something in defense of parents. "Pastry?" she said instead, with a sweet smile.

Inocencia chose a sugared pastry, daintily coating her fingers as she lifted it to her lips.

"When I was about your age," Doña Lola continued, "women weren't expected to know much about anything. A few of us did, of course. I certainly did, being as headstrong then as I am today!"

She laughed amiably at herself, an exuberant, deep chortle that scattered a family of *reinitas* pecking at tiny insects at the base of a large, potted colocasia plant.

"Oh, look, Inocencia! I love to watch the golden warblers play! They bring such joy to my garden, I wouldn't know how to live without them. See how they flit in and out of the fountain?"

Caught completely by surprise, Inocencia giggled. "Oh, yes!" she managed to say with a mouth full of pastry. "They're beauties. I didn't notice them before. There are so many things that slip right by me."

*I didn't even notice her garden. She seems to love it!* Inocencia looked around at her surroundings, studying the burst of bougainvillea, dahlias, frangipani and blood-red hibiscus blooming around a stone fountain of gurgling water. *Why hadn't I noticed all this before?* She berated her lack of awareness and added "gardens" as a topic she should study.

"Well, as I was saying," Doña Lola droned on. "I could tell you many stories about clever women. Bonocio and I surrounded ourselves with people who thought as we did—writers, artists, musicians—people whose opinions mattered. My literary salons began as a way to bring women together . . . to put our energies into trying to rid our country of a colonial government."

Inocencia had never attended a literary salon. She wondered if Lola's rambling narratives were meant to educate her. Not quite sure how to respond, she felt uneasy and shifted position leaning more towards the plants.

*I think she's telling me to prepare myself. Well, it's too late for that. I've made a mess of things already. I should have thought before I got it into my head to go see Don Sotero. And I should be thinking now about how I'll get back to my sisters in time to meet Papá! How do I take my leave without offending her? I should have planned ahead.*

The girl's fidgeting was not lost on Lola, who guessed it had to do with her family. Not wanting to frighten her away, Doña Lola reached across the table to refill her empty glass. Curiously, as she registered the young woman's worried expression, the words of an ancient spiritual verse came to mind. *Hold on to what is good, even if it is a handful of earth. Is it Inocencia I am to hold on to?*

"Honestly, my dear, we are all in great danger right now."

Inocencia stared at Doña Lola, wondering what great danger they were in. *Is she trying to warn me about Don Sotero? About my father?* "I *do* understand. I appreciate that you're trying to tell me something, Doña Lola, but . . ." She brusquely shook her head, as if to make sense of her jumbled thoughts.

"I'm simply cautioning you to be careful," said Doña Lola, setting the empty pitcher down on the table. "This governor has spies where you least expect them."

Surprisingly, Inocencia blasted, "I'm tired of being careful! My life is slipping by, and what have I done of merit? Don't you think we have to stand firm for our beliefs?"

Stunned, Doña Lola hadn't expected such an outburst from Inocencia.

"You've been at the forefront of struggle," Inocencia persisted. "Don't you believe we must claim what belongs to us?"

"You're right, my dear. I *do* know what it means to be in the eye of the storm. There was a time when just for whistling *La Borinqueña* a person could be thrown into prison! And *because of that* I felt responsible for writing the lyrics of that anthem."

"But you're *still* so brave, Doña Lola! Every day, you stand up against this oppressive regime that tramples our *dignity* as a people. I'm just beginning to stand up for myself."

Lola could hear Sotero's words coming out of Inocencia's mouth.

"*I* believe the time for fighting is *now*," Inocencia continued, "even if all we have on our side is an *idea* of what is just!"

"My dear, I don't entirely disagree with you, and maybe I didn't express myself well. But, I was only trying to warn you that the colonial authorities are spying on liberals. People will be exiled because of their beliefs."

"Sometimes I don't know what to do. I know we need *unity*. I understand your little story about the people in the house. But, Don Sotero wants independence now. The liberals want negotiations. And I think he is right, but sometimes, I think he isn't."

"Inocencia, listen to me. All I'm saying, dear, is that even in the best of times things will fall apart. *Think*, think before you act. Plot the path for *yourself* in your personal life, and in the causes you are drawn to. Look out for your own safety in this business of liberating our people."

An interminable silence followed the blunt exchange between mentor and protégée. Inocencia remained silent, deep in thought, ashamed of her outburst. Doña Lola simply waited for the young woman to recover.

"I have a lot of work to do, don't I, Doña Lola?"

Lola caught the self-doubt in the young woman's eyes.

"Yes, Inocencia. We all have a lot of work to do. But there's plenty of time to learn. Come now. I'll call for my carriage."

Doña Lola's pixie face spontaneously lit up in a knowing smile. "You really should be getting back, before your family begins to look for you."

❦ ❦ ❦

Lola watched the carriage taking Inocencia to meet her sisters, and mused about the unexpected visit. *It's difficult for her, so in love and brimming with expectations, to shape her destiny. Her ideas are different from her father's. He might be a good soul, but he is a civil servant in the employ of the colonial government his daughter seems determined to despise. It won't be an easy road for her . . . nor for any of us.*

# 7

# MAYAGÜEZ, 1887

When the bells of Nuestra Señora de la Candelaria began to toll Vespers, the time for evening prayers, Lola stopped what she was doing to listen. She loved this time of day, when she could enjoy the clanging of the bells from across the marble plaza to the walls of her home and on to the mountains that surrounded the valley. She stepped out onto the tree-shaded veranda and wondered if the ancient bones of the Taíno Indians and the Spanish *conquistadores*—buried in the ground long before it became the public plaza—vibrated with the tolling of the bells.

It was the late afternoon of Lola's salon. She looked up and down the streets anticipating an early arrival of her guests. *No one, not yet.* Then she looked in the direction of the setting sun, hoping the evening would break the heat that was sucking the life out of every living thing. The russet clay jug on the bench against the far wall, half-filled with rainwater, caught her attention. She lifted it and began to pour water into the planters. *Cool ripples of water for thirsty plants,* she thought, which triggered an image in her mind of the patriots imprisoned in El Morro. *Does anyone care if they have enough water to drink, a tin of water to pour over their heated heads?*

As she returned the water jug to the bench, Bonocio joined her on the veranda.

"You're looking cool enough," she said, wiping wet hands on a rag.

Pressing down the folds of his flounced neck wear under the collar, he responded, "There is a light breeze, thank goodness." He chuckled softly under his breath.

"Now, why are *you* laughing," she huffed trying to place behind her ear a gardenia she just picked."

"Because, love, if you want to wear flowers in your hair, you're going to need longer hair than what you've got to secure them."

"*Humph!*"

Lola settled herself in the white Victorian rocker, folding her skirt neatly beneath her legs so that it would not wrinkle. She rested her eyes and tried to catch the occasional breeze that came her way. *I should be glad I don't have to argue with Bonocio over my hair styling. Most men would complain like stuck pigs if their wives decided to cut their hair as short as mine. He doesn't remember my hair style began as a sign of my love for him. How quickly men forget.*

Standing at the balcony's balustrade, Bonocio observed the first flickers of the lights around the plaza. Illumination in the ten lampposts surrounding the fountain seemed to catch fire, one globe after the other, until the glow of the lamps grew brighter and brighter. Each evening, he watched the same scenario play out before him, as if it were the first time. And each evening he grinned, awed by the magical display.

"Bonocio," Lola murmured dreamily, "do you remember when Aurora told my mother about our romance? You were eighteen, I was fourteen. I can still picture us at that age."

"There was no romance to tell about. We were little more than children, if you remember."

"No, you're the one who denies, refuses to remember what happened. Aurora wanted to nip our romance in the bud and said she'd tell Mamá I needed a reprimand. She scolded me that I was only a young girl."

"*Uh huh,*" he responded, his eyes riveted on the bustling street scene below.

"If you'd bothered to notice, you'd agree that Aurora was a big tattletale . . . always tattling about something or someone. She told Mamá I suffered from delusions! I'd been allowed to grow long braids and thought I was already a young lady." She knew without looking at him that Bonocio wasn't paying attention to her.

"I can't believe it! You really should admit when you can't remember something."

"*¡Mujer!* How can I forget? You mention it often enough."

"Oh, *bosh*! I was afraid of Mamá, but I decided the next time the barber visited our home, I'd ask him to cut off my braids. Papá was scandalized. I remember lying to him, told him it was Mamá's idea."

A pensive look saddened her expression. She paused for a moment, then resumed her back and forth rocking.

"When I saw my beautiful brown braids on the floor . . . Oh, how I cried."

She cast a sheepish glance in his direction. "Do you at least recall I was punished, kept home for a week! You came to see me, asked why I cut my hair, and I said, 'for you.' And I told Mamá if I married, it would only be with you."

Bonocio still wasn't paying attention, distracted by the activity in the street below.

"*¡Demonio!*" He snorted deep in his throat. "Lola," he whispered and tightly gripped hold of the railing. He leaned over as far as he could to peer underneath the balcony. "Oh yes, we can expect two, no, not two, maybe three uninvited guests this evening."

"Where are they?" Lola left the rocker, moved to the railing and looked below with a practiced air of nonchalance.

"Look, look to the southwest corner of the plaza. See, there! Near the wall of the Alcaldía. Do you see the man there? See the broad felt hat bordered in white? As dim as the lamp lights are, that white border reflects the light. There. See the pale glint of light on his rifle? And the second one is . . . yes, there he is, just on the other side next to the tramway rail"

"Oh, yes," she sighed, worried for the safety of their guests. The guards, she knew, took note of who visited and when.

"Now I see him and . . . Ay, Bonocio! A very brave chap, I'd say. See how close he is to our carriage port? I'm tempted to ask these spies into the house." She gave a high-pitched laugh, the blood suddenly draining from her face. "Maybe they could use a lesson in civility to go along with their surveillance. Those guards are practically crawling all over our house."

Bonocio furrowed his brow and tightened his jaw in anger. Lola, on the other hand, appeared jovial and serene, but felt once more the impertinent stare of the guard. She had not forgotten him since the insulting interrogation she had suffered.

*This guard will find evidence to exile us, unless I crush the slimy life out of him like a cockroach underfoot!* But, how was she supposed to do that?

She didn't want to think about him . . . or the sixteen liberals locked up in San Juan's fortress of El Morro, marked for execution. Sixteen dissidents caned and tortured. *What if Bonocio were chained in that dungeon with the others?*

Quickly, she reached for her husband's hand, felt his warm fingers with her own, his nails, his skin, and gave his hand a loving squeeze. There were no bruised fingers, no jagged bloody stumps shorn of torn fingernails, *Thank God.* Still, she couldn't rid her mind of the others. It was as if invisible threads bound her to the prisoners. She imagined the oozing blood, smelled the metallic odor from lacerated hands roped tightly into wooden slats bristling with sharp, pointed nails.

Much too late, she realized the images had seared themselves in her mind, like unbreakable chains.

# 8

## MAYAGÜEZ, 1887

In the end, Lola and Bonocio did not need much coaxing to move. Once the colonial government shut down *El Anunciador Colonial* and *La Propaganda* his newspapers, Bonocio lost valuable channels for demanding justice. The couple had no intention of giving up the battle, but hounding repression, surveillance and dwindling business were hurting the family. There had been substantial financial losses. Lola and Bonocio realized they were trapped.

"Lola," Bonocio would whisper in the dead of night. "What'll happen to you and the girls if I were suddenly seized at gunpoint . . . thrown into the dungeon with the other liberals? How would it be for you without me?"

"Shhhhush," Lola would respond, holding him close. "Tomorrow is another day. Who knows what it will bring? We need to remain strong, not lose hope, Bonocio. Try to get some sleep."

But then Lola would lay awake until morning.

🌺 🌺 🌺

Leaning against the veranda's arched doorway a week later, Lola soaked up the sights and sounds of her city. She inhaled the intoxicating scents of flowering trees, of acrid, still waters sheltering scampering frogs and crabs, of humid earth mixed with nature's musk. She breathed in deeply to find the peculiar odor of dry heat rising from the street pavement, and inhaled again, as if she could lock Mayagüez into every pore of her being. Exile was ever on her mind. Once, she'd described exile as a wrenching loss of one's self, not easily forgotten. This move felt much the same.

"*Ay*, Mamá," Patria interrupted her mother's train of thought. "It isn't as if San Juan was a foreign country."

"We'll just have to get used to it," she answered.

*Get use to a garden without reinitas; to noise, filth and congestion; to not seeing my beloved green mountains fade into purple hues at dusk. But I'll return. Each year on Mercedita's birthday I'll return to place a rose on my child's grave.* She thought of Mercedes, the frail three-year-old daughter she'd lost. *They can't stop me from doing that! That would be the final insult.*

"Besides," Patria spoke gently, "we'll all benefit from a change in our routines. It'll be like a new adventure. And all of us will share it together, Mamá . . . you, me, Papá and Laura. That's what's important, isn't it? We'll all be together?"

"*Ay*, of course, *niña*! We'll have our family."

Lola turned away from the veranda and studied the formal parlor she'd decorated with her own hands. Then she pictured the Sunday afternoon salons. Populating the space in her mind's eye, she rekindled pure, crisp piano melodies, laughter, Bonocio and the girls performing skits or singing at salon gatherings, the distinct voices of friends reciting verses, debating or arguing. *So many memories. Patria is right. I'm grateful we'll all be together.*

When Patria mentioned her name, Laura wiped her wispy, blond bangs away from her eyes and glanced up at her sister. Lola and Bonocio had raised the seven-year-old child from birth as their own. Laura felt something was amiss and she retreated to a shady corner of the veranda. There, she was safe and began to play a game of stacking small seashells into piles according to size and color.

# 9

## SAN JUAN, 1887

"*¡Estúpido!*" thundered General Romualdo Palacio as he brusquely booted the frightened barber away. While trimming the general's mutton-chop whiskers, the barber's razor had nicked the general. "If you want something properly done, you've got to do it yourself," huffed the general as he ripped off the bloody towel wrapped around his neck.

It was the eleventh day of November, and Palacio had been stripped of his command. The general finished dressing on his own, cursing the audacity of the overseas minister who had heeded the complaints against him from the Puerto Rican liberals. Ordered to return to Madrid on the first available ship, the general was forced to obey against his will.

After dressing in his finest uniform, Palacio left his residence and made his way to the waiting carriage that would take him to the harbor. Along the route, Palacio waved nonchalantly at the conservative well-wishers who lined the streets of San Juan to see him off.

When finally he stood on the deck of the very same ship that had brought him to Puerto Rico, the white plume on his helmet gently swaying in the ocean breeze, he brooded. "I don't deserve this public humiliation."

He consoled himself with the thought that in a matter of hours he would be gone from this backwater hell hole. In a matter of weeks, he'd once more bask in the limelight of the worthy social classes of Madrid, a highly civilized, enlightened European metropolis.

Palacio pictured himself enjoying the full bodied *vino* of Rioja, or sherry from Jerez de la Frontera, smacking his lips to remember the hint of almonds in the wine. He tried to replicate in his memory the smells and flavor of the succulent, golden roasted pig cooked to perfection at an inn he frequented under the Roman Aqueduct in Segovia. But only a bitter taste remained in his mouth: the foul and lingering regret that he had not condemned the wretched liberals to a slow and painful death while he still held the reins of power.

When they heard the news about the general, the Tió family was already on its way to a new life in San Juan. When the news hit Ponce, Inocencia Martínez dropped a clay pitcher full of *guanabana* juice, her face glowing with a resplendent smile.

"Sotero is coming home!" she rejoiced.

# 10

## PONCE, 1887

"Absolutely *not*," bellowed an ashen-faced Antonio Martínez, slamming the palm of his right hand on the dining room table! The knowledge that Sotero Figueroa had resumed his life in Ponce stuck in his throat like a chicken bone. Until that moment, Don Antonio's easy-going demeanor had served to mask the unsettling anger he had so carefully managed to restrain. Now, he'd reached the end of his patience.

"*I am* the *head* of this family," he stammered, trying to control his tone. "I am *responsible* for this family's honor, young lady. And I say you will *never* meet, or speak to, or be seen in the company of that man from this day forward!"

The four women sat frozen around the dining table. Doña Alejandrina Santaella de Martínez, shy and retiring, gripped her handkerchief tightly in both hands, as if the mere square of lace were enough to keep her anchored to her seat. Tears of frustration verged on the brink of spilling onto her pale cheeks. Ambivalent, Doña Alejandrina longed to wrap her daughter protectively in her arms. But, loving wife that she was, her place was to support her husband's decisions.

She hated every rumor compromising Inocencia's reputation and shuddered at the thought of their daughter's repeated indiscretions. *What was that child thinking . . . to meet a man unchaperoned . . . alone in the countryside, no less. Since his return, she's been seen everywhere with him. It's undignified! Doesn't she for one second consider her reputation, the family's honor?*

Eyes downcast against their father's wrath, Kirina and Doly sat stone-faced, afraid their role as accomplices in Inocencia's secret romance would be discovered. The girls dared not look in their father's direction. Instead, they stared at the floral patterns on the plates in front of them. Every now and then, Doly's gaze slid to the untouched dishes of rice, white beans and pumpkin, wondering when she'd be able to fill her stomach.

Defiantly, Inocencia glared at Don Antonio. Her flushed cheeks and tightly sealed lips spoke volumes, but she held back a torrent of denials and justifications that she dared not unleash out of respect for her father.

Finally, just when she thought she could bear it no longer, Don Antonio thundered, "You dare show no remorse for your deceptions . . . or setting a bad example for your sisters? You should be ashamed! Leave the table and give your unruly behavior some serious thought!"

"*¡Papá!* You're sending me to my room to reflect on *my* behavior? It is *you* who plays the tyrant, refusing to understand my side of the story!"

Inocencia sprang to her feet, knocking her chair over onto the black and white tiled floor. She flung her napkin on the table, and with a forward jut of her square jaw, left the room in a huff.

At twenty-one, Inocencia was no longer a child. In the Ponce of the 1880s, women were claiming their rights to act in all sorts of ways, even to fall in love without a parent's approval.

※ ※ ※

He hated to lose his temper, but Don Antonio could think of nothing else. *¡Basta!* he declared after sitting alone with his thoughts for almost an hour. He stepped over to the cabinet where he kept a wooden box embossed with forest creatures on five sides. As he opened the lid, the strong smell of tobacco hit him immediately. He removed a black leafed cigar from inside. Holding the cigar to his nose, Don Antonio took a long whiff, but he didn't feel the usual heady anticipation of taking his first, sweet puff. His stomach grumbled with a loud *Burrrp*, bringing a burst of sourness to his mouth.

"*¡Ay, ay, ay!* Three daughters! It's a wonder I don't have ulcers," he mumbled, moving to the patio rocker nearest the flowering Jasmine bush. Don Antonio sat in solitude, smoking the cigar and thinking about the cruel tricks fate manages to play. He listened to the serenade of the tiny tree frogs, their random chirps of *coquí, coquí* soothing his troubled spirit.

Don Antonio recalled the day he first met Alejandrina, his wife-to-be. He was to audit ledgers for her father and accidentally dropped them all when she entered the room, so taken was he with her beauty. And that was the start of his good life with a winsome wife and three beautiful daughters.

Back then, it was a proper world, a world of manners and decorum, a world without generational strife, where children dared not oppose their parents. He had known better than to have met Alejandrina anywhere but in the sanctity of her own home surrounded by parents and relatives. He would never have endangered her reputation as a virtuous, protected young woman, and when he asked her father for her hand in Holy Matrimony, he promised to care for her in the style to which she was accustomed.

Cigar smoke filled the evening air, and Don Antonio's contemplations drifted to his own daughters. Imagining his three girls overwhelmed his heart with tenderness, bringing a sudden stab of remorse.

*How could I ever turn my back on them, bar the doors of my home to them if any one of them ever acted against my wishes? No*, he thought sadly, *there's got to be a better solution than turning my back on Inocencia, on my own flesh and blood.*

When Don Antonio had exhausted himself trying to figure out a solution to the matter of his recalcitrant daughter, he rose wearily from the rocker, his tired bones protesting. He dropped the cigar on the ground and ground it out with the tip of his shoe. The heavy weight of his decision rested on hunched shoulders, as Don Antonio walked along the perimeter of the courtyard to his wife's bedroom.

As was her nightly ritual, Doña Alejandrina sat before the mirror at her vanity, brushing out the braids in her long hair. When she caught sight of her husband's reflection in the mirror, she spun around, and cried, "Toñito! *Dios mío.* What is the matter? You look like you're about to collapse!"

"Ale," he murmured, using her pet name as he carefully closed the door behind him. "I've been thinking. This man . . . this Sotero Figueroa . . . perhaps we should respect Inocencia's wishes and allow him to visit her in our home. We should learn more about him, about his values, his sense of honor and duty. See how he behaves towards her and her family . . . you know, give him a chance . . . give *them* a chance?

# 11

## SAN JUAN, 1887

Lola fluffed out the seat cushions. "Rosa," she called. "Please come to the parlor! Help me throw open the window shutters to catch the morning breeze!"

Suddenly, the room was filled with dancing dust motes against the brilliant sun rays. Lola stepped out onto the narrow balcony and faced the ocean. She inhaled the crisp morning air and felt the energy coursing through her body. A flock of gulls glided from sky to sea to snatch the ocean's bounty, their raucous call in harmony with Lola's sensuous feelings. For the moment, schedules and agendas disappeared from her mind.

Lola's house stood under the shade of an old ceiba tree, a stone's throw from the San Juan Gate in the massive wall surrounding the city. From where she stood, she could see the street below curve to the ornate iron gate she knew was directly under her balcony. Four stout, rust-colored planters stood guard at the walnut door to her residence. Unlike the openness of their previous homes, dark planks and wooden banisters lent the house a closed-in feeling. Still, Lola loved the illusion of spaciousness the high-beamed ceilings gave the formal rooms.

"*Ay, mira*, Rosa," Lola said as the housekeeper appeared in the doorway. "You take care of the house chores. I'll see that the piano is ready for Patria's lesson."

She gazed longingly out of the window once more, wishing she was as free as the gulls, before she remembered the weekly gatherings. *Friends and acquaintances have made a world of difference,* she mused. Her precious salon had survived the move, its acclaim drawing the cream of the city's intellectuals to the house with the rust-colored planters.

᪥ ᪥ ᪥

"Lola! 'Pride goes before destruction, and a haughty spirit before a fall,' so says the Bible," Bonocio cautioned one afternoon. "We must be careful." The attention showered on Lola in San Juan for her poetry book, *Mis cantares,* had emboldened her. She began to feel invincible, protected by her readers and supporters. And she had begun to take what she considered "minor risks."

"*¡Hombre!* Do you think I can't control my own affairs?"

"Sometimes you tend to get ahead of yourself . . . move too fast," he called out to her.

"*Hummph!* Publicity brings influential people to the cause," Lola murmured, glancing at her husband as she passed by. She carried her diary to the small desk in the parlor where she could see the ocean while she wrote.

"We might have to use them." She shot her husband a playful, smirk. "And Bonocio . . . " She waited to see the expression on his face before she spoke. "We have an important mission."

"And, what is that?"

"When the moment is ripe, we will free the prisoners."

Bonocio looked startled, then smiled. In twenty-two years of marriage, Lola was still feisty, the same outspoken bundle of energy he had married.

"I'd like to be here when that happens. Will it wait till I return from New York?"

"I'm afraid not, love. I'll just plod on without you." The quick smile she gave her husband could not hide the disappointment in Lola's eyes. She so wanted him to be with her when she freed the prisoners.

A few days later, Lola appeared before the Commission of University Academics. Governor Contreras Martínez, land owners, colonial officials and professors were among the invited guests. Lola was to give the toast at the reception that followed.

Elegantly dressed, two swooping, iridescent peacock feathers on Lola's cream colored turban delicately framed her face. When she stepped to the podium at the center of the room, the guests broke out in applause. She scanned the audience to her right, graciously bowing her head in welcome. Then she greeted those assembled to her left, searching for her daughter, Patria, who was among the honorees. Bonocio, she noticed, stood at the rear of the room.

As Lola raised her glass for the toast, her gaze washed warmly over the audience. She smiled, rosy lips slightly parted. With the smallest of movements, she moistened her lips and began to speak:

*"Cuba and Puerto Rico are the two wings of one bird;*
*They receive flowers or bullets in the same heart . . ."*

It took mere seconds to utter the words that linked Puerto Rico to the Cuban liberation struggle. Before everyone, Lola had professed support for independence. And no one was left in doubt about her political convictions.

Patria raised astonished eyebrows, smiling broadly at her mother, but no other person in the room moved. There was no ovation, no applause, until Bonocio broke the silence with the first single clap. Slowly, some liberals followed Bonocio's example; others pursed their lips together, their brows knitted in consternation.

Lola wavered. *The audience is against me. I can hear them murmuring, feel their anger.* From her neck to her knees, she felt the tension ripple throughout her compact body, perspiration forming on her forehead. *No, wait! What am I nervous about? I said what had to be said! I can't remain silent . . . not when our people need to rise up against this oppressive system.*

She lifted her head, making the peacock feathers dance around her face, and surveyed the crowd like a schoolmarm would survey a class of rowdy children, without one hint of regret. As if a great weight had been lifted from her shoulders, she felt free, free as the gulls outside her window, free as the day the barber had cut off her braids.

Two days later, a grim-faced Contreras Martínez summoned Lola to the governor's mansion, La Fortaleza, but Lola refused to go.

❧ ❧ ❧

The governor was livid! In the presence of his chief advisors, Contreras Martínez could not sit still. The rows of ribboned medals pinned to his uniform brought out the grayish, purple hues of his whiskered face. It was clear the man intended to bombard Doña Lola with the *full* authority of his office.

"That woman's infidelity to the Mother Country will not be tolerated! I'll denounce her public insults . . . silence once and for all, her incendiary support of liberation! She is an embarrassment! Write this down," he bellowed to his aide. "A stiff reprimand, that's what she'll get."

To his chagrin, the governor was left to settle accounts in writing.

At the approximate hour Lola was to have appeared, Contreras Martínez received her letter bearing an embossed emblem of the bird with its two wings spread wide.

Lola's letter was eloquent in recalling a heroic Spain: "The generous Spain that has so often led the way to fame and glory; the Spain that does not oppress; does not degrade; the one that doesn't engender hatred among her people; that does not humiliate her own people, because this is the heroic Spain of my grandparents. . . ."

But it was also damning of the Spain that represented a group of egotists, a caste of mercenaries without a 'yesterday' or traditions to uphold; the Spain lacking morals and the respect that is due to a people no matter how poor and humble they may be. She closed with, "To that Spain, I am indifferent."

A pragmatist, Contreras Martínez fumed at reading Lola's letter, but was hesitant to persecute her because of her international reputation. He hoped the matter would be put to rest.

But Lola had no intention of letting the matter rest!

✸✸✸ ✸✸✸ ✸✸✸

It didn't take long before Lola set out to meet Contreras Martínez.

"Governor Contreras Martínez," Lola said, nodding her head in greeting as she entered his office in La Fortaleza. With justice and reason on her side, Lola spoke from her heart. "It would be cruel, inhumane, to let the liberals spend Christmas locked in cells, without the comfort of their families, unable to worship during this blessed season."

"I agree, Madame. It would be cruel in this sacred season, and I . . . "

"You *do* understand, sir. It is the right thing to do. With General Palacio's return to Madrid, there's no evidence against the prisoners." Earnest eyes begged for justice through wire-rimmed spectacles.

Flattered by Lola's sincerity, Contreras Martínez was glad he didn't have to argue the issue of the two winged bird with her. *For once, the woman is being reasonable,* he thought and nodded politely in her direction as he shuffled through papers and proclamations on the desk.

"I like to think that I am a reasonable man, señora, well-regarded by the people."

"Oh, you are! I've heard wonderful things about you . . . how you were thinking of issuing pardons during Christmas, as a gesture of kindness. So you do . . . "

"Doña Lola, if I may call you by the name everyone knows. I've prepared these official papers for you. Please regard these as my gift to you."

He handed Lola the folder, and for once she was speechless. She had nothing to say but to thank him profusely and fly from the room before he changed his mind.

*I meant to tell Doña Lola a new governor was on his way to head the government. Argh, why bother her?—I'm sure he'll abide by my decisions.*

And all Doña Lola could think about was *My gift to the brave patriots of Puerto Rico!* In less time than it took to accomplish the deed, less time than it took to affix a signature to a piece of paper, Lola held the prisoners' release firmly in her hand. As she left La Fortaleza that afternoon and climbed into the awaiting carriage, the smile on her face rivaled all the brilliance of Christmas.

# 12

## PONCE, 1889

Doña Alejandrina rubbed the fine lace veil between her index finger and her thumb. *This is the same velo y corona I wore, the very same veil and headpiece that crowned my head on the day I married my Antonio,* she thought. *And look how happy we've been. All these years . . . I remember it as if it were yesterday, how it poured all day. I stood by the portal in the courtyard, my tears blending in with the rain that soaked my face.*

*Suddenly, out of nowhere, I heard Toñito's voice: "Don't cry, mi amor. It will be a splendid day! You'll see." I turned around, afraid he'd bring us bad luck by seeing me before our wedding. But there was no one there! And then, just before we were about to leave for the cathedral, the skies suddenly cleared, and . . .* ¡Madre de Dios! *How many Santaella women have worn this veil?*

She pursed her lips remembering the generations of women in her family who had kept the tradition. Today it was her own daughter's turn. *Thank the Lord I've lived long enough to see this day.* Folding the long bridal veil over her arm, Doña Alejandrina gently carried it into her daughter's bedroom.

Gowned in layers of shimmering satin that had also witnessed generations of Santaella weddings, Inocencia examined her appearance before the full-length mirror. The high-laced collar, tiny seed pearls and accentuated balloon-like sleeves did recall long-forgotten fashions, but it added a special look to her aura, softening her jawline and emphasizing her cheekbones. Despite the nervous rumbling in her stomach, she looked beautiful, her crown a braid of deepest chestnut interwoven with tiny sprigs of lilac.

"Can you smooth out the train of the gown?" Inocencia asked Lucita.

The girl pushed aside the hem of her own smock, and dropped to her knees to fold the train.

"I *love* that man, José Martí," she told Lucita, swaying from one side to the other. "Even though I've never met him."

"That's a big problem, señorita. You're going to marry Don Sotero."

Inocencia began to giggle. "*Ay*, Lucita. Of course, I'm marrying Don Sotero! But the marriage wouldn't be taking place today if José Martí hadn't invited Sotero to bring his passion for revolution to New York. He's famous, you know, this Martí." She handed Lucita a pin for her hair. "Sotero says the liberals plan to free Cuba, and all the planning will be done in New York."

Standing on tip-toes, Lucita pinned the last lilac sprig into the bride's hair. She ran her hands down the skirt of her smock, stepped back to assess her labor and beamed. As she looked at Inocencia, Lucita's dark eyes misted. *There's no bride anywhere in Ponce who's as beautiful as my mistress*, she thought, holding back tears.

Inocencia twirled around in front of the mirror, delighted with her appearance. She liked to see the subtle changes in the gown with every spin as the fabric's iridescence shifted with the light streaming in through the curtained windows. Cocking her head from one side to the other, she sought the exact stride that made her look as if she were walking on air.

*This once,* she thought, *this most important once in my life, I want to be as beautiful as possible for Sotero.* She squeezed her lips, making the blood rush to them, then pinched her cheeks and looked again in the mirror. The hint of color gave her a radiant look.

When her mother entered the room, Inocencia smiled, as if to say, *Well, here we are, and here is the precious moment we've waited for.*

Guarding mixed feelings now that the wedding day had arrived sooner than expected, Doña Alejandrina's lips trembled slightly in sadness where there should have been joy. The bride registered her mother's concern, but thought it was merely anguish at losing a daughter to marriage.

"I know, Mamá," she crooned softly. "I know . . . but isn't it wonderful? Mamá, I'm marrying the love of my life!" Lifting the skirt of the gown, the bride inched carefully towards her mother, extending an arm out to clasp Alejadrina's hand into her own.

"I know it'll be hard at first, but Mamá, just think: soon, you'll visit us in New York! But I promise I'll come home as often as I can. So please be happy for me."

"*¡Niña! No seas tonta.* Don't be silly. And don't start to cry again. You'll spoil your pretty face. Happiness. That is all I've ever wanted for you, *m'ijita!*"

A sudden twinge in her heart, as if the moist air in the room was too heavy to breathe, scared Alejandrina. She coughed, feigning a guttural chuckle to hide the flutter of uneasiness she'd felt. *I know it's just nerves. What woman wants to be separated from daughters they birthed and raised to womanhood?* Alejandrina dreaded the thought of Inocencia beginning married life in an alien land so far away from home, without her, without any of her kin to help her.

"And don't ever forget your sisters." As if to imprint the message into her daughter's memory, she squeezed Inocencia's hands, imploring her with fierce, weathered eyes not to lose connections with Doly and Kirina.

"Now," she smiled. "Let's move along or you will be late for your own wedding."

On the evening of June 28, 1889, the Cathedral of Our Lady of Guadalupe was aglow. Don Antonio and Don Sotero arrived early for last-minute instructions. Ushered into a side office, the men took adjoining seats facing the church bookkeeper, an ordained priest from Madrid recently assigned to the parish.

The priest greeted the men with a slight nod of his head and began to review the contents of the brown manila folder holding all the necessary documents and fees for the Martínez Santaella and Figueroa Fernández nuptials.

"Don Sotero," the clerk lisped, exaggerating his Iberian diction to the Creole mulatto. "You understand this is just a formality to ensure that everything is in keeping with church regulations. And Don Antonio," the young man's voice raised slightly as if he were posing a question, "you will speak in the interests of your daughter?"

Both men knew the process was no mere formality. If any of the fees or documents were missing, there would be no wedding ceremony at all. The clerk's annoying nasal inflections intensified an air of superiority that was already grating on Sotero's nerves. He recognized Castilian snobbery for what it was and could feel his anger rising. Not one to suffer fools lightly, Sotero rolled his finger along the inside of his collar, relieving the irritating moisture, but managed to maintain his composure. He was eager to get through the administrative minutia, eager to marry his beloved and get on with their lives.

At that moment, married life with Inocencia should have been uppermost in his mind, but it was not. He thought of everything that awaited him in New York: the first step towards a new life in voluntary exile in a land where the revolutionary wheels of liberation were already in motion. Silently tapping his index finger on the underarm of the chair, a habitual sign of restlessness, Sotero wondered if the orders he'd given to pack and ship the ten crates of equipment for his printing press had been implemented.

Don Antonio did not seem to find the delay disagreeable, for it meant that Inocencia was *still* under his fatherly protection. *I can wait. Inocencia isn't just any woman; she is my daughter! A woman from a proud, adoring family that will go to great lengths to protect her! I'm not so anxious to give away my daughter. Certainly not to a man I hardly know!*

*Never mind that for more than a year, Sotero has visited our home and asked me for Inocencia's hand in marriage after a proper courtship. It doesn't matter that the man is honorable.*

*What kind of a life is Inocencia going to live in exile with a man whose dedication to a cause blinds him to everything else? What kind of life will she have as the wife of a Negro in New York City?*

"Ah, here it is," said the priest, interrupting Don Antonio's thoughts and addressing Don Sotero. "Now, let's see here. Your wife, *eh*, former wife that is, Mary . . . it says here Mary . . . not María? Well, in any case, Mary died of tuberculosis? And there were children, yes? Pray tell, *where* might we find these children?"

"The answer to your first question is, yes. And the children . . . well cared for, sir." Sotero answered with annoyance, not wanting to relive his wife's tragedy and his separation from his children, now in the care of his in-laws. "The bride is . . . Oh my! *Twenty-three* years of age," continued the pastor oblivious to Don Sotero's sarcasm. "And you, sir, are thirty-eight. Ahem, well, both certainly meet the legal age requirements."

"Now, Don Antonio, let's see . . . you paid for banns proclaimed on three separate holy days, the documents of certification for the bride and groom, the wedding ceremony, the sacramental fee . . . Oh, and . . . did the bride and groom provide a measurement of beeswax for the ceremonial candles?" the priest asked, raising soulful eyes towards Don Antonio as a sign of piety.

⁂ ⁂ ⁂

As the men stepped out of the office to take their places near the altar, Don Antonio turned to Sotero and spoke to him in a loud whisper. "Now we know, Don Sotero? Now we know why so many couples run away to St. Thomas for their nuptials. And the poor . . . *ay, los pobres* . . . " he chuckled, shaking his head as if in disbelief, "no wonder so many of them live outside the bonds of Holy Matrimony. They can't afford to feed themselves AND Holy Mother the Church."

Ordinarily, Don Antonio's criticism of the Church would have been added to by Sotero, but the groom hadn't paid attention to Don Antonio. Sotero was rooted to the marble floor, mesmerized by the glimpse of an angel swathed in white, who had just entered the church vestibule. Carrying a bountiful bouquet of lilacs, brilliant yellow margaritas and blood red poppies, his bride resembled a goddess.

Sotero Figueroa gazed at the woman without whom, he realized, life would be unbearable. Time stood still. He forgot about his printing equipment, his books, newspaper articles, steamer schedules and all the other mundane affairs that had clogged his head on that day. All that mattered was a bright future with Inocencia beside him, in a land where he could express his political beliefs without fear.

# PART II

# 1
## NEW YORK CITY, 1889

"*Ay*, Sotero, look!" Inocencia gushed as she looked out the cabin porthole with an unobstructed view of the ocean. "Six whole days in our own little world!" *I'll get to know my husband, the man . . . not the revolutionary.*

"Sotero, this'll be our own private hide-a-way." Amused, she set about inspecting every corner of the cabin. "Awww, look! Look, a small wardrobe! Isn't it darling?" She opened a mirrored closet door and saw six hangers, and four drawers. "Like being in a doll house!" Ignoring the fine coal dust accumulating on her white gloves that had no place in her dream world, she continued to run her fingers slowly over the smooth wood surfaces. Then, she did the same with the other objects in the room.

"It's just perfect," she murmured. Misty-eyed, she turned and gazed up at Sotero, who had patiently waited out his new wife's explorations.

"It amazes me how you can find such pleasure in the smallest things," he said.

Inocencia tossed back her chestnut curls and flung both arms around his neck. "Thank you, my love."

The newlyweds had left San Juan Harbor on board the USS *Knickerbocker,* a mail and cargo ship destined for New York City on a routine coastal run. The Cromwell Steam Ship Lines boasted the *Knickerbocker* was the pinnacle of first-class steamers. "Not more than a week," they adver tised, unless they encountered inclement weather.

On the first day at sea, Inocencia explored the steamer, thoughts about adventures and discoveries uppermost in her mind. She hadn't exactly fit into her new role as a married woman and was conscious of toning down her enthusiasm when she met other passengers. Still, she found it hard to pretend that this wasn't her first voyage, especially since there was little about this journey that did not excite the child in her.

In the late mornings, she'd walk into the large passenger lounge, called the Saloon, making sure she dressed her best by alternating cuffs and collars on the four frocks in her wardrobe trunk. Full of curiosity, she'd set forth to meet Saloon passengers who came from every corner of the Island.

"How do you do," she'd say, pronouncing every syllable. "My name is *Doña* Inocencia Martínez *de Figueroa,*" and she'd extend her hand to Spaniards, Germans, French and native-born Puerto Ricans, like herself and Sotero. She'd engage in short humdrum conversations about the weather, but the truth was she didn't much feel like a *doña.* The *doñas* she knew were ancient.

Instinctively, she was drawn to the small circle of Span- ish-speaking women and their children. The young bride felt comfortable with them, discovered she didn't have to put on airs. She soon realized that everyone, especially the children, seemed to delight in her company and could hardly wait to share such impressions with her husband.

"It seems they *do* like to include me in their conversa- tions," she told Sotero when they met at dinner one evening.

"And, please don't laugh, but the little ones are so much more clever than I expected."

Sotero did laugh. Sharing his wife's recounting of her adventures, he was amused by the subtle changes already taking place in her. *Like the blossoming of a flower to full bloom,* he thought, and quietly took hold of her hand under the tablecloth.

The Saloon also became Sotero's favorite place. As if books and the San Juan newspapers weren't enough, Sotero had stuffed a folder jammed with correspondence into his satchel just before boarding. He expected to catch up on his letter writing during the voyage.

Sotero's obsession with work was the only fly in Inocencia's perfect voyage. Her idea of a honeymoon at sea did not include his work obsession. So when she found him engrossed in paperwork, ink-stained drafts askew across the surface of his favorite corner table, she'd make it her business to distract him.

"Sotero!" she'd pout, using all the wiles of a winsome bride. "Oh! Oh my goodness. Come . . . just *look* at this view," or "Please, Sotero. Put the book down. Come. We'll take a nice long walk along the deck!"

"*Cómo molestas,*" he'd whisper under his breath in mock annoyance. But it didn't take long for his face to soften, or for his large hand to willingly extend towards his wife's.

Before breakfast, and every afternoon, the newlyweds strolled the deck arm in arm planning their future. Like mischievous school kids, they'd poke fun at the other passengers' peculiarities, accents or habits. They'd challenge each other on concocting the most outrageous stories about snobbish passengers, until the newlyweds would dissolve into peals of laughter. On occasion, they'd stroll the decks with others, but that was rare. Having eyes only for each other, Inocencia and Sotero took great care to be by themselves.

Their solitary evening walks bore their own special enchantment. Under a shield of silver stars, brilliant against a jet black sky, the lovers confided their true feelings. Like generations before them, they vowed never to part. Then, Inocencia would stretch out her arm clasping her fingers as if to grasp the stars.

"Oh, quick, Sotero! Catch me a good luck star that we can keep forever."

Sotero would chuckle softly, "Silly girl," and wrap his arms around her waist.

Before long, the ship's monotonous routine and cramped physical space began to grate on the passengers' nerves, and stories spun at mealtimes became a prime form of entertainment. Over candle light and smooth red wines, Inocencia sat wide-eyed, caught in the yarns the travelers told. Such tales held Inocencia captive at each meal, inspiring her, setting expectations for the unknown world she would find in New York.

On the fourth day, the *Knickerbocker* slammed into the storms.

Riding fierce waves on the high seas, Inocencia felt a cramping in the pit of her stomach and flew from the dining room. Treading unsteadily from deck to cabin, she was buffeted like a ragdoll at every turn as the steamship roiled about on intolerable swells. Sharp jabs attacked her intestines. She couldn't breathe. Her abdomen lurched in spasms, and she pressed her handkerchief tightly against her mouth. Stumbling into her cabin, she was afraid she would not make the berth in time to avoid public humiliation.

Inocencia looked pathetic clutching the small pillow against her stomach. "*Ay*, Sotero!" she wailed, "I'm going to die, I know it! This is what dying feels like." Sweaty and glassy-eyed, a profusion of damp ringlets clung to her pasty face. She released the pillow long enough to vomit into a metal pail beside her bed.

"*Ay*, Sotero," she cried in spurts, "now I *want* to die! Death is better than suffering what I'm going through right now!" And she vomited again.

By late afternoon, the ship's doctor staggered between deck railings and ship's walls on his way to pay the Figueroas a call. He was a portly American with a pencil-thin black mustache who wore a seaman's uniform similar to the ship's captain.

"Now, Madame Figueroa, we'll make you well in no time."

He took her wrist in his hand to count her pulse beats and searched her face for signs of serious illness. Finding none, he continued. "This treatment I'm going to prescribe is experimental. But we've had some success in using quinine for seasickness. I'll give you one dose now . . . a second dose will most likely be needed before we cure this bugger."

Inocencia lifted herself shakily on one elbow. She reached for the glass the doctor handed her. Spilling half of its contents, she tried to drink the water in spite of her trembling hand.

She tried to thank him with a half-smile that looked more like a sneer. Then, plunging headlong back into her pillow, she gave up the effort and surrendered to sleep.

⁂ ⁂ ⁂

By the seventh day of the voyage, the young bride's irritability had reached its peak. Three long, sharp blasts of the ship's foghorn signaled their arrival in New York Harbor.

From afar, she heard Sotero calling her name. Someone was shaking her by the shoulder, trying to awaken her. *Noooo,* she wanted to yell, but couldn't articulate the words because her tongue kept getting in the way. *I've barely slept after another day of retching seasickness! Now you want me to wake up!* Her weak arms flayed wildly against Sotero.

At first, he'd whispered, "Inocencia . . . Inocencia wake up! Come, love. Wake up." Then he brusquely shook his wife, trying to bring her to a sitting position. He braced his right arm underneath her shoulders in support and gently pulled her arm with his left, coaxing all the while, "That's it . . . that's it, my dear. Legs over the edge of the bed. That's a good girl, love. Now steady. Hold on to me and see if you can take a step."

When Inocencia blindly groped for the pillows, Sotero scolded, "Come now, Inocencia! You'll *hate* yourself if you miss a proper welcome from the Lady in the harbor."

Through dazed, puffy eyes, the young wife gazed languidly at her husband. Her mouth slack, Inocencia's head lolled about, as if she were half comatose. Suddenly, she turned abruptly to grasp the bucket on the floor and deposited the remainder of her morning coffee and roll.

Finally, Inocencia managed to stand up. Leaning against the edge of the bed, she pulled her dress over her head, plunged her arms into the sleeves and pulled down the long skirt. Once Sotero laced up her shoes, her legs were able to support her. She stood on her own and swayed her way to the deck, grabbing hold of every available railing, hand grip and banister.

⁂ ⁂ ⁂

She *was* radiant! There was no denying that. Neither Inocencia nor Sotero was prepared for the majesty of Lady Liberty. Standing on tiptoes, Inocencia marveled at the statue, her eyes roaming from the rays in the Lady's crown to her sandal-shod feet. The ship passed so close that the towering figure loomed over the vessel.

Completely copper clad, the gleaming woman's facial features were as clear as the folds in her gown.

"Look, Sotero. See how the Lady's torch glimmers through the mist?"

In the gloom of a steel gray sky, it seemed to Inocencia the torch burned exceedingly bright that Monday morning, the eighth day of July. She wondered if the blaze was meant to symbolize a new life.

"She is a sign," whispered Sotero, "a powerful symbol for an ideal. For a belief in freedom and liberty. And, perhaps, a symbol for our own freedom."

"Oh, yes! I agree. She welcomes everyone. And yet, look at her eyes. They seem to scan the open seas . . . almost defiantly. Oh, Sotero, she *is* a sign, isn't she? A golden inspiration."

Inocencia stared in awe at the statue for as long as it took the ship to steam past Buttermilk Channel and onward towards the North River. In the grip of the moment, her queasiness disappeared. She hadn't expected to be so enthralled by a statue. Glancing timidly at Sotero, Inocencia smiled, glad he'd not given up on rousing her from a sick bed.

Through the mist, Inocencia watched the harbor magically emerge. Teeming with all sorts of crafts and flags from all nations, large, graceful clippers vied for prominence over whalers and iron-clad frigates. A small escort tug floated alongside the S.S. *Knickerbocker.*

"Oh, those tiny ferry boats and tugboats are my favorites," she said, gripping her husband's arm. "Like toys in a sea of giants."

She glanced about at her fellow passengers, gauging their impressions of such wonders. *Why, almost every living soul on board the ship and the crew must be on this deck,* she thought. Among the ship's forty-two passengers, many of Inocencia's new friends reflected her rapture. Others simply shed tears.

*They must have left loved ones behind,* she mused.

The gray, soundless city loomed before them. Silently, the ship glided towards its destination. Inocencia and Sotero felt as if they alone drifted through the mist, drifted into the place where immigrant dreams were made or broken.

The mist shrouded cityscape, its tall buildings jutting like sabers through the haze, made Inocencia's knees feel weak. A confusion of emotions overwhelmed her. She suddenly felt like crying, where but a moment before she had been elated by the new sights and sounds. A sense of foreboding began to fill her heart.

Inocencia felt cold. She linked arms with Sotero, pressing her lithe body close to his. Suddenly, she was afraid, anxious she'd become separated from him while disembarking. Smiling broadly, he leaned his forehead towards hers. The glint of mischief that suddenly appeared in his dark eyes seemed to say, *I was right, wasn't I. You wouldn't have wanted to miss this.* She lowered worried eyelids and looked away. Reading his wife's anxiety as excitement about the city, he playfully squeezed her arm against his chest and laughed softly, unaware of his wife's inner turmoil.

# 2

## NEW YORK, 1889

A stranger in an alien land. That's how Inocencia felt as she picked up the small, red case where she kept her valuables, and followed Sotero's brisk pace down the gangplank. Once the ship's doctor had stamped their papers in their cabin, clearing the way for the Figueroas to disembark, Sotero had rushed off to find their baggage. All ten pieces of luggage and crates were duly accounted for, customs paid and inspected. When Sotero dashed after the trolley hauling their belongings through the maze of the enormous wharf, Inocencia lost sight of her husband. She was suddenly stranded in a bedlam of jostling bodies and unintelligible languages, lost among hundreds of newly arrived steerage passengers. Pushing her way through the crowds, afraid of getting mauled in the congestion, she yelled, "*¡Sotero!*" at the top of her lungs.

No response. Frantically she searched for him, peering into the faces of strangers who bore any physical resemblance to him. When she finally caught up with him, Inocencia was stunned speechless. Sotero was barking orders in English to the dock hands stacking his crates for transport. *I didn't even know Sotero spoke the English language!* There was more to learn about her husband than she'd realized.

As the couple neared the exit, a shirtless street peddler, wearing suspenders and a bowler hat over his stringy orange hair, suddenly blocked Inocencia's way. *Zoom!* He thrust a jiggling toy monkey into her face.

"*Eeh!*" she screeched, both hands flying up in protection.

Sotero rushed in front of her and shooed the man away. Shouting at the peddler, he grabbed his wife's red case from where it had fallen and handed it to her.

"These scoundrels! They hawk their garbage right in the faces of newcomers, especially steerage passengers. They rouse the greenhorns' curiosity, then easily separate them from their meager savings . . . poor devils. Why, I have a good mind to . . . "

"Please, Sotero, forget it. Let's just move on." Anxious to leave, she looked for the pier's exits and entryways. Many bore signs over the doorways. She understood "medical" and "information," but couldn't interpret the other signs. In the clash and clamor of dock hands handling crates, barrels and other containers around her, Inocencia could not deal with so much chaos. She failed to understand the questions posed in English by port officers intent on moving the passengers along in an orderly fashion.

At one point, she again became separated from her husband and found herself heading in the wrong direction. Caught in a melee between an immigrant family and an interpreter, a small child grabbed hold of the hem of her dress, thinking she was his mother. She stooped to help the boy just as a woman gruffly pulled the child away, scowling at Inocencia.

"I'm sorry. The boy was frightened . . . I was trying to help him."

Her eyes soon began to smart from fine particles of soot and dust that, in less than an hour, turned her white dress into a pale shade of gray. She tried to speak above the din, but a burst of hot, dank air filled her lungs so forcefully when she opened her mouth that she thought she was going to faint. Fatigued beyond endurance, Inocencia suddenly slumped into the outstretched arms of a summer-suited, long-bearded stranger.

✺ ✺ ✺

When she regained her composure, Sotero's arm rested gently against the small of her back.

"My dear, here's the man I spoke to you about . . . Don Juan Mata de Terreforte. Let's thank him as well for rescuing you from the mob."

Feeling disoriented, Inocencia held out a shaky, gloved hand. At first, she couldn't understand why the man standing before her seemed so dismal. Was something wrong? The worn, straw hat jauntily askew on his broad forehead contrasted with the ghostly pallor of his summer suit. His rheumy, dark eyes seemed downcast, and Inocencia hoped she'd find a hint of kindness in this tired stranger.

"Don Juan is a patriot, my dear, a veteran of the '68 Lares uprising. You were much too young to remember that time," Sotero laughed. "This old friend has made arrangements for us here in New York."

Inocencia gave a slight smile. *At least, this old timer has appeared to help us.*

As Don Juan arranged for transporting the luggage, Sotero cupped a hand under his wife's elbow and led her to an awaiting carriage. At last, Inocencia began to feel grounded. Pasting a forced smile on her face, she began to feel that New York was neither welcoming nor favorable. It was hot and dirty. Lacking the lush green foliage of her native land, it was downright ugly.

✺ ✺ ✺

A clawing humidity gripped the city in a stifling embrace. Heat shimmers rose, spirit-like, from puddles caught between the cobblestones. Throughout the carriage ride, Inocencia sat very still, taking short breaths so as not to gulp in large amounts of the foul humidity. Just then, the carriage rounded a bend, and Inocencia caught sight of the first of many sunless, garbage-strewn alleyways close to the docks. The area reeked of burning garbage. A rivulet of water running along the gutter carried rotted scraps of food. When she spied a large black rodent fishing out the scraps, she yelped in disgust.

Frenetic, street vignettes fascinated her, like accidents she couldn't turn away from watching. She gaped at a group of half-clad ragamuffins rolling hoops under a canopy of endless clotheslines. Outstretched lines of soggy wash dripped soapy water below and the hoop rollers raucously jostled against one another to receive the offerings.

She felt hot and sticky. She closed her eyes and imagined how delicious it would feel to have cool soapy water dripping on her bare skin. The narrow-brimmed hat with a fake rose on her head offered no relief from searing rays that plunged in and out of bloated clouds. Now and again she'd dab the moisture off her upper lip with the linen handkerchief she stored in the cuff of her sleeve. When she turned her attention to the conversation between the men, she found she had to strain her head forward to hear their words.

"Since the Lares uprising," Don Juan explained, "I've endured the bitter fruits of exile in this city. I can tell you, it could have been worse."

She remembered Sotero saying the two had shared a prison cell after the insurrection. So desperately did she want to ask about their friendship that she clenched her body, rigidly holding herself from rudely interrupting. Don Juan spoke in very low tones, directing his words only to

Sotero. Before long, Inocencia began to bristle in frustration. She hated being shut out, and tried again to catch their words above the racket of carriage wheels, traffic bells, whistles, shouts, horns and neighing horses.

"Yes, Don Sotero, you are certainly correct. Yes. It is the same here," she heard him say. "Our enemies here, and those who cause grief to our movement, are the same hard-headed fools you left behind. Here, you'll find support for your ideas . . . patriots like Juan Fraga and, of course, Rafael Serra. These men lead in organizing our people."

Don Juan paused for a moment to check the street names.

"Both are cigarmakers, you know, so you can count on their knowledge about the political situation and their ability to organize."

Inocencia hadn't heard those names before, but she could see at a glance that Sotero was keenly interested. *Perhaps he knows of them through their writings.*

"Tell me more about these organizations," urged Sotero raising his eyebrows in delight.

"Hah! I knew you'd be interested, my friend. Well, it is like this: Juan Fraga has organized Los Independientes. He owns a small cigar shop in Brooklyn, which is where the club meets. He's also a partner in Fraga and García, a cigar factory on Gates Avenue, but the club meets in the store on Fulton Street. Martí thinks highly of Fraga and his club."

"What is it about Fraga's club that's so special?" Sotero questioned.

"Ah! This is an important club. Martí sees it as the first of many dedicated to the independence movement of our islands.

"Serra's club is La Liga de Instucción y Recreo. It's political in the sense that one might say education is also political. Serra aims to uplift and inspire illiterate blacks, the poor, uneducated Cuban and Puerto Rican workers in this city."

"I'm impressed." Sotero wrinkled his brow. "I understand the recreation part, but how exactly does Serra's club instruct?"

"For one thing," said Don Juan nodding in approval, "the club sponsors literary forums and lectures to school our people regardless of the color of their skin or their poverty. Knowing you, Don Sotero, you'll probably want to join both. But, don't misunderstand me about the politics of education. Martí's a master at . . . "

Inocencia could bear it no longer and jumped into the conversation. "Oh, *please*, do forgive me for interrupting you, Don Juan. But what can you tell us about the women? Are there any women's associations?" She was specifically thinking of Doña Lola's women's group.

"Doña Inocencia," replied Don Juan politely, "the ladies *always* help at social functions. They bring grace and beauty to events sponsored by groups like the Hispanic American Beneficence Society, and to our many cultural *soirées*. Their feminine virtues allow them the honor of carrying the national flags in the parade of nations.

"But, let us speak of pressing issues. I believe, Don Sotero," Don Juan said as he tilted his head away from Inocencia, "that you'll find your accommodations quite adequate. Oh, it may not be as comfortable, at first, for your señora, but your printing press, inks, woodblock type and tables are awaiting you."

"How many rooms are there?" Inocencia interrupted sharply.

"Reams of printing paper of the highest quality, mind you," continued Don Juan, ignoring Inocencia's question. "Of the very best wood pulp. The club committee is investigating the rolling press and metal type which I'm told is the height of modernity."

"Sotero," she scolded. "Ask about the rooms!"

"Ah, the rooms. Small, but clean, decently furnished, but as I said before, you, señora, may wish to make changes."

"If Martí spoke honestly," said Sotero, thinking of his imminent publishing enterprise rather than domestic comfort, "and I mean without his usual flowery exaggerations, the print shop is a short walk from the newspaper publishing district, right? I recall he mentioned 'Park Row,' where the *New York Herald* and other newspapers are published?"

"Martí! Leave it to Martí! He knows what he wants, and what he's talking about," replied Don Juan. "Within a few short blocks, there's a thriving commercial district . . . with paper sellers, advertisement agencies, photographers, printers and printmakers. Your shop will be right there with those others, but not so close that you'll lose out to the competition."

"I appreciate all these efforts," Sotero said as he gave his wife a quick smile of inclusion.

"My friend, you'll be catering to a distinct international clientele . . . French, Germans, Italians . . . not just the Spanish-speakers."

*José Martí!* Inocencia beamed. That was a name she recognized!

A short ride brought the group to 284-286 Pearl Street, a building in a bustling commercial district of lower Manhattan. As the carriage came to a stop, Inocencia's face fell! She had never expected to see what stood before her.

"No! Oh no! This can't be!" Her eyes round in amazement, she alighted from the carriage onto the sidewalk, gawking in complete disbelief at what appeared to be two enormous storefronts with windows. The door between the storefronts was the one and only entry.

"This can't be our new home . . . it's nothing more than a store! A commercial establishment! How could this possibly be a home?"

Suddenly, her eyes welled up. About to spill all of the day's frustration, she turned towards Sotero for an explanation.

At that instant, a fast galloping horse pulling a wagon load of produce crates careened around the corner, spraying buckets of filthy gutter water onto the sidewalk in front of Number 284. As if to anoint Inocencia's disillusions even further, remnants of gutter filth, slop and horse manure suddenly drenched the bottom half of her once white travel dress.

Instantly, both men reached out to grab her by the arms, but they could only stare, helpless to mend the naked expression of humiliation on Inocencia's stunned face. Sotero stifled his impulse to grin. But, Don Juan understood the pain of displacement better than the newlyweds. He also well understood the ways of the city.

He extended a fatherly arm towards Inocencia and said, "Come, Doña Inocencia. Welcome to this unforgiving city of New York." At that moment, Inocencia's tears spilled freely down her cheeks. Still, these were hot, angry tears, a sign that she wasn't crying because she felt sorry for herself. "I *hate* this awful city," she declared, and picking up the hem of her soiled dress, she marched over to the carriage and collected her small red suitcase.

That night, flashes of light unleashed rolling thunder. The gray clouds that hovered over the city for most of the day spilled a torrent of pounding rain that settled into a steady downpour, its patter pulsating against the concrete sidewalks and dirt-filled alleyways.

Inocencia lay in an unfamiliar bed strangely comforted by the rhythmic, snoring of her husband beside her. She thought about all that had transpired: the beautiful wedding in the candle-lit cathedral, the smell of beeswax and incense, the subtle fragrance of flowers, the steamship making its way to New York's North River and the Lady in the harbor.

In the darkened room, illuminated now and again by waning stabs of light, Inocencia examined her new life. *That kitchen with that awful coal-burning stove . . . That closet of a sitting room. . . . No, it will never do to smother myself in cooking smoke in such a cramped space. But let's face it: I've never cooked a meal in my life! I'll write to Mamá, ask if she could send someone to help out.*

*First things first. I'll learn to speak English! How can I do that? Oh! Sotero spoke of a bookstore . . . Brentano! There's a Brentano Bookstore somewhere on Fifth Avenue. I'll go there, buy four, if I can afford it, maybe six, Spanish-English dictionaries. When I meet someone who doesn't speak Spanish, I'll hand that person a dictionary. Then I'll just open a second one for myself. This is so simple. It'll work . . . I know it will.*

Drowsily, Inocencia began to trace shadow outlines on the ceiling. She listened to the rain, to the noises of the night. An image of the street rat popped into her head, and she wondered if insects and unknown small animals were in the bedroom with them. Suddenly, she heard the sharp screech of an alley cat and jerked her head towards the midnight blue window.

Alive with silvery threads of rain, the room's back window faced a picket fence between an unassuming backyard and a narrow alleyway. On Inocencia's side of the fence stood three tall enclosures, dark, silent sentinels on nightly watch. Each one housed a public latrine.

# 3

# HAVANA, 1890

Lola slumped against the pillow she'd placed on the back of the armchair and chuckled, "So! They're married!"

She noticed the newsletter she held in her hand was dated Winter, 1889, the same year she and her family had arrived in Havana. *Goodness! That's almost two years already.* She pulled the fine silk shawl wrapped around her shoulders closer to her body to ward off the night's coolness, and chuckled again, recalling her own harried courtship.

It was close to midnight. The household had settled in till morning. Sounds from the nightly chorus of frogs and crickets surrounded the house, and the dim light of a kerosene lantern on the table next to Lola's armchair gave the sole pinprick of illumination.

*I've got to stay awake,* she thought stifling a yawn. *Hope Don Eusebio isn't late.* She strained to hear the distinctive snap of the burro flicking its tail, or hooves climbing the dusty trail behind the house. Silence. She returned to reading the newsletter of Los Independientes.

*I could easily have missed the reference to Sotero and Inocencia buried among a long list of events.* She scanned the rest of the contraband paper to see if there was other information about the couple. Finding none, she folded, then hid it among a batch of fashion clippings in the large straw, sewing basket by her feet along with other tidbits she was saving for Bonocio. She pictured her husband's broad smile when she'd hand him the concealed bounty, and heaved a deep sigh, counting the days until his return.

Lola read everything she could get her hands on about the liberation movement. She searched everywhere for news about her compatriots. Letters and Bonocio's trips connected her to the movement, guiding her underground activities in exile. Not a day went by that she didn't post three or four letters to patriots in Florida, New York or Paris.

Thinking again of Inocencia, Lola reflected, *That girl! In such a hurry to liberate the world. Hope she has an easier time of it in New York. How does she plan to free Puerto Rico from there. I wonder. I should write, tell her that here we've been thrust into the fiery cauldron of Cuban politics.*

Then, she yawned and thought of Patria and Laura asleep in their rooms. *At least my daughters are getting a good night's sleep, even if I'm not.* Shifting her shoulders to puff out the back pillow, she decided instead not to make herself too comfortable in case Don Eusebio arrived later than expected.

*Well, I guess it doesn't much matter where you end up. Exile takes an invisible toll on everyone's spirit. The anguish of separation cripples the entire family.*

An image of San Juan sprang to mind, and Lola's hand suddenly clutched her chest as if to grasp hold of an elusive memory. *That day! The day I freed the prisoners . . . Oh, what a glorious day it was!* The prisoners' letters full of gratitude were locked safely in her secretaire. She'd hand-tied the bundle with a striped yellow ribbon herself, but she was forgetting the *feel* of how it happened. That onset of forgetting frightened her, and she rushed to remind herself, *There's still much work to be done here . . . and in Puerto Rico.*

※ ※ ※

It was two in the morning when the soft bray of Don Eusebio's burro woke her up.

"Don Eusebio," Lola called out from the door in a loud whisper. "Is that you?"

"Sí, Doña Lola, it's me."

"What happened? Did you run into trouble?"

"No, señora, I didn't, but the *muchachos* bringing the boxes met up with a roadblock." Lola wrapped herself tightly in her shawl, picked up the lantern and went out to help the short, wiry man wearing a wide, red bandana tied firmly around his bushy hair. As craggy as a walnut, his face sported a large brush mustache that he wore with bravado. He grunted as he unloaded a barrel, then turned to unpack two smaller crates. All the while, he muttered soft sounds to keep the small beast still.

"*Ay*, Don Eusebio! You look exhausted. Wouldn't you want to stay in the shed until morning? Give yourself and the burro some rest?"

"I would, Doña Lola, believe me, I would." He spat out the black, road dust from his throat and wiped his lips with his hand. "But they're on the prowl tonight. I don't want to draw them to your house."

"Then, let's hurry."

Holding the lantern, Lola led Eusebio to the storage shed in the back of the house off the kitchen. He quickly rolled the barrel towards the side wall. Setting it upright under a shelf holding baskets of *yuca*, *yautía* and other root vegetables, he pulled off the heavy lid. Lola placed the lantern on the wood floor and quickly thrust her arm up to the elbow into the fragrant, shiny coffee beans. Midway, she felt the butt of a rifle.

"How many?" she asked.

"Two. Two precious Remingtons. The barrel is too small for more than that."

"Precious enough! Our poor Mambises have only machetes to defend themselves."

"One by one, Doña Lola. Without help from the exile communities, we build our arsenals very slowly."

Once Eusebio secured the lid back on the barrel, he scurried to the rear wall and lifted a plank from the floor. In the hollow space beneath it, he hid two crates of dynamite. Then he covered the crates with an old, soiled burlap bag and replaced the plank.

"Can't say exactly when someone'll come to get the goods," he said, dusting off his hands.

"Let's hope it'll be soon."

Within the half hour, the job was done. She had begun to catch Don Eusebio's nervousness, and when he refused her offer to have a cup of coffee with her, she knew with certainty how worried he really was. As Don Eusebio disappeared with the burro into the night, Lola breathed a sigh of relief.

Wrapped in her shawl, Lola stood alone in the dark, left to worry about the insurgent cause. It had pulled Bonocio away to foreign shores and left her to suffer his absences in silence, to guard their family and to temper the winds of war that were swiftly sweeping towards No. 52 Calle Virtudes, the family's home in exile.

# 4

## NEW YORK, 1892

On a blustery Sunday morning, the city of Brooklyn lay captive under a fierce January freeze. Dashing along the several blocks from Gates Avenue to Washington Street, Don Juan Fraga stole a furtive glance at the large clock by the barbershop. *Time is of the essence*, he admonished himself as he tried to quicken his pace. Bundled in a thick, woolen overcoat, Fraga was on his way to an important meeting. He bent his head forward to shield his face from the razor sharp headwinds, all the while holding on to his relic of a homburg with one gloved hand. He sported worn, but serviceable, brown leather gloves that he refused to trade in for a newer pair.

"It's a matter of comfort," he'd tell his wife, "not fashion." To which she would respond, "It's a matter of being a stubborn, old fool!"

In his haste, Fraga paid scant attention to the unusual morning's exertion. Before long, he was winded. His breath became labored and began to form puffs of steam on the checkered scarf he wore covering his mouth and almost all of his thick handlebar mustache. *All right,* he thought, *this is an important meeting, but I must slow down.* A moment's rest, and Fraga continued on his way, convinced it was far better to be a target on the move than to stand still and surrender to the elements. He hugged the wool cloth tightly around his neck. The closer he came to the East River, the more fiercely the winds swept around him.

On days like this, when the East River became a solid sheet of ice, the cigarmaker would brave the cold and wait in line to board a horse-drawn trolley across the Brooklyn-Manhattan Bridge instead of taking the cheaper Fulton Ferry, as was his custom. He thought briefly about the coming meeting. As he passed a newsstand, he glanced at the headlines and shifted his attention to the morning's news. An unanticipated decline in the stock market. Bold headlines in both the *Sun* and the *Tribune* confirmed that 1892 had begun on a dire note. There would be a break in diplomatic relations between the United States and Chile, stated other headlines, causing the impending slump in the market.

*Heavens forbid,* Fraga mouthed to himself. *News like this might deter some of the wealthier Cubans from attending the meeting and donating to the cause.*

Their great leader, José Martí, had requested that Don Juan, one of his most trusted allies, arrange a special meeting of their club, Los Independientes.

"It's time to discuss the mission and bylaws of the new revolutionary party," José Martí had confided in him just days earlier.

Without a moment's hesitation, Fraga had agreed. As he was president of that organization, the man felt a keen responsibility to arrive early and confer with Rafael Serra, the club's secretary. Nothing should be left to chance.

Aboard the trolley, Fraga removed a glove to search for the keys to the meeting place: the offices of Manuel Barranco and Co., known for marketing the popular El Progreso brand of tobacco. Once his thumb and index finger locked upon the cold metallic keys in the left-hand pocket of his overcoat, he relaxed until the trolley car unloaded its passengers on the Park Row side of the bridge. As the doors opened, Fraga tightened his checkered scarf, grimaced at the blast of icy air that smacked his cheeks and plunged towards the cavernous maze of small, brick streets and alleyways leading to 281 Pearl Street.

By midday, Fraga and Serra stood at the doors of the import-export company to welcome club members, friends and family. The crowd inside was electrifying. Over and over Fraga heard the same comment: "Don Juan, what is so important that you're calling a special meeting on a Sunday?" And always, his response was the same polite, "¡Compatriota! I can only assure you that you'll not regret joining us today."

Anticipating insider information about what was to transpire, early arrivals gravitated towards one another full of questions and speculations. Soon, the entire membership had assembled. Every soul in the room expected something spectacular was about to happen.

The source of such anticipation was no secret; it centered on one individual, José Martí, and what he had to say.

The man was of medium stature, but to everyone in the room, José Martí appeared to be larger than life. A slender figure clad in black, he entered the room and quietly stepped up to the podium. His fine-featured, pallid face stood out among his compatriots; its contours accentuated all the more by an overly broad forehead and thinning black hairline. Except for a dark, brush of a mustache that drew attention away from his thin lips and small chin, the leader was clean shaven.

For those who followed him, defended his ideals, it was the intensity of his dark eyes that defined the man. His were the eyes of an ancient soul or visionary who had been everywhere and had seen everything.

As soon as the assembled took note of him at the podium, they fell silent. Key members of Los Independientes— Juan Fraga, Benjamín Guerra, Gonzalo de Quesada and Sotero Figueroa—all expatriate leaders in their own right, stood behind Martí, forming a supportive column for the principles he would express that afternoon. Flanking each side of the podium, they took their seats.

Martí's gaze washed over his audience for what seemed to be an eternity. Juan Fraga began to fidget, showing signs of nervous impatience. He raised inquisitive eyebrows towards Sotero, silently questioning why Martí hadn't begun to speak. Giving an I-don't-know shrug, Sotero hoped he'd quelled Fraga's jitters.

Martí remained pensive, treating the moment with the respect it deserved. His gaze swept over the audience, dark eyes darting from one person to another, quietly seeking the woman from whom he would draw strength and resolution. What he was about to propose required great sacrifice and commitment from the people, even the shedding of their blood. He needed to know that she was there to lend him support, validate the courage of his convictions.

At last he saw her. Carmen Miyares de Mantilla sat small and inconspicuous in the last row. A thick, black fur scarf covered her neck. Her face was partially shielded by the veil of her black hat. These were flimsy protections for the lady, but she wished to remain unrecognized. Still, when his eyes found hers, she subtly touched her gloved fingers to her lips, offering a distant kiss as if she could wipe away his fears. The dark-eyed beauty was the love of his life, mother of the child whose image he carried in the inside vest pocket nearest his heart. She could never conceal her presence from him. In their private life, she was his muse, his inspiration. Their hearts, as he imagined in his poet's mind, had long ago chosen to beat as one, even though both were married to others.

Martí maintained eye contact with Carmen for as long as he could, drawing energy for the task that lay before him. When he turned towards the audience and began to speak, his lean, honest face expressed the solemnity of the moment, but his voice pulsated with raw, steadfast courage.

"We are here," Martí quietly declared, "to unify and reorganize the revolutionary Cubans in exile . . . and to encourage compatriots sympathetic to our cause to join in our efforts."

His eloquent, disciplined manner held the audience's undivided attention. Martí expressed realistic concerns about the mission they were preparing to embrace, the obstacles they were sure to face, and the historical significance of their sworn commitment. His soft intonation, as those assembled knew from experience, would slowly begin to rise until the force of his ideas seemed to overwhelm the very physical space in which they were gathered.

Some club members would later say the Master was bathed in the patriarchal aura of Old Testament seers; others saw a fiery visionary awakening symbolic flames of insurrection in the hearts of every Cuban and Puerto Rican seated in the room. As he presented the Articles of the Cuban Revolutionary Party, the party platform, and its Secret Bylaws, the philosopher of liberation evoked the essence of the revolution. Martí symbolically cloaked himself in the glorious flags of 1868: of the Cuban declaration at Yara and the Puerto Rican declaration at Lares. Raising his voice, he reached a stirring crescendo:

"The glue that will unite us is . . . the Cuban Revolutionary Party! With the support of all men of good will, *our party will forge the path to independence!*"

The audience rose to its feet as if it were one body and erupted in wild applause, and with its unconditional support, Los Independientes became the first of hundreds of patriotic associations to declare itself integral to the party.

The Cuban Revolutionary Party was going to war.

# 5

# NEW YORK, 1892

Inocencia cradled the hot brick wrapped in a thick towel and taking quick, cold steps, rushed towards her side of the bed. Using the iron footboard for leverage, she leaned forward and lay the bundle on the mattress. Quickly, Inocencia turned back the heavy quilt and slipped the towel wrapped brick underneath. Then she picked up the bottom of the pink cotton nightgown that covered her from neck to toes and slipped herself under the covers.

When she heard a soft whimper coming from the adjacent alcove, she cringed. "Oh, no," she said, creeping quietly out of her bed. Careful not to disturb the covered brick, she replaced the blankets and tiptoed to the small room where her children slept.

Inocencia gazed at the two little heads wearing night caps. Nothing was amiss. Reaching into Alexa's crib, she pulled the wool blanket up to her chin. Then, turning to Julia, Inocencia found the baby curled up into a ball, a bundle of bedding clutched in her tiny hand.

*Oh, you poor babe. No wonder you were whimpering.* Once Inocencia had covered the child, she rushed back to her own bed and dove under the quilt.

*Good! Everything is toasty warm. I can read the revolutionary papers comfortably until Sotero comes to bed. Except for my hands. And my head. They'll be cold.* She wondered if there was a way to read the papers Sotero had left for her without exposing her hands. There wasn't. Had she not missed the meeting, she wouldn't have to read about it with cold hands. On that day, Inocencia had decided it was much too cold to take the children outdoors; there was no one she could leave them with. *Now I wish I'd been there. It is the cause that counts, but still, couldn't I have bundled the children up?*

Against a mountain of pillows, Inocencia began to look over the new party's mission and bylaws, but images of Sotero at the meeting without her, probably surrounded by adoring women, would not leave her mind. In her mind beautiful women floated around her husband, while she was ugly, terribly uncoordinated. Worn out by household and children, she knew she looked like a pink balloon. A bloated pink balloon.

*Those early years in New York, how lovely they were at first. We went everywhere together: to meetings, lectures, to delightful restaurants and dances. Every day, a new adventure, an unexpected discovery! We laughed as we worked side by side. I'd keep an eye on Alexa in her carriage and proofread copy, helping him in the print shop. And now, now what? Two babies and a third on the way. Well. Nothing in life comes easy.*

*Oh, puff! I'm feeling sorry for myself even though I'm married to the most generous husband in the entire world. Didn't he rush to find us this house when Alexa was born? And when Julia arrived, he was the one who wrote to Mamá asking that she send my sisters to New York.*

Unable to sleep, Inocencia read the documents into the night, looking for the ways she'd play a role in the coming revolution. The first part called for the "united efforts of all men of goodwill to gain the absolute independence of the Island of Cuba and to promote and aid that of Puerto Rico." *Did they forget to stick in the word, "women"? Well, I'm sure they* mean *women as well as men. We've also been fighting for liberation.*

The second section was about the organizations that would make up the body of the party. It stressed the groups' allegiance to the party's mission. *Surely, they'll include women's clubs. And that means I should make haste to organize the women. It's my patriotic duty. We women must be equal partners in shaping our future.*

Much too cold to plan strategies, Inocencia dropped the pile of papers to the floor and scooted awkwardly under the covers to savor the remaining heat from the warmed brick. *You'd think I'd be used to the cold by now after spending three winters in this city.*

*⁂ ⁂ ⁂*

Within weeks, the fundamental principles of the Cuban Revolutionary Party were read, discussed and put to a vote in dozens of clubs from New York to Key West, from Philadelphia to Washington, Haiti, the Dominican Republic and Jamaica.

In Paris, the aging leader of the Lares revolt, Dr. Emeterio Betances, glowed with pride to learn the details of the party's founding. As dawn broke out over the rooftops of Rue Chateaudun, Betances dipped his pen into the inkwell, and wrote to Sotero.

*Amigo y compatriota,*

*I have read your letter with profound emotion, and it has been a great comfort for me: in it shines a sovereign faith more powerful than despotism, and because of that, capable of assuring the triumph of our sacred cause. I now have my reward— that the seed has not perished, and that the luxuriant tree of liberty lives on.*

# 6

# NEW YORK, 1892

A sharp stab of pain flashed across Inocencia's left ankle. She could not take one more step. She had finally located 1730 Broadway, but her poor feet felt like icicles. She'd discovered that Moroccan leather, the height of New York fashion, tended to stiffen in cold weather. *I would have been better off if I'd wrapped my feet in thick cardboard,* she mused as she held tightly onto the iron railing leading to the building's entrance. Inserting her gloved fingers in the narrow space between the shoe and her stockinged ankle, Inocencia pushed down to dislodge the rigid leather fold away from piercing her skin.

She had suffered for blocks walking along unforgiving pavement. Even the simple act of crossing streets had been fraught with unexpected dangers: Horse-drawn carriages zigzagged this way and that, moving in whatever direction best suited the drivers. There was no mechanism to control traffic in the city. She knew of people who had lost limbs, even their lives, in needless accidents. At one intersection, Inocencia thought she'd board a Broadway cable car, but the crowds so recklessly shoved their way into the vehicle that she did not have a chance of boarding the car. She'd not forgotten her traumatic encounter with crowds at the pier when she arrived in New York three years earlier and decided to continue on foot.

That frosty morning, Inocencia had mistaken a building numbered 1780 for 1730. Without thinking, she'd asked the carriage driver to let her off. Once she realized her mistake, there wasn't another carriage in sight. And so she'd clutched her fur-trimmed cloak tightly against her body and began to count the number of drab, dirty streets she'd have to walk.

As she made her way along Broadway, she looked for a respectable tea room or beer garden. Aching to rub the warmth back into her toes, she dreamed of slipping out of her shoes under cover of an ample tablecloth. One German Lager House, its polished oak walls and tables beckoning, drew her attention. Women and children, she noticed, intermingled among the customers. Slowly negotiating three narrow steps, Inocencia looked for an inconspicuous table where she might sit, imagining the delicious feel of the warm interior. But when she caught a whiff of the cured liver sausages set out on a corner counter and the odors of hard boiled eggs, breads, luncheon meats, cheeses and pickles, she began to gag. Bolting out of the lager house, she tried not to vomit. But she couldn't help but double over in the narrow alley next door to the beer garden.

Finally, Inocencia had arrived at her destination. The building on Broadway turned out to be an upscale multiple family dwelling. The words, "The Rockerham," were chiseled over the front doors. This time, Inocencia made absolutely certain this building bore the numbers 1-7-3-0. She wiped her lips for any tell-tale sign of moisture, entered the building and asked the doorman. "Which flat belongs to the Villaverdes?"

Two crusty, battle-scarred warriors of Cuba's Ten Years' War, Cirilo and Emilia Villaverde, had lived in exile for most of their lives. Don Cirilo, a lawyer who'd been writing political tracts for years, claimed it was the most effective tool to voice his outrage against the atrocities of the colonial system. And Doña Emilia penned articles and letters to the newspapers in the expatriate community. She was also known for her feisty temperament, a reputation she put to good use in political organizing. A woman of action, she bowed before no one. Her attitude had always been, "You are either with me or against me," and while she would never admit to it, her greatest flaw was a stubborn inability to compromise.

One of Emilia's great successes was establishing the Liga de las Hijas de Cuba, the first women's group of the war of 1868. Las Hijas supplied munitions and volunteers for the Cuban Army of Liberation, and throughout the course of the war, the army came to rely on the club's donations of weapons and ammunition, medicines, clothing and money.

Because of these and other revolutionary activities, Doña Emilia and her husband Cirilo were targeted as "enemies of the state" by the Spanish government. And that's exactly what they were to the Spaniards who controlled Cuba. Cirilo was one among many dissidents attacking the Spanish empire, but Doña Emilia was a new sort of irritant. At a time when women were shunned for meddling in the public affairs of men, this courageous woman persisted defying male authority.

⁂ ⁂ ⁂

On the morning of Inocencia's visit, the housekeeper answered the door. Mary McDonald's shock of fading red curls, upturned nose and dark blue eyes hinted at the comely young woman she'd once been. But on this day she did not present a welcoming figure. As severe as the black dress and starched-white apron she wore was her disdainful scowl at the caller. *Perhaps I've made a mistake,* Inocencia wondered, as Mary McDonald's cold glare took stock of the store-bought quality of the fur trimmed cloak, calculating the visitor's modest means.

Mrs. McDonald hadn't set out to be rude. She simply felt it was her duty to screen visitors before letting them in to see the Villaverdes, of whom she was extremely protective.

"Please, Madame, excuse me, but I may please see Doña Emilia?" Inocencia was nervous, not quite sure if she'd pronounced the English words correctly. Her strong Spanish accent and mispronunciations worried her.

"Madame Villaverde does not usually entertain visitors at this hour . . . but I'll see what I can do," She said after accepting a calling card from Inocencia. "If you like, you may wait in the library. It's warmer there."

The library enfolded Inocencia like a woolen blanket. Inhaling the pungent fragrance of burning mulberry logs, she dropped her muff on a side chair and hurried towards the *pop, pop, crackle* sounds of the hearth. It wasn't long before Inocencia had actually slipped off her shoes, allowing her stockinged feet to sink greedily into a soft Persian carpet. Wiggling her toes into the fiber, she imagined digging her feet into the white sand beaches of the Caribbean.

"Mmmmm," she moaned softly, aware only of tiny tingles spreading like needles throughout her body. *I'll just quickly step into my shoes if I hear someone coming.*

As feeling returned to her limbs, she began to explore the room. She reached for a figurine on a shelf, then fought the impulse. She would not peek into cabinets, thumb through books, or pick up the framed pictures on the mantle. But she did run her fingers along the back of a green velvet armchair, noticing how it sat, just right, in front of the roaring fire. The white coverlet casually draped over its armrest raised images of the armchair's ample embrace on wintry afternoons.

*If only Kirina and Doly could see me in this amazing space, they would love it. Sotero, too. Our home is always so cramped with people, but this . . . this room is so special.* She smiled, wondering what it would be like to hear the boisterous laughter of Alexa and Julia romping before her on the plush carpet. How rosy their cheeks would be as their chubby arms reached out to her.

Carefully treading towards the tall windows, Inocencia pushed the drapery aside. She craned her neck to view the street below. Dozens of people were braving the windswept, bustling thoroughfare. A woman swept by, huddled stiffly in fur capes. Her gloved arms were tucked into an oversized fur muff. She took tiny steps, like an ungraceful dancer without a partner. Two young men, bank clerks from the looks of their somber dress, crossed Broadway. They reminded Inocencia of stringless marionettes, struggling to maintain their balance. One held tightly to the brim of his black, bowler lest the wind sweep it away. The other held tightly to his partner. Inocencia laughed, then caught a glimpse of an enormous feathered monstrosity of a hat, beneath which a young lady clung to the arm of an older woman. *Is the older woman her mother?* wondered Inocencia, loving the street theatrics displayed down below.

Suddenly, Inocencia caught her breath. The scent of gardenias filled the room. She heard the rustle of a taffeta gown, followed by the soft click of the door's brass latch. Someone had entered the room. To her embarrassment, Inocencia was too far away from her high-cut shoes to slip unnoticeably into them. She turned slowly towards the door and faced Emilia Casanova de Villaverde.

The older woman was of medium stature, neither lean nor plump. She wore a black, crisp day dress that hung loosely over her matronly frame. Spider-veined lids shaded rheumy, brown eyes. Wisps of graying tendrils escaped from the confinement of an unadorned *chignon* at the nape of Doña Emilia's neck. Along with a fringe of frizzy bangs, errant curls helped dispel the otherwise stern appearance of the feisty *doyenne* of the revolutionary clubs.

*So this is the patriot the Spaniards burned in effigy,* thought Inocencia, somewhat stunned to find the famous woman so unassuming.

Emilia dropped her gaze and read the name on the calling card. She studied the young woman bathed in the window's anemic morning light. Then she saw the shoes. One stood upright, the other rested on its side beside the fireplace. *Emilita loved to take her shoes off just like that, in front of the library's stone hearth at the Casanova Mansion!* Doña Emilia hadn't thought of her daughter's pranks in decades!

She had met Don Sotero through José Martí, but not Inocencia Figueroa. Still, the *doyenne* hardly expected her to be standing barefoot on the priceless Persian rug in her library. *What sort of woman is this, who defies propriety? Who would dare to engage in such unladylike behavior so soon upon meeting me.* She grimaced, not a wide gesture, for that was not in Doña Emilia's character. *There's a vulnerability about this woman . . . so much like my beloved Emilita.*

"*Por favor*, Señora de Figueroa, make yourself comfortable. It is a pleasure to finally meet you. I've met Don Sotero, of course, and now it is my honor to make your acquaintance. Oh, but Mary should have taken your coat and hat. I'll have her take your things and bring us some coffee and warm rolls."

"*Gracias*, Doña Emilia. May I call you that? I feel as if I've known *you* for a long time. I've wanted so much to ask for your guidance. The pleasure is all mine, I assure you."

Inocencia spoke more rapidly than usual, hoping to distract the lady with words while she thrust her feet into the discarded shoes. Then she attended to removing her outerwear.

Doña Emilia waited patiently, a glint of amusement in her fading eyes. Her hands folded in front of her, she remained standing while Inocencia fumbled with her things. Without a sound, Mary McDonald had entered the room carrying a tray of steaming coffee, warm cream and sugary sweet rolls. She too awaited Inocencia's hat and coat. As Inocencia handed hat, cloak and muff to Mrs. McDonald, Doña Emilia noticed the slight bulge around her visitor's waist. *She doesn't wear stays, this one*, reflected Emilia, and smiled to herself, pleased that in the matter of corsets this young lady had a mind of her own. Then it dawned on her. *No, Emilia! This woman is pregnant!*

# 7

## NEW YORK, 1892

"I like 'Mercedes Varona,' don't you? As the name for my club?" Inocencia turned towards Doña Emilia with a radiant smile that erased all traces of her initial shyness.

"My dear Inocencia, the club will bear whatever name *you* decide. You are its creator," responded Emilia.

"Well, then I've decided! My club will be 'Mercedes Varona!'"

Brimming with all sorts of ideas, she confided her plans to Doña Emilia as if they had always been friends. She shifted excitedly in her seat, carelessly unbalancing the cup and saucer she held in her hand. Saving the china, Inocencia could not save the small silver spoon that toppled into her lap. Quickly, she glanced up at Doña Emilia in embarrassment.

*Inocencia's enthusiasm will get the best of her yet.* Doña Emilia pretended not to notice the potential mishap. Her guest managed to place spoon, cup and saucer on the side table next to her chair without further incident. Recovering her poise, Inocencia settled back, thinking herself to be the luckiest person in all of New York. She was spending time with the famous Doña Emilia in the exquisite library of her home. After the incident of her misplaced shoes, she was surprised to feel so much at ease. But the *doyenne* had shown exceptional patience. She seemed to like Inocencia.

"Mercedes Varona." Inocencia savored the melodious sounds and syllables of the club's name. "Yes!" she affirmed. "The name honors the movement and honors women as patriotic as yourself, Doña Emilia, who sacrificed so much for Cuba. But, I must confide, the whole thing seems daunting to me."

"Are you sure you're ready for such an important step?" Emilia arched an eyebrow.

*What if I fail?* Inocencia thought, secluding her fears in the flickering of the burning logs. The shape shifting orange and gold flames held her rapt attention. She thought of the wives and daughters of the expatriates coming to join her club. Women's faces shimmered in the glow of the fire, inquisitive voices rose, all speaking at once. For the first time in their lives, the club women would share in a process of reasoning and debate.

*Here, we all work as equals for liberation, reach accord about fundraising events,* she imagined herself saying in her most professional voice. *We discuss editorials, add our opinions to the political arguments of the day according to our own beliefs.*

"This club could be like Doña Lola's women's group, where ideas are discussed and exchanged, except that 'Mercedes Varona' will have rules and resolutions."

"Inocencia, I do believe you're ready," Emilia laughed as she rose from the green armchair.

At the lady's desk near the door, the *doyenne* was in her element. She pulled out a sheet of paper from the center drawer, opened the small crystal bottle of black India ink on a silver tray on top of the desk and, after dousing her pen with ink, began to jot down the steps needed to form an organization.

Inocencia joined Emilia at the desk, and the two heads bent over the document. Together, they crossed out unworkable ideas—no, the club will not rotate its meetings—replacing them with fresh ideas—yes, there will be a yearly gala. Emilia handed the notes to her new young friend. "Now it's up to you to write the club's mission statement." Inocencia read the document in silence, visualizing the club's formation. *What an important asset for the movement,* she thought, holding the paper by its corners as if it were made of gold. Smiling at Doña Emilia, she said softly, "Thank you." She knew that without Doña Emilia's help, her club would still be on her wishlist.

They spent the morning drawing up bylaws, calls for meetings, lists of activities and other details. Neither woman seemed aware of the number of hours they'd devoted to the business of organizing until Doña Emilia humorously quipped, "Doña Inocencia, in my country there's a saying, 'my stomach is beginning to think my head has been cut off.' In other words, it is appropriate to entertain the notion of a mid-day meal! You can re-visit the mission statement after we've nourished our bodies and given our brains a chance to rest."

Over the meal, Inocencia discovered Doña Emilia's softer side. She'd heard much about the woman's stern character, but she didn't know Doña Emilia was also known for generosity. Her private fortune had gone towards helping refugee families, but hardly anyone gave her credit for that.

Inocencia told tales about her life, her children and her friendship with the Serra family.

"It's all very casual, you understand . . . our visits. They're like family outings. We sit around the kitchen table—nothing like your elegant dining room . . . "

Emilia interrupted, "I do know the Serras, Inocencia. And I admire the work they're doing for the expatriate community."

"Then you know Consuelo, their daughter. She wants to be a school teacher. Imagine that!" Inocencia beamed.

"I must say that while I'm impressed with Don Rafael's writings about justice and discrimination," continued Inocencia. "I'm more impressed with his wife, Doña Gertrudis. She's an *educated* woman, you know. A midwife. She brought my babies into the world."

"And, a person of high ideals," said Doña Emilia. "When we talk about creating organizations to help promote a cause, an ideal, we're also talking about committed women, Inocencia. *You* are a committed woman."

Feeling a blush creeping into her checks at Doña Emilia's compliment, Inocencia lowered her eyelids and dabbed her lips with a napkin. She didn't know quite what to say, but she was relieved of saying anything when Doña Emilia suggested they take their coffee in the library.

🌸 🌸 🌸

"It's . . . I don't know, difficult to explain even to myself, who lived through the experience," reflected Doña Emilia, taking small sips of black coffee. "Can you imagine my euphoria, my dear, from that moment when I first saw the flag of liberation waving freely in the breeze of a dawning day? I felt such reverence, such powerful emotions that I knew right then, right at that moment, that I would commit my life to fighting for independence.

"I heard the rapid fire of rifle shots—rat, tat, tat, tat—and awoke with a jolt. Can you put yourself in my shoes? Visualize my fears? All mixed up with a sense of exhilaration like nothing I'd ever felt before, being a girl of eighteen. I threw open my bedroom window and, there it was, the beautiful flag of liberation! And I *knew* the wait was over. The insurrection had begun in earnest."

Chills rolled up Inocencia's spine. She overflowed with admiration for this woman who had done so much in her lifetime, but there was no equivalent Puerto Rican flag story in Inocencia's experience. *Perhaps, the flag of Lares, but she was only two years old in 1868.*

Listening to Emilia's story, Inocencia began to understand. Dedicating a club to the valor of one young woman had enormous implications. *Through 'Mercedes Varona,' we honor all the women who've struggled . . . maybe for a personal kind of liberation, or equality for oppressed groups of people on a much grander scale! But hadn't I known that from the women's group! Hadn't I always thought of women's equality in the past? Why had I forgotten?*

Not since the days in Puerto Rico, when she discussed such matters with Doña Lola, had Inocencia felt so alive, so in control of what she wanted, and not what others expected of her.

Suddenly, the seeds of liberation sprouted endless possibilities: *liberation for the masses, no matter your class or the color of your skin, not even your sex. "Freedom means equality!" How many times have I heard Sotero and Rafael Serra say that? Of course, they mean racial equality and justice, but doesn't that also extend to women?*

All of this she related to Doña Emilia in a rush of words that caught the older woman by surprise.

"And who better than Serra to explain justice and equality?" declared Inocencia. "Dedication to a cause? Don Rafael throws himself into educating the working poor, the black and the white, swears it will improve their lot in life. *That* is commitment."

*Why had I forgotten? Three years of listening to compatriots in the movement must have prepared me for something ... for forming 'Mercedes Varona.' What was it Martí and Don Rafael always said? Oh yes!* Inocencia locked wide eyes, ablaze with excitement, with those of Doña Emilia, and recited aloud, "We must fight for a freedom that is with all, and for the good of all!"

"I agree!" Emilia shouted, recognizing Martí's words.

"Doña Emilia, this time, our movement will succeed. This time, it's different. Martí and my husband have made a difference. The newspaper, *Patria,* will unify our efforts. And hundreds of organizations! They continue to form, committed to the struggle. And not just here in New York, señora, but everywhere, in Tampa, Key West, Philadelphia and other cities, and the revolution will be supported. This time, señora, it is different."

Energized by Inocencia's exuberance, Doña Emilia's dark eyes also glistened with excitement.

The woman who sat in the hansom cab bound for home that afternoon was a more mature and independent Inocencia Figueroa than the timid lady of the frozen feet who'd sat in the Villaverde library that morning. Aglow with a mission and the promise of bringing new meaning into her life, she no longer feared the stone-cold streets. She felt giddy, anxious to get home to share her impressions of the day with Sotero.

Inocencia had thrust her gloved hands into the fur muff as she mulled over everything that had happened, when her hand came across a slip of paper. *What's this? Oh, it's that slip of paper I picked up on the front steps before I entered the carriage.* Slipping it out of the muff, she began to unfold the note. It was difficult to read in the wintry light, but she slowly made out the scrawled message:

"Have you considered, Doña Figueroa, where your husband spends his evenings away from home?"

Inocencia froze. Disgusted by the note's insinuation, she crumpled up the slip of paper. Then she reopened it to tear it into pieces. Turning to fling the scraps out of the cab window, Inocencia gasped and dropped them on the floor. As a flutter of butterfly wings filled her abdomen, her right hand moved quickly to shield her unborn child.

# 8

# HAVANA, 1892

As exile settled into a routine, Lola and Bonocio's living room became the frequent setting for literary and political salons. At one lazy afternoon meeting devoid of more serious political plotting, Lola felt inspired to recite a few verses from her new collection. She stood by the piano so that she could glance at her pages without interrupting the performance. Quickly scanning the verses, she selected a poem about personal survival in the midst of upheaval. When the only sound in the room was the subtle swish of her taffeta skirt, she began to recite.

Her eyes glimmered like river stones, and a reverent hush fell over the guests. Reaching the last stanza, Lola gazed dramatically around the room and passionately recited, *"Porque la patria llevo conmigo"*—because I carry my homeland within me. Eyes closed, chin slightly raised, she slowly dropped her head to her chest and repeated in a stage whisper, *"Porque la patria llevo conmigo."*

*"Brava, brava!"* Shouted the guests bursting into loud applause. Lola simply smiled, a round faced, dimpled smile that endeared her even more to the appreciative audience.

"I'm so gratified by your response. You see, this collection, *Mi Libro de Cuba,* is special. Here, let me read the dedication aloud. *Cuba y Puerto Rico son/ de un pájaro las dos alas*—Cuba and Puerto Rico are the two wings of the same bird.

"*Ay*, how contentious these words have become . . . and perhaps they should be because we should never forget them. I have always felt that I am a child of the Antilles. In my heart and mind, I've never felt a stranger in any of the places I've lived. *Because I carry the nation within me.*"

Breaking into raucous chanting, a few of the guests joined in repeating the closing line of Lola's poem, "*I carry the nation within me.*"

"Doña Lola," shouted one of Patria's young admirers, "you can't leave us with only one recitation. Give us more, give us more . . . "

Now, a chorus of "*give us more, give us more*" caught fire, rising to a crescendo of voices. And Lola selected one more poem. It was a four-stanza poem entitled, *Absent,* which obviously referred to Bonocio's frequent travels.

"And how is it that your family ended up in Havana?" asked one of Patria's colleagues.

"Well, if you haven't heard the story . . . My goodness it was recited everywhere! As it happened, Bonocio had been invited to give a speech during the intermission of a new play at the public theater in Cabo Rojo.

"Bonocio's presentation was on liberty, mind you, a fiery indictment of the colonial government."

"Hear, hear!" echoed the guests.

"My poor husband poured his heart and soul into it. Everyone cheered and clapped and stomped their feet, but the town mayor found it infuriating, meant to provoke mayhem, and shouted, 'Bring down that curtain!'

"I jumped out of my seat, ran up to that stage and grabbed the curtain's edge, lifting it as far as I could with my short arms, way up in the air to keep it from dropping, all the while yelling at the top of my lungs, 'Aren't there any *men* here?'

"A number of our compatriots scrambled to their feet and came to help me. Poor Bonocio was in total shock. He never expected me to react so, so . . . physically! He completed the presentation amid delirious applause.

"Oh, I can tell you." Lola sighed wistfully, her gaze more in the past than with her friends. "I can tell you we had a number of narrow escapes in Puerto Rico.

"The next day, when I came home, the house was empty. Bonocio had fled some two hours before the authorities knocked on our door with an order for his exile. I closed up the house, prepared my daughters, and we followed him here, to Havana."

Her forlorn note resonated with countless tales of others who'd fled on a moment's notice, and others who hadn't made it at all.

"¡Ay, basta! Enough about my family's perils. Let's get on with the business of the afternoon. Pichardo!" Lola turned to the founder of the literary review, *El Figaro*. "Would you like to share something from your magazine?"

Pichardo chose a short poem to bring the afternoon salon to a close, but promised to deliver some interesting, controversial works at the next meeting.

⁂ ⁂ ⁂

The following Sunday, the salon met again. Pichardo had forgotten his promise to bring something controversial to read aloud, but circulated flyers announcing a literary contest his magazine was sponsoring. Some guests discussed literary styles; others pondered elements of abuse in law and order.

In one corner, Lola peered over her spectacles. She got up from her rocker to wander about and chat with one group, then another, gathering news and commitments. Her pleasant face was a perfect cover. She had eyes and ears everywhere, alert to where everyone was, and what they were saying. To an outsider, it seemed to be a perfect, leisurely event. But at the core of Lola's social afternoon, conspiracy bloomed like a tropical garden. Everywhere, information buzzed. Requests made and granted that afternoon vied with news of arrests and near captures. Money neatly stitched into the hems of ladies' garments exchanged hands, and contraband newspapers passed from one reader to the next.

"Our strength," argued a well-heeled revolutionary, "is in the eastern provinces. There, rebel generals are winning every battle. But, I ask you, where are the volunteers? Why must our supplies come through Havana and not through secure coves along the coast?"

"*Cálmese,* señor," responded a recently arrived expatriate, "I think we should be demanding weapons, not volunteers. Weapons are easier to transport than groups of inexperienced well-wishers!"

Lola registered all this while inching her way towards the women writers.

"The quinine *must* be transported to secret destinations. Otherwise, the rebels will never receive the cargo." Quick to realize the high cost of quinine was also an issue, Doña Aurelia suddenly cried out, "Jewelry! We must sell our jewelry if we're serious about raising such large amounts of money!"

"But, my dear," responded Doña Mercedes, "the problem is in the *lines* of communication between New York and the Cuban rebel cells. The rebels can't seem to protect them."

Lola stood at the cross hairs, mindfully attentive, capturing every word and nuance. That night she'd play the pivotal role of covert correspondent.

Suddenly, insistent pounding rattled the front door. Lola signaled for silence, placing her index finger over her lips. With a slight shift of her head, she signaled Rosa, the housekeeper, to open the door. There stood two members of Havana's *Guardia Civil*, the police!

"*Buenas tardes*," said the one in charge.

His slow-moving subordinate mutely studied the house, taking visual inventory of its surroundings and counting the number of carriages awaiting their passengers.

Lola came to the door.

"Ah, Doña Lola! Someone reported a commotion coming from your house."

"No, señor. *¿Cómo puede ser?* That can't be true. But please excuse whatever noise we *may* have made. You see, my daughter invited some university students for afternoon coffee. . . . Well, you know how it is. We were laughing, enjoying ourselves, perhaps talking too loudly, just having a small celebration."

Her mirthful words tumbled one against the other in a ploy to keep the policemen at bay with easy chatter.

"Ay, señores," she laughed, "thank you for stopping by, but I can assure you, everything is as it should be. Perhaps a drink of water before you depart? Or something stronger?"

The policemen, whose arms cradled rifles almost as tall as themselves, glanced around again, but didn't attempt to gain entry. "*No se moleste*—don't bother yourself, Doña Lola. We'll keep watch for a while . . . for your own safety, you understand."

# 9

# SANTA CLARA, 1892

Several days after the Guardia Civil disrupted Lola's gathering, Doña Marta de Abreu sat in the drawing room of her Santa Clara estate. On her lap was a letter from Havana. A deep furrow appeared between her thick dark brows. She narrowed her eyes, curious about the letter's content, and smoothed back an abundance of steel gray hair piled high on top of her head. She fussed a bit with the envelope, then she reached for the *lorgnette* that hung around her neck on a black ribbon. Doña Marta's keen dark eyes and insightful intelligence were known to cut through a conversation like a knife sharpened for the kill. She had the same skill with the written word.

She felt the weight of the letter in her hand and wondered if it was short and to the point, or if it involved complications. Opening it, she found a delightfully chatty account from her dear friend in Havana. Doña Marta's young son, Pedro Estévez, was living with the Tió's in Havana while he attended secondary school. And Lola wrote to report that he was doing just fine, that Patria and Laura sent warm embrace, and at that very moment, were on their way to the dentist. As for Bonocio, he was once again traveling abroad.

Regarding the political situation in Havana, "nothing much is happening here of interest except that Bonocio and

I attended a lecture recently and the *only speaker worth his salt was Sotero Figueroa.* He came from New York *especially to make a presentation.*"

On the heels of that pointed observation, Lola jumped into matters of health. She had not been at all well, afflicted with very high fevers. "As you well remember, my dearest Marta, how important it is to have the quinine on hand because these wretched fevers are just intolerable."

Doña Marta carefully refolded the letter and placed it in the pocket of her house dress before storing it under lock and key in the strong box with the others. She gazed pensively at the yellow primroses blooming outside on the veranda. After a while, a sparkle appeared in her dark eyes. She'd figured out exactly how to arrange what Doña Lola was asking her to do.

# 10

## NEW YORK, 1892

On the day Inocencia prepared to open the Club Mercedes Varona, she dreamt about Doña Lola. She recalled Lola saying something about finding your own path in your personal life.

"*Ay*, Lola! Today I need your strength, not your advice." *I'm a bundle of nerves and can't seem to do anything right. I must concentrate only on the club.*

"Anita!" Inocencia called from the upstairs bedroom. "I asked you to please help Alexa change her dress." *That girl infuriates me! Makes me want to send her back to Mamá in Puerto Rico!* Before leaving the bedroom, Inocencia stuffed a clean handkerchief into her sleeve, then glanced at her image in the mirror. She sighed. Letting out the seams of the soft gray dress she wore did nothing to hide the fact that she was almost full term.

*Suppose the women decide not to come,* she thought as she descended into the parlor. *Maybe liberation doesn't run deep in their veins . . . their husbands may have told them not to attend. What then?*

She had good reason to worry. Even in these modern times, Inocencia knew that Cuban or Puerto Rican woman couldn't always express a will of their own, nor could they come and go as they pleased. Besides, expatriate families knew enemy spies lurked among them. Pinkerton agents had wormed their way into their ranks. There were also rumors of shady characters in the pay of the colonial government out to destroy the independence movement. Most of all, Inocencia worried no one would come because it was she, and not the more mature and well-known women leaders, who called the meeting.

By early afternoon no one had arrived. Whenever Inocencia heard a noise outside, she'd rush to peek out of the front bay windows, her eyes eventually wandering up to a cloud-covered sky threatening rain or snow. *I wish they'd get here. I did say early afternoon. . . . I did say "my home at 235 E. 75th Street," didn't I? If they missed the Second Avenue El, I'm certain they know to take the Third Avenue train.*

Calling again to Anita, Inocencia closed the curtain and turned away from the window.

"Oh, there you are. *Por favor*, child, pay attention. They'll be here any minute now! See that the parlor is in perfect order. And tell the children to play quietly in their bedroom. Oh, and Anita, ask the señoritas Doly and Kirina to join me in the parlor as soon as they can."

"Sí, señora," responded the exasperated girl, not masking a disgruntled undertone in her voice. *How many times is the mistress going to say the same thing? Does she think I'm deaf?*

Anita trudged up to the second-floor bedrooms, festering with annoyance at each step. When she heard a high-pitched squeal coming from the children's room, Anita lingered on the stairs. Turning her eyes to slits, she painted a matching scowl on her lean, birdlike face and marched into the children's room to quiet them down.

Suddenly, the women were at the door!

"Inocencia! My dear, you look lovely," gushed Laudelina Sosa, removing her hat and gloves in the crowded foyer. Everyone was speaking at once. Eva Betancourt gave Inocencia an unexpectedly forceful hug that would have thrown the hostess off balance, if Doña Gertrudis Heredia hadn't grabbed her arm and kept her on her feet. Gertrudis smiled warmly, whispering in Inocencia's ear, "My dear friend, despite everything, you've moved forward! I'm very proud of you."

They arrived in three separate groups. Some had traveled together, others came in cabs and one or two found it more convenient to ride the elevated trains. To Inocencia's delight, the recalcitrant Anita suddenly embraced the challenge of transferring cloaks and wraps to the hall closet, as if she had been born to the service class. Impressed by the dress and demeanor of the women, Anita behaved with dignity.

Inocencia ushered her friends into the modest parlor.

"Please, make yourselves at home," she said, invoking the familiar, *"Mi casa es su casa,"* and gesturing graciously towards the brown plush sofa and chairs she had recently bought on sale at Macy's. Glancing towards Anita, she signaled the girl to prepare hot chocolate for the guests.

"I just adore these quaint, row houses," Doña Eva whispered to María Acosta, as the women took seats in the parlor. She had already nosed about the formal spaces of the Figueroa home, and knew this simple house had survived the wear and tear of several generations. "They're quite a distance from the city, but elevated trains are such a convenience. I know quite a few families—respectable Negro families—that have homes in this neighborhood."

"And does it surprise you that families come here to live?" quipped María Acosta, irritated by Doña Eva's snobbery. When it came to issues of working-class self-improvement, Doña María had no patience with well-to-do women who never ventured beyond their privileged lives.

"Who wouldn't want to live here instead of the tenements? Tenements are congested breeding grounds for disease!" She took a steaming cup of hot chocolate from the serving tray Anita held before her and continued lecturing Doña Eva.

"I can't imagine how the steady stream of immigrants, fresh off the boats at Ellis Island, manage to live in those tenements, families of ten or twelve stuffed into two rooms. The ones who move up to the row houses on Third Avenue are the lucky ones. Still, there should be laws to regulate health and sanitation in this city."

Doña Laudelina's ears perked up. "*Ay*, Doña María. My children told me the most amazing story. It seems the hippopotamus at Central Park has improved, but the poor rhinoceros, the darlings' own favorite, suffers from rheumatism. They come out with the strangest things, my little ones."

At the mention of health, some women turned pale. Illness of any sort, even among animals, was not idle chatter. The idea that contagious illnesses could also be contracted from animals was not far from their thoughts.

"*Ay*, Laudelina, don't even mention such things," murmured Dominga Muriel, her pudgy double chin trembling as she spoke. "Not four weeks ago, nineteen cases of typhus fever were traced to a boarding house on E. 12th Street."

Inocencia glanced anxiously at Doña Gertrudis, the only woman in the room she trusted with medical knowledge.

Gertrudis smiled. "There's nothing to worry about." She leaned over and patted Inocencia's arm. "City officials found the cause: infected immigrants from Marseilles, who had disembarked on Ellis Island."

🌿 🌿 🌿

The time came to move onto the day's work, and Inocencia slid open the pocket doors to the dining room.

"Please, my friends, take a seat around the table. My husband kindly prepared a packet of materials for each of us."

Each woman brought special talents to the table. Señora Alvarez, the American-born wife of a Cuban physician, socialized among the wealthiest expatriate families, many of whom were philanthropists. She was comfortable in the white, professional class made up of physicians and bankers, factory owners and sugar barons, all essential connections for the fundraising that lay ahead.

"At this moment," said the bubbly señora, "the Sociedad de Beneficencia Hispano Americana is raising money to build a hospital. We *all* should pledge our support for this worthy cause and buy tickets for their next gala!" The lady's dark brown eyes sparkled brightly, a cloud of curls and ringlets bouncing to her every move. She innocently gazed around the table expecting enthusiastic support from the women.

About to bulge out of her head, Doña Gertrudis' coal black eyes stared at the speaker. *The nerve! Does she honestly believe it's that easy for some of us to attend the galas of the wealthy?*

Doña Gertrudis and Dominga Muriel understood life among the poor. They lived in working-class neighborhoods where people earned their wages in cigar factories, small bodegas, neighborhood restaurants, barber shops and boarding houses. Their neighbors often didn't know if there would be work from one week to the next. Gertrudis and Dominga had organized racially integrated groups, and both could testify on that subject to the ladies at Inocencia's table. As a black woman, Gertrudis had encountered painful confrontations in her political organizing efforts.

"Ahem, if I may be so bold . . . " Doña Gertrudis folded her hands on the table, her gold wedding band brilliant against the darkness of her skin, and proceeded to enlighten the group the way she did when teaching the student midwives at her clinic. "Before we move ahead to form this club, all of us must be aware that this will be a club composed of white, black and *mulata* women. There will be more than one hotel, restaurant or hall that will not allow us the use of their space *because* there are colored women among us."

Eva Betancourt and Adelina Sánchez lowered their eyes, uncomfortable with Gertrudis' account of discrimination, but the rest focused intently on the woman's every word.

"It saddens me to say," she continued in her quiet, articulate manner, "that I have suffered such embarrassments in the past. When making arrangements at one place and paying them our hard-earned deposit, we've found out on the day of the event that we were not welcome!"

Most of the women present sympathized with Gertrudis' cautionary tale. She was, after all, a woman who commanded respect. Midwife to many of their families, Gertrudis was also the one they sent for to prepare their deceased for burial. Because she kept their secrets, she had earned their trust.

"It means," Doña Gertrudis continued softly, "that we, who are gathered here today, are also committing to become one in a family of mixed-race *compañeras*, understanding that prejudices and discrimination directed at one of us are directed at us all."

She hesitated before she spoke again. "Are we willing to take that step?"

No one responded. Inocencia froze wondering if that spelled the stillbirth of the Mercedes Varona club.

All of a sudden, all of the women raised their voices to support Gertrudis and the Mercedes Varona club. The ladies committed themselves to the cause of liberation, offering their special talents to make the club a success.

Next, Inocencia's sisters, Kirina and Doly, spoke.

"We know how fundraising in political groups actually works," Kirina offered. "In Ponce, we were involved with the Puerto Rican Autonomist Party."

Quickly, Doly added, "It was for a short time, at least for me, but we learned how to organize activities that brought in lots of money for the association. Didn't we, Kirina?"

"What Doly and I mean to say is that we're willing to work as fundraisers for Mercedes Varona."

Laudelina Sosa told the group of the many associations she'd worked with. She accepted the office of vice president. María Acosta was to be secretary. Eva Betancourt, Adelina Sánchez Dávalos, Doly and Kirina Martínez and Dominga Muriel were to be members-at-large.

⁂ ⁂ ⁂

"The next order of business," said Inocencia, "is a reading of the Bases and the Bylaws of the Cuban Revolutionary Party. After that, we'll have a discussion. Doña Adelina, would you please honor us by reading aloud?"

The former teacher agreed. Then, placing her index finger under each word, she read, 'The Party is constructed to gain, with the united efforts of all men of good will' . . . "

"Men?" Doly raised her head quizzically and looked at Inocencia.

"I had the same reaction," laughed her sister. "It just means 'mankind,' all men and women."

Once the Articles and Secret Bylaws were read and accepted, the women did something they had *never* before done in their lives. They *voted!* They voted in a political organization. They voted to affiliate the Club Mercedes Varona with the Cuban Revolutionary Party and endorse the people who would head the club, the Party and the New York Council of Organizations.

"It's done!" Inocencia brimmed with an indescribable sense of accomplishment.

She scanned the faces of her compatriots. It was an emotional moment for her, and she was sure her companions felt the same way.

"My *dearest* friends," Inocencia said, "we've taken great strides today. We're organized, united and prepared for action! Isn't that *extraordinary*?!"

"Living proof is what we are . . . living proof of Martí's words about unity," gushed Dominga Muriel.

"And all the oaths we've taken today are of our own free will," added Gertrudis Heredia, a knowing smile playing at the corners of her mouth.

María Acosta signed her name to the minutes, dated the document, February 21, 1892 and handed the papers to the club's president for her signature.

"Well done, my friends!" Inocencia beamed.

Still feeling euphoric, she embraced Kirina, extended her hand in a firm grip to Laudelina and then, through misty eyes, looked for the place in the documents to sign. She wrote: Inocencia Martínez Figueroa.

"And now, to the business of planning the very first grand event to raise funds for *our* revolution!"

# 11

## NEW YORK, 1892

In the season of blooming lilacs, Inocencia sat at the kitchen table one afternoon clipping an article from the newspaper, *Patria*. She smeared the back of the clipping with glue and pasted it into a scrapbook labeled Club Mercedes Varona. *There! That's done,* she thought and pushed herself away from the table. Inocencia yawned, stretching her arms up high, then turned to massage her lower back with both hands. She heard a tiny squeal from the cradle by the table and quickly reached over to rock the crib. "Shshsh," she whispered soothing the baby she nicknamed 'Lily Bit.' Frail and small since the day she was born, Inocencia worried about this child. She worried about the club, too, and wondered if she would ever sleep through the night again.

Suddenly, something startled Inocencia. There was a face at the window behind the Lilac bush. She left the cradle and rushed to close the back door. A red-bearded man in a dark brown suit and straw hat was already there, spying on her through the window in the door. Quickly, she slammed the palms of both hands against the door. Then, wondering if she'd been too hasty, she opened the door a crack using her foot as a stopper.

"May I help you?"

Removing his hat, the stranger held it waist high with both hands. "I'm so sorry, Madame. I may have the wrong house. Is this number 237 . . . the home of Mr. Murray, the blacksmith?"

His English, Inocencia noted, was as accented as her own.

"Oh, I can't help you there. This is number 235, and my *husband*, who's in the other room, doesn't know anyone named Murray."

As he took his leave, Inocencia shut and latched the door, thankful she didn't have to call out for her invisible husband. She began clearing the mess of newspaper from the table, when something odd struck her. *I've seen that man before. In the park, or was he strolling in the neighborhood? How curious. There aren't any blacksmiths on this street.* Awakened by the slammed door and voices, Lily Bit began to wail, driving all thoughts of strangers out of Inocencia's head.

# 12

## NEW YORK, 1893

Sotero Figueroa was late. He rushed towards the marble stairs leading up to his office, intending to climb them two at a time when, without warning, he collided with a man in a checkered, brown suit.

"Oh, I'm so sorry, pardon me, sir," Sotero said, bending to pick up the stranger's straw hat, which had flown off his head in the collision.

"No problem, Señor Figueroa," the man responded gruffly. As he placed his hat on his head, he stared intensely at Sotero, as if he were memorizing the man's features.

"Do I know you, sir?" Suddenly, Sotero felt uncomfortable.

"Well, we've never been introduced, formally that is," the bearded man responded.

"I'm sure I've seen you, probably coming and going in this very building." Sotero laughed amiably. "So, again I beg your pardon. Good day, sir."

Irked by the encounter, Sotero continued towards the stairs. *Something peculiar about that fellow. Seems on edge about something.* He tried to remember if perhaps he'd done business with the man before, but nothing came to mind. *Hm, I certainly would've remembered so striking a character.*

❧ ❧ ❧

Annoyed by the delay, Sotero raced up the two flights of stairs to the third floor. Alone and breathless on the landing, he gulped in mouthfuls of air, placing both hands against his thighs, knees slightly bent until he regained his wind. All the while his eyes feasted on the bold black lettering that announced his print shop on the door's window. Situated just to the left of the third floor landing, Sotero's pride and joy read:

IMPRENTA "AMERICA"
Propietario S. FIGUEROA
Traducciones del Español
A los Idiomas Inglés, Francés, Alemán e Italiano
O vice versa

He was delighted with the sign, the location and the building. In fact, for a fleeting moment, he wished that his personal life could bring him as much pleasure.

Inserting a large brass key into the door lock, Sotero found it was already opened and let himself into the press room. He heard the soft rhythmic *thunk* of the gordon jobber platen press printing the next issue of *Patria*. He loved the vibrations and constant din, the scent of newly unwrapped paper fresh from the mill and the musky odor of printers' ink. Here, in an atmosphere of male camaraderie, everyone worked together to get *Patria*, Jose Martí's revolutionary paper, out on time. The momentum never ceased to excite him.

Sotero wielded influence with Martí. He offered him advice and even edited the newspaper when Martí was out of town. In the mechanical aspects of the printing press—layout, ranking and positioning copy, and choosing the appropriate fonts—Sotero exercised complete control. Every layout of *Patria* received his scrupulous inspection and final approval before going to press.

Sotero employed a full-time compositor and press operator, Juan Feliciano, and a printer's apprentice, Pancho Vázquez. Of course, Sotero could easily run every aspect of the business by himself, as he had done in Ponce, but Imprenta América had grown. The job of producing *Patria* alone had more than doubled. Now, he also published *Nueva York Ilustrado* as well as posters, leaflets, advertising and other odd printing jobs.

No sooner had Sotero set foot in the door, when Juan Feliciano rushed over to him, excitedly waving a copy of the *New York Herald* above his head. A scraggly fellow, small and lean, from his first day on the job the compositor had been called "Juanito." Sparse facial hair, fine sandy bangs and an untamed cowlick gave Juanito a boyish look that belied his artistry as a typographer.

"*Buen día,* Don Sotero! And a smashing good day it is. Have you seen the *Herald? Pues, ¡mira esto!* Look. And we have telegram confirmation from Key West of an uprising! Saturday night. In Cienfuegos, Santa Clara province . . . twenty-five men declared '*¡Viva Cuba Libre!*'"

"What? Are you sure?" Sotero exclaimed as he snatched the telegram from Juanito's hands to read for himself. "It says here they encountered resistance . . . they captured the police headquarters. Took more than . . . *¡Demonio!* . . . more than one hundred weapons! Reinforcements. And casualties! On both sides!"

"And the *Herald* says Santa Clara is now free of disorder, but . . . Look here, Don Sotero, fifteen cities near the center of Cuba have declared themselves anti-government. The *Herald* says this is the start of the rebellion!"

Juan handed the newspaper to Sotero with a broad grin pasted on his boyish face.

"Ay, Juanito, if I had a small bottle of rum stashed away somewhere, now would be a good time for a toast!" Hoping against hope that Juanito might magically produce one, Sotero made a mental note to keep some fine spirits in the shop for such occasions.

From his contacts, Sotero knew the war had begun to escalate. Rumors spread like forest fires. Every day, Sotero thrust himself into the movement at Imprenta América working with the revolutionary societies: Borinquen, Los Independientes, the Sociedad Literaria, Pinos Nuevos and the Cuban Revolutionary Party's New York Council. But in his heart, the press was his mistress. He loved her without reservations. He *knew* his worth, *knew* the contributions his press made to the war effort were invaluable.

# 13

## NEW YORK, 1893

As Sotero Figueroa left the building after work, engrossed in the articles he had just edited for *Patria,* he did not notice the stranger wearing a brown suit who stepped from a neighboring doorway. Inconspicuously, the man raised his right hand and adjusted the brim of his straw hat so that his face was in its shadow. Then he began to trail Sotero Figueroa. When Sotero rounded the corner of Sixth Avenue and 34th Street, something caught his eye and he suddenly stopped dead in his tracks. Instinctively, he slowed his pace, walking gingerly into Madison Square Park. All at once, he jerked his head around hoping to catch sight of . . . of someone. Scanning the faces in the crowds, he only saw unfamiliar men and women enjoying a summer's walk. The park's cool green shade attracted passers-by eager to escape the sun baked streets. Nothing appeared out of the ordinary.

He chose a park bench close to the entrance and sat down. Casually, he crossed one leg over the other. A minute or two passed before he bent down, pretending to tie his shoe laces. He straightened up, lazily giving himself ample time to assess passers-by. No one approached him, nor did anyone look in his direction. Still, he couldn't rid himself of the uncomfortable feeling that he was being followed.

*A waste of time,* he thought. *And I'm going to be late. For no reason.* The meeting of the Club Borinquen was to take place in a brownstone monstrosity known as Chimney Corner Hall on the corner of Sixth Avenue and 25th Street. Irritable and hot, his brow a sea of furrows, Sotero turned his thoughts to the Club Borinquen and decided to continue on his way.

*How in the world will we deal with the economic woes besetting our clubs?* Sotero held little hope that solutions would miraculously appear at this meeting. Espionage and finances topped the list to be discussed. Suddenly, someone gripped Sotero's arm. He spun swiftly around, a clenched fist prepared to pummel whomever had waylaid him.

"Whoa, Don Sotero! What's the matter?" Juan Fraga's raised hand protectively covered his face. "It's me! Take it easy!"

Almost a head shorter than Sotero, the humble cigarmaker had narrowly escaped Sotero's wrath.

"*Ay,* Don Juan! Forgive me." Sotero reached out to steady the man. "I thought you were someone else."

"All's well that ends well, Don Sotero. But you seemed to be consumed by the devil himself."

"You might say so. I was off in a hellish world of diminishing returns: lack of funds, *compañero,* lack of funds! And especially now that liberation efforts have heated up in Cuba . . . Any ideas for raising money?"

"Seriously? I tell you, it's not a good time for a revolution. Money-wise, that is. Last year, well, that was different. Rebellion was in the air. Everyone was excited, wanted to give us money for the war chest."

In spite of the humidity, the two compatriots walked briskly towards 25th Street. Glad to have Don Juan by his side, Sotero relaxed his overactive imagination.

"How would you describe the situation?" Sotero questioned. "You're a cigarmaker, a businessman, the same as myself. I've got thoughts about raising morale, but raising money . . . "

"Here's the problem as I see it, Don Sotero. Right here, where the transportation and building trades are good, where the docks are never idle, where commerce always thrives, they're already closing tobacco factories."

"So, Don Juan, what you are going to tell me next is that cigar workers, who donate a day's wages to the cause, won't be in a position to part with the funds, is that it?"

"Once you close factories, Don Sotero, yes, you put people out of work. It's a downward spiral. Creditors aren't sure they'll get paid. Merchants lose confidence. There's no gold or silver to secure the currency."

As the compatriots caught site of Chimney Corner Hall, they hastened their pace. Both men stood at the curb waiting for a lull in the traffic to cross the street to the hall.

"Cigarmakers are a major source of our revenue!" Sotero yelled above the din as a horse-drawn wagon passed by. "Borinquen and Los Independientes must take the lead to raise morale, Don Juan!"

"What we must do, Don Sotero, is use our unity, our valuable united front. That's a powerful weapon. We help our people now, and they'll help us when they're back on their feet."

"You and I both know Martí is not going to put the revolution on hold. This'll be a short meeting, Don Juan, now that we've ironed out all the points we have to make," laughed Sotero.

As he entered the building, he thought he saw a movement. Out of the corner of his eye, a familiar figure seemed to stir. *Where have I seen that man before?* But nothing came to mind.

❀ ❀ ❀

Following the club's meeting, Sotero decided to take the shortest route to Broadway and return to the print shop. Briskly, he pounded along the heat-soaked pavements, thinking only about the work he wanted to complete. Although it was late, the streets were filled with all kinds of people desperate to escape the inferno of their tenement rooms. Some lounged about on front stoops playing games or musical instruments; others made chairs of upended barrels. Too tired to sleep, they traded stories and secret fears about losing jobs and facing uncertain futures. Families spread blankets on the fire escapes, and Sotero imagined the rooftops would be jammed with people hoping to find a few hours of comfort before sunrise.

Flashes of dry lightning appeared sporadically against the charcoal sky. This time, no red bearded, straw-hatted man trailed Sotero. The stranger had followed Juan Fraga instead. Still, Sotero was startled when a cloaked figure suddenly appeared out of nowhere. Another time, the urgent clanging of speeding fire trucks set his nerves on edge. Scurrying rats gnawing their fill of rotted garbage in pitch-black alleys filled him with disgust. He could not wait to get back to the print shop.

Old newspapers strewn along wet gutters and doorways added to the night terrors. Sotero skirted such nuisances and failed to notice the screaming headlines in yesterday's tabloids. The bold letters announced the scourge of typhus continued to grip the city.

# 14

## NEW YORK, 1893

Alexa flinched. The child's bleary hazel eyes flew wide open! Someone had made a scraping noise close to her hiding place. Terrified she'd been discovered, she sat very still, breathing heavily but trying not to make a sound. From her spot behind the overstuffed chair, she could see the room's dark shades had been drawn, but instead of keeping out the suffocating summer heat, the heavy drapery intensified it. Hot air seemed to rise, like vapor from a boiling tea kettle, throughout the parlor, bathing her in a clammy film of sweat. She felt chilled, and the downy hairs on her arms and the back of her neck stood on end. After a while, she relaxed and began to take in short, quick spurts of the room's warm air.

Alexa tried to move her cramped legs away from the claw feet of the bulging plush chair, but found her black stockings were wet and stubbornly clung to the oak wood floor. She tried to pull her smock underneath her to make a cushion between the stockings and the floor. It too was wet. It was more important to remain hidden than to be dry, so she pushed herself back with all her might against the corner, the heels of her black Mary Janes leaving skid marks on the gummy floor. *I'm safe here. My hiding corner. Safe behind Mamá's chair, behind the plant,* she thought, *big enough for only me. No one will know I'm wet.* Searing, hot shame filled

Alexa with remorse, bringing sorry tears streaming down her cheeks. Silently, she tried to stifle her sobs. The child had peed in her underwear. She was three years old and should have known better, Mamá would say. But she didn't know where Mamá was. She whimpered. Closing her heavy eyelids, she began to doze.

*Were the black monsters still in the room?* Alexa wondered when she awoke. She waited a second before she peeked through the narrow slit. She saw them. They were still there. She watched from her hiding place as they gyrated, like lost souls, on the walls, taller than they were before. *They must have grown 'cause I didn't keep watch!* Now they were huge. Soon they would creep over her. Their bloated bodies swayed on the bit of floor that she could see from her hiding place. Big monsters could do whatever they wanted. They crept over the base boards, shimmied up the walls and folded onto themselves on the ceiling. Her heart pounded so loudly in her tiny chest, she was certain someone had heard and would discover her. She closed her heavy eyelids once more, pretending she was invisible.

Alexa's braids became undone. Colorful plaid ribbons dangled on a few strands of her long brown hair. Pushing matted tendrils away from her swollen eyes, Alexa spied again and saw the monsters dancing furiously to the flicker of the lit candles in the room. The demons were everywhere! Their eyeless faces bounced here and there, on the fireplace mantel, on side tables, even stretching up the drapery and window shades. Nearby, two candles began to sputter. In special holders she'd never seen before, the candles had been placed on tables and scattered throughout the room.

*Oh no,* she cringed. *The demons are enraged! Some are shrinking—they're disappearing and . . . Oh no, they're growing taller again in other spaces.* Suddenly the child heard murmurs very close to her hiding corner. She wondered why the people spoke in whispers. *They're scared of demons too. That's why they talk in whispers. If they talk normal, they'll frighten the monsters away. I'll tell 'em: talk normal!*

She wiped her runny nose on the sleeve of her smock, trying to make sense of voices speaking in a mixture of Spanish and English. Swallowing the mucous filling her throat, she listened closer. *The people aren't talking; they're sobbing. Why are people crying? Are they sad 'cause I was a bad girl and didn't use a potty? Maybe they're sad 'cause Mamá will punish me.*

Cramped into her soggy triangle, Alexa's thin arms wrapped tightly around her legs and drew them up to her chin. She started to doze again, giving in to the swollen eyelids, when she heard piercing, wrenching wails. She swept her hair away from her eyes and peeked. It was Mamá! *Mamá, I'm here,* she said to herself. *Come find me. Why's Mamá screaming so loud?*

Aching to fly into Mamá's arms, Alexa suddenly stopped short. She remembered Titi Doly was looking for her. She wanted Alexa to do something bad, and Alexa wouldn't do it. *Don't scream, Mamá! Please, please, please don't scream! You'll wake the babies. It'll all work out! Ask Papá!*

Her forehead began to hurt, pressed against the chair's plush fabric. She saw Doña Gertrudis tightly grip her mother's wrists. Mamá lashed out at the older woman, trying to free her wrists, but Gertrudis held on to her tightly until she was able to wrestle the screamer onto the sofa.

"¡Cálmate, mujer!" Alexa heard her say to Mamá who was yelling and weeping uncontrollably. "Let me be, Gertrudis! ¡Ay, Dios mío! Leave me alone. I want to hold her, I want to . . . "

Gertrudis did not let go of Mamá. For a brief moment, Alexa was shocked at the sight of Mamá's contorted face, all twisted in pain. *Ohhh, someone's hurting Mamá,* she whimpered and covered both ears with her small hands.

"You must calm yourself! The children need you, Inocencia."

Doña Gertrudis was crying too. She stroked Mama's hair, then hushed her like a child. "Your newborn son, Inocencia, think of him. He needs to feel his mother's arms around him, now. Your little girls need their mother, Inocencia. Calm yourself, woman. Look at Sotero. Your husband is destroyed! He needs you right now."

"*Noooo!*" screamed Inocencia with the eyes of a mad woman.

"Let me go! *He wasn't even here!* I tried and tried to find him, but *he wasn't even here!*" Inocencia allowed her head to slump against Doña Gertrudis' shoulder and wept softly. "Where was he, Gertrudis? Why wasn't he with me?" She began to sob all over again.

"Hush, child, hush. Inocencia, hush."

Gertrudis held Mamá, rocking her from side to side, and gently allowed Titi Kirina to put her arms around Mamá. They sat together, Titi and Mamá, one with arms around the other, the other like a limp ragdoll. They sat and swayed together on the sofa. Then Alexa saw Gertrudis walk over to a side table and fill a glass with ice water from a pitcher.

*I want water, too!* Suddenly Alexa was so thirsty her tongue felt fat, too large for her mouth. But still, she would not reveal herself in case Titi Doly was in the room. She watched Gertrudis drop liquid from a small blue bottle she'd taken out of her pocket into the glass of water.

"Here, drink this," she said to Mamá and stroked her head again. "It will make you feel better. You'll be able to sleep for a while."

When Mamá was taken upstairs, Alexa withdrew her damp head from the peeking slit. Her neck hurt. Tired of pressing against the prickly plush covering of the chair, the child squirmed back into her hiding triangle. She felt hot and achy. As she used to do when she was as little as her sister Julia, Alexa jammed her thumb into her mouth to make saliva.

✷ ✷ ✷

The weary child's eyes slid sideways to peek through the opening. The dancing shadows on the walls, floor and ceiling had elongated. There were more people in the room, but she couldn't see Mamá, only a small sliver of Papá sitting motionless. He was sitting in a side chair by the fireplace, holding his head in his massive hands. *Papá doesn't want to talk to the people,* thought Alexa, *and see? Papá isn't afraid of the demon shadows.*

After a while, Alexa decided she too would not be frightened. She would not wet herself when she looked again at the two dining room chairs in front of the parlor's bay windows. Mamá didn't like it when people took chairs away from where they belonged. The chairs faced each other, but they weren't for the people to sit on, and they weren't for games, or for sewing like when she and Mamá sometimes knitted together. They were there to hold Julia's casket that stretched from one chair to the other, where a white dove slept tranquilly.

*Julia!* Alexa whispered harshly yet low enough so that no one else would hear her. Using all the power of concentration a three-year-old could muster, she called again. *Julia! Come out of that box! You don't have to sleep there. We have a big bed all for ourselves! Julia, wake up! Wake up!!!*

"Alexa, where are you, my precious?" Titi Doly called from the kitchen. "Come, darling. Come to Titi Doly." The child's aunt walked towards the parlor, thinking that something familiar had caught her eye as she came down the stairs.

Hot tears spilled down Alexa's cheeks. She began to gasp for air. *Titi's going to find me, I know she is.* Alexa's head was swimming in pain. She almost wished her aunt would find her. It was so hard to hide. She was thirsty, and wet, and hungry, and she longed to be smothered lovingly in someone's arms.

"There you are, my love!"

Doly moved the chair away, allowing enough room to enter the hiding place and scoop the child up in her arms. Alexa began to wail out loud. An incomprehensible feeling of sadness tugged at her heart so that she could hardly breathe. She cried, caught her breath and gasped until her sobs settled into a series of weeping hiccups.

"It's all right, love. I have you now. Don't cry, Alexa. Julia's playing with angels. Come, love." Doly soothed the weeping child, rocking her gently. "My goodness, Alexa, you are burning up! Come, child. Come and kiss your sister goodbye."

Alexa suddenly tensed her frail body, arching her back away from her aunt's embrace, and flung her skinny arms and legs in every direction.

"*Nooooo!*" Alexa screamed! "No, Titi . . . *Noooo!* Don't . . . don't make me kiss Julia!"

Alexa leaned closer towards her aunt as if to share a secret. "No Titi, no. If I kiss my sister, the people will take her away!" Alexa whispered, "She doesn't want to go, Titi!"

🌾 🌾 🌾

Before the year's first frost, Inocencia's three little girls had died from typhus Only her infant son, Mario, remained to mend his mother's broken heart.

# PART III

# 1
## HAVANA, 1895

On moonless nights they lingered at the primroses, two gray headed souls leaning in towards each other as if they were discussing soil and fertilizer. The garden had become the safest place to confide their secrets.

Bonocio lifted his head and looked around making sure none of the servants were nearby. "Lola, there's news," he whispered. Lola froze. Her hand, extended towards a yellow buttercup, hung in midair. Even before he'd said a word, she knew something was wrong. All through dinner he sat across the table from her in stone-faced silence. The 'news' was bound to be unpleasant, and cold fear was already rising throughout her body.

"Juan Gualberto Gómez was thrown into jail."

"*Qué sin vergüenzas*, Bonocio," Lola said in disgust. "If they dare imprison a man as influential as he is, who unites the races with his writing, they'll imprison us too."

"You're very right, Lola. We can't afford to take any more chances."

"Well, it's better to leave the country than be thrown into prison. But if we go," Lola said in despair, "who'll be left to speak the truth?"

*Patience,* Lola told herself. *I have my family's safety to consider.*

❊ ❊ ❊

On May 19, the world, as Doña Lola knew it, turned upside down. On a lonely stretch of Cuban beach in Dos Ríos, a sniper's bullet snuffed out the light that was their beloved leader, José Martí.

Under the weight of hopelessness and haunting nightmares, Lola's bravado began to melt.

❊ ❊ ❊

*La Correspondencia de España* was the Spanish newspaper of record. No one dared question the paper's unwavering support of colonial policies. No one would ever suspect that insurgents could plant copies of José Martí's newspaper, *Patria*, within *La Correspondencia's* pages. But that was exactly what they had done. The bundles were to arrive in Havana Harbor that morning and Lola lost no time in sending Lina to buy the newspaper.

Shielding her eyes with her hand, Doña Lola's maid, Lina, scanned the congested harbor for the *Seneca,* the American ship carrying the contraband cargo. Rowboats taking passengers to and from the ships caught Lina's eye, and she wondered if the bundles of newspapers were still onboard. Suddenly, she spied *The Seneca,* its cargo haphazardly dumped into piles on the dock. Bundles of *La Correspondencia* lay unattended.

*I could walk off with a newspaper and no one would know*, Lina reasoned, *but Doña Lola said, "Lina, don't bring attention to yourself."*

Lina decided to wait in the shade of a warehouse, lazily shifting her weight from one leg to the other, until someone appeared to collect the bundles. Before long, crowds began to gather around the person assigned to the business of selling the newspapers.

Lina was shrewd. She walked casually towards the dock, scanning the crowd. When she saw an elderly gentleman who might fit her plan, she focused on his actions and hesitant gait. By the look of his white suit and fancy riding boots, he was a planter. The man's ruddy face was partially shielded from the morning sun by a broad, straw hat. In one liver spotted hand he held a cane with a wolf head for a handle; the other hand casually raised an unlit cigar to fleshy moist lips.

As the planter fished in his pockets for some coins to purchase a paper, Lina slipped in behind him as if she were his servant. When the planter stepped away with the paper tucked neatly under his arm, Lina stretched out her small, sweaty fist full of coins.

"Master needs another copy," she said dropping her gaze demurely.

The planter turned in her direction, and Lina held her breath.

But Lina already had the paper in hand, and no one took note of the skinny, shapeless girl wearing a loose bandanna over her frizzy hair.

The folds of her oversized apron concealed the newspaper, and Lina strolled away maintaining the illusion that she was somebody's servant. As she reached the first residential home beyond the harbor, Lina began to run, carefully pinning the paper against her small body with her bony elbow. Panting for air, she felt exhilarated, free as the wind that lifted the kerchief right off her head like a kite in flight. Lina was quickly learning the fine points of subterfuge. *I'm just like Martí when he sent that message inside that cigar,* she thought. *Doña Lola'll be proud of me.*

🌾 🌾 🌾

Far into the evening, Lola read and re-read the homages and condolences to the deceased Martí in *Patria*. She peered at the paper's date. June 25, 1895. *Less than a month ago,* she thought. Her wire-rimmed glasses bore smudge marks of dried tears and ink-stained fingerprints from the pages of the newspaper. Framed in a black border, Martí's image dominated the front page. He seemed to stare at her, smoldering eyes reaching out from beyond the grave. *What message can I detect from these eyes,* she wondered. Eventually, her gaze would wander from the image to Sotero Figueroa's opening article. There she'd remain, a captive of the word: ¡**INMORTAL**!

# 2

# NEW YORK, 1895

Unaware that he was holding his breath, Sotero stood quietly outside the room listening to Inocencia hum softly to their son. Tension spread across his shoulders, but he continued to listen until the muffled secrets between mother and child gave way to smothered giggles. He envied the easy way she had with the child. Picturing his wide innocent smile, apple cheeks and halo of dusty curls, Sotero wished he could get the boy to respond to him the way she did.

*She must be in bed with him.* He imagined the two huddled up in quilts against the wintry draft that he knew bled in through the porous window frames. He had intended to fix them.

"*No. Mi amor . . . no.* No more play tonight, or I'll have to tell the Cuco you won't go to sleep." The words to the children's lullaby drifted in and out of her humming. "*Duérmete, Ma-r-i-o . . . Um umm . . . Que viene el cuco.*" The threat of the bogeyman evoked honeyed memories.

Sotero felt a tinge of loneliness. He wished he could shed his worries and become the boy Inocencia sang to. The truth was that everything was falling apart for Sotero. He worried about himself, about party unity, about the void left by Martí's death. But he couldn't bring himself to share his troubles with his wife. Two short steps. That's all he had to take to be on the other side of the door and huddled in warm blankets with his wife and son.

147

*No. I won't bother her when she's with the boy. I'll deal with my troubles, stand strong as I always have against these . . . these . . . dogs who betray the cause.*

"What we need to do is to pull together the Puerto Rico Section of the Cuban Revolutionary Party, and move on towards liberation!" Sotero had advised his old compatriot, Rafael Serra.

Don Rafael nodded slowly, his full lips scrunched tightly beneath a well-groomed mustache. He read Sotero's clouded face and reached across the kitchen table to refill their glasses.

"This amber rum comes from the islands, my friend. It'll work magic . . . nurse away any ills and pain you may have." Don Rafael clinked his glass against his guest's, taking one sip of his to Sotero's massive gulp.

For much of the evening, the two had toasted each other's health. One minute Sotero wallowed in the movement's problems; the next, he'd pound his fist on the table, sending bottles and glasses into spasms of tinkling against the enamel table top.

Don Rafael took it all in stride. Quietly, he studied the lazy smoke patterns curling up from their cigars. *Best to let the man fight it out with his demons,* he thought.

"Well, now tell me, Figueroa . . . How do you propose to trim these thorny issues, once you've finally identified the beast?"

"Argh, Don Rafael. I can't fix anything anymore. Now, I'm merely a visitor at *Patria*. The new staff fight each other for power. You know they're selling out Martí's revolution, don't you?"

"Bringing Cuba under the American fold, you mean?" Serra's cynical laugh echoed deep in his chest.

"Outrageous! Martí is in his grave less than ten months and . . . Argh! Let them all go to hell!"

"*Oye*, Figueroa, you're not alone. We're not blind. Annexation used to be a dirty word . . . now it's regularly in *Patria*'s editorials."

As the rum took effect, Sotero spewed out his discontent. His prickly tongue pressed against his dry cottony mouth.

"'Annexation' and that other word, 'negotiation' . . . let's not forget that one. The new leaders are far too friendly with the American government for my taste. And I'll tell you, my friend, I'll have none of it."

"Patience, man!" Don Rafael seized the opportunity to speak before the glassware slipped off the table in another Figueroa tirade.

"You *may* have to play the most important card in your hand, my friend. Listen to me."

Don Rafael leaned closer to Sotero's chair to make certain his slightly slurred words didn't diminish his council. "My advice? Sit at their table, Figueroa. When you speak for us, the workers and the liberationists at *their* table, the conversation changes. Stay the course, *compañero*, stay the course and save what we've achieved. Change can come from within just as easily as from without."

Sotero rubbed his thumb against his lower lip, mulling over Don Rafael's advice.

"You may be right, old friend."

His raspy words hung in the air for a long while. Gradually, his temper began to ebb, floating into a realm of uncertainty. He studied his hands spread out on the table in front of him, then his gaze slid over to the empty glass. But even he knew he needed courage from the heart, not from the rum, and he turned his thoughts to his next move.

From the kitchen, Sotero could hear the mantel clock in the Serras' parlor strike the hour. Time was running out. Except for the scraping of his chair against the wood floor as he rose from the table, there wasn't another sound in the room.

"Tomorrow, old friend. Tomorrow we choose a leader for the Puerto Rico Section," Sotero said, preparing to take his leave. "I dread to think we may be inviting a new colonial master into my homeland."

꙰ ꙰ ꙰

*Serra gave me learned advice,* Sotero mused, remembering last evening's conversation. Now, he stood in the small foyer of his home preparing to leave for the dreaded meeting. Listening for sounds from the upstairs bedroom, he only heard the wintry silence of a still house. *Inocencia and the boy must be sound asleep.* In the foyer's beveled mirror, a tall, angular figure reflected Sotero's motions. The visage was a fraud, he knew. He could feel it in his bones, feel it in his red-streaked eyes. Dark pouches had rearranged the contours of his face, and the fleshiness around the eyes accentuated hollows beneath his chiseled cheeks.

He had lost the battle to lace his necktie, so it did not fit neatly under the wings of his collar. Sotero had almost called for Inocencia's help, but decided against it. He'd tried to properly knot the cravat by making his mind a blank slate and concentrating, but each twist and turn of the silk cravat brought forth *Patria's* original mission statement. That mission might have been lost by now, he knew. He pulled out his pocket watch and checked the hour. It was time to move along. Sotero slipped the key and timepiece into his waistcoat and checked the clasp on his gold cufflinks. He wore the lucky ones with the Masonic emblem. He shrugged into his coat. Before darting down the front stoop to the street, he lit the small lamp in the foyer. It was a bitter December evening and he dreaded coming back to a cold, dark house.

Turning up the collar of his great coat Sotero walked briskly in a westerly direction towards the bright lights of Lexington Avenue.

*I would rather be anywhere else tonight than in the home of Dr. José Julio Henna.*

# 3

# NEW YORK, 1895

A shock rippled throughout Celia Santiago's body as the cold metal stethoscope touched her bare skin.

Unflustered, the doctor listened to her breathing. "Cough, please," he requested, closing his eyes. Behind his lids Dr. Henna saw the pulmonary networks in and out of her lungs, listened to the reedy sounds and ragged whistles.

"Take a deep breath," he said, thinking the air flows sounded like a rumbling train.

Celia inhaled deeply, then slowly exhaled, then gagged. Something had caught in her throat.

"It's all right. Let's try again," he murmured, his brow furrowing into a map of lines and creases.

Celia filled her lungs and exhaled as often as he requested.

"Have you noticed any sign of bleeding during your bouts of coughing," Dr. Henna asked? Removing the stethoscope from her back, he let it hang casually from his neck. "Have you seen discoloration on your handkerchief?"

"No, Dr. Henna." Her voice faltered for an instant. She shifted her gaze from his light blue eyes to his right ear, and to the reddish fringe of bristly hair that framed the sides of his baldpate like a partial crown of thorns. "I don't think I spit up any blood, but coughing leaves me so weak I can hardly roll enough cigars at the factory to make a living."

"Not to worry," Henna mumbled under his breath. The threads of concern on his forehead seemed to slacken as he gently took her dainty wrist in his bear paw of a hand, registering a quick reading of her pulse. He flashed a smile to put her at ease but it was almost lost beneath the robust walrus mustache he wore.

*Hmm, poverty is the culprit here,* he mused. *Poverty in Puerto Rico that forces you to leave, and poverty here, compounded by the harshness of the elements.*

"What you're going to do is rest . . . a week free of all the cares you carry on your shoulders." He spoke the words he often used with patients knowing the futility of asking a worker to find time to rest.

"I'm going to send the Health Department a sample of your sputum for analysis. You may get dressed. Now, Señorita Santiago . . . Celia . . . don't you worry, you hear?" He gazed earnestly at the patient. "Do you trust me to get to the bottom of this?"

She nodded her head and hastened behind the screen to slip into the blouse and jacket she'd left beside her handbag on the enamel table. Smoothing the upswept bun of dark hair on the top of her head, she pinned a small black hat into it. Before stepping back into the examining room, she wiped nervous perspiration off her hands on the white hand towel that rested on top of the table. Then, she pressed down the front of her woolen gray skirt.

Dr. Henna had folded his large, six-foot frame into a swivel oak desk chair and rolled from desk to the file cabinet and back again. Opening the folder marked "Santiago, Celia," he began to record the patient's history.

*November 17, 1895. Celia Santiago. 25 years of age. Small framed, dark haired woman. Appears younger. Slumps her*

*shoulders. Has an intermittent gait when she walks. Employed*
*as a tobacco roller in the Fraga and García Cigar Factory.*

*Patient presents with a hacking cough, obstructions in her*
*breathing, dark circles under the eyes. A slight tinge of redness*
*around the tip of her nose. Patient's eyes are rheumy, fingers*
*stained, probably from handling the tobacco leaves, but show no*
*sign of clubbing.*

The doctor pulled out a notepad, pausing to think for a
second, then scribbled a prescription in the undecipherable
code of his profession.

"Take this to Don Domingo Peraza. His pharmacy is on
the corner of Third Avenue and 23rd Street," he said rolling
the chair towards the patient. "Ask him to call me if he has
any question about the prescription. The number is in the
upper right hand corner. Until we know the status of your
condition, we'll continue to treat you with cough tonics, perhaps some iron drops to give you added energy."

He rose from the desk chair and handed her his office
card. "My hours are listed on this card. See? Here's the telephone number if you need to call me. And please, señorita,
don't hesitate to call or come to the office if you need me. Or
I'll make a house call to you, day or night. Do you understand?"

She nodded and glanced at the card he placed in her
hand.

Telephone: 2264
Dr. J. Julio Henna,
8 West 40th Street,
1 to 2 p.m. And 5 to 6 p.m. Sunday, 1 to 2 p.m.

*Except for Sundays,* Celia realized, *I'm at work all the other*
*times. If I get worse . . .* She knew she could not take any more
time off from the factory. Celia would have to rely on cough
tonics.

☙ ☙ ☙

By the time Henna examined the last patient in the waiting room, winter darkness claimed the dimly lit streets of the West Side, numbing the bones of faceless souls on route to their myriad destinations. Bathed in a pool of pale yellow lamp light, he could hear the street noises outside the window from where he sat hunched over patient records.

A soft growl at the pit of his stomach reminded him that he'd missed his afternoon coffee, and images of crisp potato omelets floated into his head. *Perhaps Mrs. Riley could make up a plate for me before the meeting,* he mused, lazily rubbing his right temple with the tip of his pen as if there was something else he wanted to do but had forgotten. *Well, I wish I could forget the meeting,* he thought, troubled by the notion of adversarial politics.

He removed his glasses, rubbed irritated eyes until they were rimmed with red and gave a wide, noisy yawn. Henna's blurry gaze slid sideways to the small painting of an attractive woman he kept near the desk.

"Ada Henna, love of my life, it is time for you to come home. I'm beginning to talk to myself."

# 4

## NEW YORK, 1895

*Tap Tap.* Mrs. Riley's feather-like taps fell softly on the mahogany door. Hearing no response, she pressed her ear against the door, then checked the grandfather clock in the foyer. It was almost eight o'clock. She could see the time from where she stood outside the doctor's office. Quietly, she turned the knob, opening the door just far enough to peek into the darkened room. As she expected, the room reeked of stale air. A sour scent of spoiled food caught Mrs. Riley's attention, and she glanced about for its source. The roast beef sandwich, pickled relish and potato salad she had brought in for the doctor hours earlier sat untouched on the small lacquered side table near the sofa. The doctor still sat at his desk transferring handwritten notes from house calls he'd recently made to his Chinese patients.

"Ahem . . . Dr. Henna . . . excuse me, but the Committee of Patriots has arrived. I've accommodated them in the library." She picked up the tray, covering the contents with a linen napkin, and mumbled something under her breath about Mrs. Ada's return.

"I'm on my way, Mrs. Riley. Oh, how many gentlemen are there?"

"Five. Five gentlemen, Dr. Henna."

"Hmmm. Seems like we're in for an interesting meeting. Did I ever tell you I was a revolutionary in my youth?"

"No, sir."

"Yes, yes, Mrs. Riley, I was. Even went to prison because of it. But, that was a different time. I was a different person then. Oh, well, those stories are for another day."

"Yes, Dr. Henna." She stepped quietly out of the room, her face devoid of all expression. Only the flicker of her light eyes showed her surprise at the doctor's strange revelations.

Henna stopped writing and straightened his back. He was agile enough to stretch both arms high above his head. Pressing his back from side to side into the chair, he tried to release the cramped position his shoulders favored when he wrote his notes. Then he withdrew a white handkerchief from his pocket and wiped the Waterman's pen before replacing it in its holder beside the matching inkwell.

# 5
# NEW YORK, 1895

The smell of tobacco mingled with that of fine spirits overwhelmed the doctor as soon as he opened the library's French doors. *I mustn't drink anything this evening,* he told himself. *Need to remain sharp, concentrate on the factions I'm sure to find in this room.* A gregarious man by nature, Henna greeted the five committee members warmly, quipped about the nasty weather and welcomed them to his home. When he came to Sotero Figueroa, Henna nodded in welcome, but grew wary. *He wears defiance like a cloak, this one. He wants me to know he'll not compromise his principles. Well, neither will I, my friend, but perhaps we can learn to work with one another.*

At that very moment, Figueroa was thinking about Serra's advice: *stay the course,* compañero . . . *change comes from within just as easily as from without.* He knew what course he wanted to take that evening.

Unlike Figueroa, the pharmacist, Gerardo Forrest, appeared buoyant. He helped himself to a snifter of brandy from the console table and moved eagerly to engage Henna in conversation. Both men belonged to the Martí Charity Association, and Forrest felt entitled to take certain liberties in Henna's house, like filling his glass with brandy without invitation.

At sixty-three, the stocky, barrel-chested Manuel Besosa was the committee's elder statesman. A cigar manufacturer by trade, he sat uncomfortably in an elegant antique side chair comparing notes with the dapper young lawyer, Roberto Todd. As Dr. Henna joined their company, Besosa gratefully rose from his chair.

Todd, who was a personal friend of Henna's, took the lead in presenting the purpose of the meeting. "It's time, my friend, to form the Puerto Rican revolutionary party."

The fifth member of the committee, Juan de Mata Terraforte, supported Todd's declaration with a solemn, "Hear, hear!"

Before anyone else had a chance to respond, Sotero moved to frame the discussion from his point of view. "Let's get one thing straight, gentlemen. Before we get into the crux of the matter, we must all agree that we *will not* sever the union with Martí's party. The war in Cuba makes it difficult to liberate Puerto Rico, but not impossible, gentlemen. The Cuban Revolutionary Party will honor that pledge."

When he requested each of the members to voice their agreement or rejection for the record, not one gentlemen disagreed.

"Well, I guess we should amend Todd's declaration accordingly," huffed Besosa.

As he prepared to reframe the group's purpose, the cigarmaker's expression suddenly changed, showing a sheepish embarrassment. He gazed blankly at his companions as if he had lost track of what he was going to say. "Ah!" he murmured, trying to find his train of thought. "Ahem, *compañeros*. I beg your indulgence. You see, it's about my boy. I promised my Harry . . . he's very much interested in history . . . I promised I'd report to him the details of this very important meeting." He looked around at his compatriots, a bemused smile playing on his lips.

"Now, gentlemen. My memory is not what it used to be. If I appear to stumble, it's only because I'm trying hard to commit our deeds to memory. So . . . may I count on all of your young memories, for Harry's sake?"

Without intending it to happen, Besosa's confession became a welcomed respite. It reminded the expatriates that they were all on the same side.

"We're resolved to take matters into our own hands," Besosa continued. "Under the auspices of the Cuban Revolutionary Party, of course, as Don Sotero has cautioned us. And, we're committed to raising an invading army."

"With respect to everyone. I've said all this before, but I believe it's worth repeating so you won't underestimate my priorities," interrupted Sotero, more subdued this time than before. "If the United States decides to support the Cuban cause, they must also support the liberation of Puerto Rico. Americans will respect us more if we stand firm on this issue. We've got to make them realize that we Puerto Rican people are a people that can and should be free of all outside pressure."

Henna observed Figueroa with renewed interest. The journalist's words sparked an opportunity the doctor could justifiably embrace. "And, it seems to me," he bellowed, "that it should be an American citizen who negotiates. An American speaking about these truths to fellow Americans. An American who speaks their language . . . an educated, enlightened person with social standing and prestige, don't you agree?"

*And here's where we muddy the waters,* Sotero realized, knowing that Henna was not only an annexationist but also a U.S. citizen.

Feeling the tension rise in the room, Manuel Besosa launched into the speech he had prepared.

"Dr. Henna. We, the Committee of Patriots, with the sanction of the delegate, Estrada Palma, offer you the position of president of the Puerto Rico *Section* of the Cuban Revolutionary Party."

A loud crack from a shifting log in the roaring fire abruptly broke the stillness in the room.

Henna stepped towards the corner table where he'd placed an untouched goblet of Burgundy. He clasped both hands behind his back and rocked slightly on his toes. As if he were weighing the pros and cons of Besosa's request, he waited before responding, letting the tension continue to grow.

"*Paisanos,*" he said, speaking to the committee members with grave sincerity, "you do me a great honor. But I must be honest. I am a convinced annexationist. I confess to you that over the years, I've come to believe that a union between our homeland and the United States is the best solution. To achieve *my* personal goals, I know it is first indispensable to wrest Puerto Rico from Spain's control."

Only Sotero flinched at the finality of his words.

"Nonetheless, I accept this honor and promise to abstain from annexationist propaganda during my term as president. And to leave to the free will of the Puerto Ricans the final decision as to what form of government they'll choose once the island is free of Spain."

Resisting insistent pangs of distrust, Sotero congratulated Dr. Henna. Extending his hand towards the man, he said, "I'll do whatever I'm called upon to achieve our goal of liberation."

To Henna's credit, Sotero Figueroa was a man of his word.

# 6
## NEW YORK, 1895

The picture postcard fluttered to the kitchen floor. She'd forgotten it was there among the loose papers. When Inocencia opened the Mercedes Varona scrapbook at the kitchen table, the card had fallen out. She stooped down to pick it up and dusted off its surface. She examined the details of the Currier and Ives print as if she'd never seen it before. *All of them ice skating in Central Park . . . look how happy they are!*

Inocencia allowed her mind to drift into the wintry scene. She hummed the music of the skating waltz in her head and watched handsome men and pretty ladies come to life, laughing, falling and holding on to each other as they twirled around on a snowy afternoon. Then, it struck her. *Expatriate families ice skating in Central Park! What a wonderful way to raise money for the club.*

She began to write a note to Doña Emilia, relieved that she'd come up with something for the club, even if it was only an idea. Emilia was club president now. When Inocencia complained about fatigue, the *doyenne* had graciously taken over the presidency—"But only until you feel well enough to come back," Emilia had said.

In return, Inocencia promised to help in whatever way she could. That promise hadn't amounted to much. She just didn't have the energy or the will to move on anything that required her attention.

Except for Mario.

Mario was the reason she got out of bed in the mornings, the reason for devoting all her waking hours to his happiness and protection. She could no longer bear to think about her lost girls, or to speak their names out loud. It was as if they had only existed in her dreams.

Suddenly, Inocencia heard an unexpected bang from the upstairs bedroom. *It's nothing, just a toy crashing to the floor,* she told herself. *Maybe that wooden horse he loves so much.* Young Mario had refused a nap, but agreed to quiet time in his room. *I'll ignore it. Besides, I need time to jot down my thoughts, or they'll fly right out of my head. Time to call for a messenger to take this note to Doña Emilia. Where does it go . . . the time?*

As she wrote, she glanced quickly at the dates on the calendar pinned to the wall near the pantry. There was a big red circle around the 22nd day of December.

*What is so special about today? It must be something Sotero needed to do.*

☆ ☆ ☆

That evening, Sotero rushed home to tell Inocencia all about the grand event: the Puerto Rico Section had held its first general assembly at Chimney Corner Hall.

"Finally, Inocencia. We're on the road to victory!"

"Oh, Sotero, isn't that nice." She smiled and then returned to the balls of yarn that she was sorting.

"Fifty-nine patriots, Inocencia! We elected the directorate of the Puerto Rico Section of the Cuban Revolutionary Party. And I'm one of them!"

"Uh hum. You'll be excellent, I know."

"Woman! Do you know what that means? We didn't leave Martí's party! We *all* swore allegiance to the section's liberation platform! *All* of us, even the conservative Don Tomás Estrada Palma."

"Oh, that's wonderful," she smiled, closing the lid on the basket. "I can see how happy you are."

"There's more, Inocencia. I was saving this bit especially for you. We finally have our flag: a white star against a deep blue triangle. And the stripes are red and white, the reverse of the Cuban flag. Imagine that: *we* have our own flag. Can you believe it?"

"Oh," she responded, a wisp of a smile on her pallid lips. "I'm glad it all worked out."

Sotero's jaw dropped in utter amazement.

*Where is the excitement, the applause? Did Inocencia forget our mission? Forget that we're at war?*

# 7
## HAVANA, 1896

Lola awoke in a cold sweat. She thought she'd heard whistles, short and shrill and closer to the house than she would have liked. A thin film of humidity clung to her bare arms. She had worn too much clothing for a warm June night. That was Bonocio's doing. He'd insisted that they wear some street clothing to sleep in. *Just in case,* he'd said, and Lola had bristled at the idea. Then, he'd insisted they move into the back bedrooms with easier access to the streets, and that, for Lola, spelled the end of a good night's sleep.

As she turned over on her side, thinking to catch a wink before daybreak, she stopped short. *Voices? Was she hearing muffled voices?* Blindly, she groped for her spectacles on the night table. Before she could reach them, Bonocio roughly dug his fingers into her upper arm.

"Hush," he whispered. Alarm rang in his voice. "Lola, quickly, get ready. Don't make a sound."

The door flew open! Patria rushed into her parents' room. "*¡Virgen Santísima!*" Out of breath, she rapidly began to gather her parents' things and throw them into a canvas bag.

"*Dios mío,* where's Laura?" In that frenzied moment Lola had forgotten her younger daughter had been sent to visit the family in Puerto Rico.

"Hurry, Lola. Hurry," Bonocio pleaded.

"Leave it!" they commanded as Lola reached for a bag of books. "Faster, hurry!"

"Mamá, take only what's essential, leave everything else behind!"

"Papá, where's. . . . "

"The bag, under the mattress. Patria, hurry."

"Passports?"

"In the bag, Patria, for you, your mother and Rosa. Money too, and papers and keys for the apartment."

"For Rosa . . . ?"

"We can't leave her, Patria. They'll throw her in jail."

The three of them stumbled towards escape, barely making it out the back portal with all they could carry before they heard the crash of the front door. Lola's heart was thumping like a drum. Her feet felt encased in cement blocks. Much too late, she realized she had left her wire-rimmed glasses on top of the manuscript by her bed.

Bonocio fled behind them, shielding his wife and daughter with his dark-clothed body from the rifle-carrying shadows that swiftly invaded the house. He ran for his life, and theirs, until Lola and Patria reached the horse and buggy that he'd arranged for every night a short distance from the house. When he saw Rosa and her godson beside the buggy, he knew his overbearing caution had paid off. That morning, the U.S.S. *Orizaba* was anchored in Havana Harbor, preparing to embark for New York City.

A silvery dawn spilled against the dark horizon as Bonocio dashed away from his family. Shrouded in mist, he sought escape in the opposite streets and alleyways, praying the armed shadows would follow in his tracks, and not in the women's.

There was no time. No time for an embrace. No time for a farewell kiss. Lola felt the searing pain of his departure as if someone had cleaved her in half. For weeks, the women did not know if he had made it safely to a waiting ship, or if Bonocio was dead or alive.

*New York, July 29, 1896*

*My dearest friend, Marta!*

*. . . We are now in New York. It became impossible, regardless of our strong motivation, to remain in Havana, and we left, actually were forced to leave, before confronting greater persecutions. That suffocating and malevolent atmosphere! Lately there had been a rash of incarcerations, imprisonments of distinguished persons. The low morale continued to spread. Thank God I had the good sense to send Laura to my sister in Puerto Rico.*

*We are modestly installed in New York but at least we live in tranquility and can anticipate better days. Here, triumph of the revolution is expected momentarily. They say that General Máximo Gómez assures the end of the war within four months if he receives ten thousand rifles to arm one thousand men . . . and that is the great infusion we all aspire to. God willing, we will soon be able to sing the hymn of victory. . . .*

*Patria and Bonocio join me in sending you and your family our warm wishes. I bid you farewell with a big embrace,*

*Lola,*
*138 West 116th Street*

# 8

## NEW YORK, 1896

Inocencia let out a high-pitched squeal! Her hands flew up to her open mouth. She hadn't expected to see such a spectacle, certainly not like the one unfolding right at her own front door. Doña Lola stood on the landing draped in the most outlandish layering of mauve face veils that Inocencia had ever seen. She couldn't help but to laugh at her old friend's frivolity.

At the curb, a liveried driver waited beside a black ladies' Phaeton partially shielded from view by Lola's rotund figure. The carriage was hitched to a team of white horses.

"Oh, Lola! Phaetons are so *risqué!*"

"My dear, that's us!" Lola laughed through the haze of veiling. "Outrageously flirtatious. We'll dash about town without a worry in the world." She smiled impishly. *It's time,* she had decided, *to jar Inocencia back to her fighting spirit! Time to rejoin the revolution.*

"Well, come, come, come! Aren't you ready? I promised you a day full of surprises, and I am delivering on the first of my promises. Get ready, woman! We are going on a day of adventure!"

Inocencia shrieked again, this time accompanied by a flurry of gleeful hand clapping.

A three-year-old, sandy-haired boy peeked out at Doña Lola from behind Inocencia's skirt. Confused by the commotion, the boy was not quite sure what to make of his mother's unusual behavior. Ogling with eyes as dark as midnight, Mario stuffed his index finger into the hollow of his cheek, dribbled saliva, then distorted his mouth into grotesque shapes. The boy peeked at the visitor, first from one side of his mother's skirt, then the other, until the moment he noticed the white horses with fancy headdress. Then, he pointed his chubby body down the ten steps toward the horses at the curb.

"Oh, no, no, no," commanded Lola, quickly grasping the child's arm. "Not so fast, young man. You must be the young master Mario, I've heard so much about," she said, looking up at Inocencia.

"Sí, Doña Lola, that's him! This is the young tyrant who rules this house!" Inocencia smiled. "This tiny mite has his parents, aunts and everyone else trained to jump to his whistle."

"The boy is a blessing, isn't he? A beautiful, healthy child. But, come, come, let's not tarry! We've much to accomplish today."

Everyone knew Inocencia doted obsessively on the boy, never letting him out of her sight. At her slight hesitation, Lola innocently inquired, "You do have someone to stay with the child, don't you?"

After entrusting Mario's care to Titi Kirina, the women were soon caught up in the bustle of the congested city. The Phaeton stopped as close as it could get to the northeast corner of E. 26th Street and Madison Square so as to allow Lola and Inocencia to step down from the carriage. Linking arms to cross the street, they narrowly escaped an encounter with dozens of lady cyclists. In bright, puffy-sleeved jackets and calf-length skirts, the wheel ladies tooted their horns along Broadway as they cycled towards the park.

One impatient biker, her wild red hair flying askew, shouted at Lola, "Bloody hell, madam, move out of the way!"

Astounded, the friends looked at each other and burst out laughing, only to find themselves surrounded by a ring of wheel ladies. Lola labored to quicken her pace, picking and capering her way through the group with Inocencia in tow.

"¡Madre mía! This parade of wheel ladies'll never end," roared Lola.

The friends ran to the sidewalk, breathlessly joking about women and bicycles.

"Lola, just tell me," laughed Inocencia, "why would anyone in their right mind purposely put herself in such danger? I'd have to be *insane.*"

"Humpf," snorted Lola, invigorated by the encounter with the lady bikers. "Not I! I'd be the first one to ride a bicycle! Think of the convenience, the ease of traveling it gives women! Bicycling gives women the utmost independence . . . and *healthy* exercise. Inocencia, you could never live in Europe because women ride bicycles everywhere!"

Lola was in her element! Her gloved hands flying in all directions, she emphatically added an air punch to her arguments.

"You're so right, Lola! I'll never live in Europe if I have to ride a bicycle to get around!"

"Wasn't it you, Inocencia . . . ? Yes, *you* were the one who wanted women to be on an equal footing with men back in the days when we were in Puerto Rico."

Inocencia stared blankly at Lola as if her friend were speaking about someone else.

When Lola grasped the younger woman's elbow, guiding her to the gilded doors of Delmonico's, she said, "This is where we are expected for lunch today."

Inocencia blanched! "Doña Lola," she gasped, fingering her drawstring purse for the twenty cents her husband had given her to splurge that afternoon. "I can't afford to eat lunch in such an elegant place."

"Nonsense, my dear! Didn't I tell you that *this* day would be full of surprises? Come, my friend. This is my treat. It'll be a new beginning for us both."

After entering and waiting to be seated, Inocencia studied the restaurant's tasteful interior. Wondering if she was properly dressed for such elegance, she fidgeted nervously with her purse and gloves.

Lola leaned over and whispered, *"Mira,* Inocencia, the different seating arrangements let the patrons either be seen, if that's their preference, or find seclusion behind the ferns and giant palm fronds. Makes you wonder how many of the patrons are engaged in secret liaisons, doesn't it?"

Captivated by the music, Inocencia's attention wasn't on the placement of tables, or the restaurant's decor, chandeliers or velvet seat cushions.

"Listen, Lola! They're playing a Viennese waltz! Do you hear it?"

Strains of "The Blue Danube" drifted softly throughout the room, folding the tinkling sounds of the diners' silver forks and spoons into unintended punctuations. Violins struck a chord for Inocencia, filling her heart with a sensation she could not describe. Inocencia could not remember when she'd been so engaged, but she knew if she gave in to the rapture, she'd melt into tears.

Lola ushered Inocencia to a table in the ladies' section of the restaurant. She'd requested a corner table. After being seated, it didn't take long before the two friends were deep in conversation.

"A dirty, frigid city," Inocencia remarked about her impressions of New York.

Recalling how a wayward horse had covered her in manure, Inocencia confessed, "Ay, Lola, it was so painful. And I'm still mutilating the English language! You're so smart. Can you tell me why Americans smother their words. Why don't they pronounce each syllable in a word?"

"Oh, before you know it, you'll be speaking like a New Yorker. . . . ," Doña Lola assured her young companion. "Well, exile has been a recurrent nightmare for us . . . our family . . . Maybe not the shock it's been to you . . . but living in Cuba became dangerous. And I have to say it frightens me to think that I might never again live in Puerto Rico. I've become so melancholy, sometimes overwhelmed with a feeling of loss. You know . . . the strangest thing? I miss the spirits of my ancestors.

"My salons anchored me, gave me purpose! I was doing something important for the movement. *Our meetings!* Oh, Inocencia. You would have loved them. Fraught with danger, intense, productive . . . they were all of those things. And up until the end we were effective. I can tell you that."

Sharing feelings erased the passage of time. Yet, in the funny stories and anecdotes deep-seated emotions began to stir. Lola listened politely, smiling and nodding her head, but she could not shake the feeling that Inocencia's spark was missing. *And is it any wonder,* she thought, *after all she has been through?*

"We don't ask for insurmountable burdens, do we, my dear? But in this life we all have obligations to meet, no matter what obstacles stand in our way."

Lola daintily bit into a watercress sandwich. "Look at your own club! What an impressive contribution you've made with Mercedes Varona, even though you were going through so much in your personal life."

Inocencia stiffened in her seat, tension settling over her face. About to savor the sweetness of a Napolitaine biscuit, she placed the cake back on the plate and brought the linen napkin to her lips. After a moment, she reached for her bag and withdrew a letter from a creased white envelope.

"This is the letter Martí wrote to me when the troubles first began." Her words were barely audible. "I carry it with me always. It's silly, but the letter makes me feel he's still with us . . . makes me feel I was the leader he thought I was."

A dull green stare fixed itself in Inocencia's eyes. Lola wasn't quite sure she'd heard correctly when her friend whispered, almost to herself. "I kept Martí's change of clothes in a cardboard box in the attic, with his cup and saucer. I couldn't bear to wipe away his memory as if he'd never existed. You see, in the afternoons, he liked to stop by the house on his way to meet Sotero at Imprenta América. I'd make him a fresh cup of coffee. Then I'd sit with him in the kitchen, holding my own cup in my hand. We'd talk."

She paused, weaving together invisible threads of memory. "He was like a little boy looking forward to his favorite afternoon treat. You know, he loved a dish of ice cream with chocolate.

"Sometimes, I'll hear a noise as if someone has opened my front door. I turn around expecting to find him smiling broadly at me. 'My lady and dear friend,' he'd say with that joyful enthusiasm he had. 'I've come to see you and your husband, but mostly to borrow your esteemed husband's books again.'

"Then, when the children . . . everything changed."

Without a word, Lola connected with the sorrow in Inocencia's eyes and reached across the table for the letter.

Through misty glasses, she read:

*New York, April 24, 1893*

*Madame President of the Club Mercedes Varona,*
*My distinguished Compatriot,*

*This evening I received a notice from the directorship of the Club Mercedes Varona at the very moment when I plan to embark on a trip which I hope will not be useless for our country. I am not sure, my sisters, if my health is sufficiently vigorous to attend to all of the duties of my trip.*

*If the Club Mercedes Varona were to cease to exist, it would deprive us of its example and its spirit and, most assuredly, that catastrophe would deprive me of my health. And I will maintain my health if during my arduous tasks I were to receive word that the club continues to exist. There is much wrong-doing in the world and many obstacles before reaching true liberation. I will visit the Club Mercedes Varona before any other club to give an accounting of my work and intentions.*

*Proudly, I salute you, my sisters of the club on this election day.*

*The Delegate,*
*José Martí*

Lola re-read, "There is much wrong-doing in the world and many obstacles before reaching true liberation." *Was Martí talking about the couple's marriage, or the obstructionists within the movement?*

"Ay, Inocencia!" Understanding the inconsolable burden Inocencia carried in her heart, she felt a surge of affection for her old friend.

"He had faith in me," Inocencia said, just above a whisper, "that I'd continue the work of the club. It set an example for the other groups, you see. So, I tried. But the children were too ill. And Sotero . . . well, I guess Sotero couldn't let him down either. You see, he worked such long hours, felt he had to do everything, be everywhere, especially when Martí was away on his travels. And my suspicions about my husband began to grow. I blamed him for *everything* . . . the death of our girls, the club, everything that had gone wrong, even the *typhus*. I knew we were being watched. Our enemies used every opportunity to destroy us! But, instead of relying on each other, we became like those ships that pass each other, drifting in opposite directions. And I began to doubt our marriage.

"In May, my boy was born. Healthy. Thank God, he was that, but so demanding! Before year's end, the girls were . . . *it's so painful to remember* . . . Oh Lola! You would have *loved* my little Julia! And Alexa . . . "

Inocencia fell silent. Knowing she had to finish her story, she lowered her glassy eyes to the napkin on her lap, studying it intensely as if she might find a different ending to the tale instead of reliving the truth.

She spoke again in a strained voice that could barely be heard. "Those huge dark eyes just swallowed you up and wouldn't let you . . . Oh, no! *Ay*, Lola!"

Inocencia suddenly reached out and squeezed Doña Lola's hand

"*Ay*, Lola," she moaned. "Alexa had hazel eyes!!! I've forgotten my own children." And she began to weep quietly into the crumpled linen napkin.

Somewhere, a haunting violin intermezzo echoed the sorrow of Inocencia's story, rising and falling in intensity. Dusting away her layers of guilt, the music awakened the buds of a new beginning.

# 9

# NEW YORK, 1897

"Buenos días, Doña Lola," Flora and Leopoldina Quesada offered their greetings as soon as Lola arrived at the fundraiser. Organized by the various women's clubs joining together for the cause, the event was expected to bring in lots of money.

"Such an exciting day, *profesoras* . . . the biggest fundraiser of the year! Your patriotic duty is exemplary." Lola's words trailed off as she breezed her way into the school's auditorium.

Club banners appeared everywhere! In waves of excitement, the women noisily called out to one another in the frenzy of last-minute preparations. Thirty-six booths were prepared to sell bonds, jewelry, paintings, books, bric-a-brac and raffle tickets. Amid the hubbub, Lola searched for Inocencia and their own clubs' banners.

Caught in a crossroad, Lola collided with Blanche Baralt, the woman who had given a rousing speech at the Women's Congress of Patriotism the previous year. A group of younger women surrounded Madame Baralt, all of them standing close to a club banner that read, "The Daughters of Cuba Club."

"My dear Lola," Blanche droned in a sugary tone "we must catch up before day's end." She turned and ordered the young ladies surrounding her to take command of their posts.

"Why, of course, my dear lady," Lola answered, knowing they'd probably not cross paths again amid all the activities. "The Daughters have a *great* location," she called out over her shoulder.

Women lugging tote bags, boxes, baskets and crates spun a heady beehive of activity. Gingerly, Lola stepped from one group to another, adjusting her glasses so she wouldn't miss a thing. She took in current fads in fashion and flitted from table to table as maids carried trays of colorful containers. These were full to overflowing with flyers, pinwheels, balloons, artwork and table coverings.

The method to their madness was making money, and the hustle-bustle atmosphere in the auditorium raised Lola's adrenaline sky high. She wanted nothing more than to jump into the fray. When she saw the red and white banner of her clubs, Caridad and Oscar Prinelles, Lola was thrilled. They were positioned in booths not far from the food stalls. *Excellent. Anyone going to buy food or beverages will pass by our booths.* She made a mental note to relieve the club officers after she'd met with Inocencia.

*Why raising money excites me, like playing roulette at a casino, I don't know. Has to be the exhilarating blend of avarice and gentility. I can already smell it in the air.* She reminded herself to share that observation with Inocencia. Out of habit, Lola pushed her spectacles up high on the bridge of her snub nose, knocking her hat to the side of her head just as the first trickle of customers began to stroll leisurely among the displays.

She squinted her eyelids to see if they had begun to mill around her booths yet. Then Lola stopped short. She smelled the aroma of freshly baked goods. Without giving it a second thought, Lola took off in the direction of the aroma.

Low rumbles rose in intensity from the floor to the rafters, reminding Lola of parishioners at Sunday prayer. As her thoughts returned to money and profits, she soon encountered a gauntlet of women selling their wares. *They sound like carnival barkers*, she thought, darting from the curiosities of one booth to the next.

"Señora! Come. Look here. A box of fine lace . . . from Spain. Perfect for evening wear!" Another lady suddenly cried out as if she were in an open air plaza, "Come! Come and see this fine gold bracelet donated by a wealthy Cuban refugee. Forced to leave everything she owned behind when she sailed from Havana, she is sacrificing her bracelet for the cause!"

Lola laughed, amused by the woman's ability to spin a yarn, and dove into aisles festooned with patriotic flags, garlands and bunting. Women displayed bejeweled necklaces, rings, earrings, bracelets around their necks, arms, ears and hands. They wanted to sell everything before day's end.

Some ladies aggressively hawked clothing, books, ceramics, raffle tickets, even musical instruments at passing gawkers and buyers; others handed out brochures advertising their club programs, hoping to spill the day's momentum into increased membership.

*Wait until I tell Inocencia about the cunning wiles women are using to sell their wares!* Lola couldn't help but smile. Fascinated, she watched daughters or nieces of club women flirting shamelessly, using their pretty faces, pouts and smiles, to draw in customers . . . their mothers or aunts standing guard nearby.

*Ay, madre*, she thought. *Each club is pledged to raise funds for the same cause, but the undercurrent of competition can't be denied.*

"Oh, there you are," Lola barked above the din when she spied Inocencia pinning red, white and blue bunting around a booth marked Club Mercedes Varona. "Where's Laudelina? Wasn't she assigned to this booth?"

Lola handed Inocencia a pineapple puff pastry wrapped in a folded napkin that she had bought from the food concession. Then she took a bite out of her own.

"*Ay*, Inocencia. We'll need more tables to lure customers. Got to show our wares more artistically. Right now, everything is bunched together," Lola said, licking sticky fingers.

"Well, buenos días to you too, Doña Lola." Inocencia chuckled, not surprised that her friend would enter the booth bellowing orders. "Doña Laudelina is delayed. I'll be taking care of business at Mercedes Varona until she arrives. And, don't worry. María Acosta will preside at the Hermanas de Rius Rivera Club until I can relieve her."

"Do you realize there are only eleven women's groups in this city?" Lola fired enthusiastically. "For an exile community, we take on the greatest burdens. But, let's face it, we need more . . . more tables, more action, more visibility if we're to make any money today!

"The truth is, my dear, we need *experienced* women whose hearts and souls are with the cause! Imagine how unstoppable, how *effective* we would be if we could double or triple our club activities."

"Yes, yes, Doña Lola! But not today. Today, we're here to make today's money."

"And what is that infernal pounding?" Lola asked, turning to the source of the racket.

Strapped to a wooden chair in the square formed by his mother's four booth tables, Lola saw a very unhappy child. Sullen-eyed, young Mario's lower lip pouted. Lest anyone assume the boy was happy, his high-cut leather boots banged annoyingly against the legs of the chair. He wore his first set of short pants, and Lola guessed the dirt-soaked stain on the green sailor suit was the cause of his grounding.

"The young scamp is being punished until Doly gets here. Please ignore him. No, no, Lola! Pretend you don't see him, or he'll find a way to get you to help him escape. He was rolling hoops. Rolled right into the gutter."

"Humph," snorted Lola, finding it difficult to show displeasure towards the child.

"I shouldn't have let him go," fretted Inocencia.

"Well, if Mamá didn't want you to play, why did she dress you in short pants and stockings, my sweet?"

Mario offered a dimpled smile, bonding with the one person who understood his dilemma. When Inocencia turned towards the table arrangements, Lola slipped the boy the rest of her pineapple pastry.

By the time Inocencia relieved Doña María Acosta at the Rius Rivera booth, she'd already strolled the aisles comparing prices and merchandise at surrounding booths with her own. *My prices are too low,* she mused. *The bonds seem to set the standard at five dollars a bond. But jewelry can sell for any price depending on the quality. What about books? Crafts or baby clothes? These are valuable items. I'm going to price higher.* She decided to allow the buyers to bargain for better prices if it came to that.

By noon, Inocencia had sold the last of Lola's collection of poems. Beaming a radiant smile towards Doña Lola, she held up a dollar bill in her hand, then turned to inserting a stack of Rafael Serra's essays between a tray of ladies' hand soaps and a set of infant caps and booties. She grabbed a pencil from the table and labeled the essays and the soaps at five cents. The price for the infant clothes, she set at three cents, reasoning that children's clothes were usually passed down from one child to the next.

"I could have told you my poems would sell out," chided Lola as she joined Inocencia in the Rius Rivera booth. "They also sold out at the Congress of Patriotism last year."

"Well, let's see how well the hand soaps do. I'm pricing those as high as I dare," laughed Inocencia, delighted the Rius Rivera Club was making money. It was the first club she'd created for the Puerto Rico Section.

At the close of the day, when the party atmosphere had finally begun to wane, Inocencia heard a loud whoop from the direction of the Club Caridad. Lola came rushing towards Inocencia's booth, waving a sheet of paper in the air.

"You'll never *believe* it, Inocencia!" Lola shouted, stopping to catch her breath. Caridad made one hundred and sixty dollars!"

"Oh, Lola! How magnificent!" Inocencia blurted out excitedly. She lifted her long blue skirt and twirled around to give Lola a congratulatory hug. "Your good fortune makes it all worthwhile. It's a good sign, Lola, a sign that God is on our side. We *will* win this war."

Without warning, the skin on Lola's arms and neck prickled. *Someone is walking over my grave,* she thought superstitiously. She gazed soberly at her friend, wishing she could pluck Inocencia's words from the air and put them back into the genie's bottle. *Some things are better left unsaid.*

She glanced about at the debris that was left from the morning's displays. Ripped up wooden structures reminded her of naked bones. Remnants of multi-colored booths became swaths of destruction, the kind she'd witnessed in the ravaged Cuban countryside. She paused and stared at scattered busted balloons, pinwheels and discarded bunting. She listened to the absence of noise. When all was said and done, *this* was the epitome of the club women's hard work. This was what their labor had accomplished.

*How it pales in comparison to the fallen patriots, the young generals who've lost their lives on the battle front,* she thought. Turning soulful eyes to her trusting friend, she murmured.

"What if we don't, Inocencia? What will we do then?"

# PART IV

# 1

# NEW YORK, 1897

When he heard the swish of Lola's skirt, Bonocio stopped packing his briefcase. *Uh, oh. I may be too late,* he thought, anxiously. *I'm in for it now. Lola's litany of questions and farewells grows longer every day.* He patted down his thick head of silver hair and reached haphazardly into the usual drawers for gloves. *Oh? Things are never where they're supposed to be any more. And I'm running late for the meeting. No time for idle chatter.*

And then, Lola stood before him. She was not in a mood to be rushed. She tilted her head, silently inspecting his appearance from head to toe. Using her *lorgnette,* she searched for anything amiss. When she settled for straightening his cravat, her snub nose wrinkled as if she would have done a better job of tying it.

"Lola, *por favor,* I look perfectly handsome. Please stop dressing me," Bonocio mumbled in annoyance.

Lola ignored the outburst, then stepped towards the coat rack to retrieve his hat. The kid leather gloves, she lifted discretely from the console. *Right under his nose,* she thought, handing them to him. Without saying a word, she began to brush imagined bits of dust off of his lapels.

"Bonocio," she finally said, giving him the raised eyebrow he knew meant business. "Temper your remarks at the

185

meeting today. I'm serious. And while I'm at it, there are some points I wish to make before you rush off in such a hurry, so please hear me out."

"Of course, love of my life. How can I possibly escape without points?" He attempted a bit of levity. "What is it the generals say about you? With women like Lola, you can make a revolution!"

"*Ay*, Bonocio. Be serious. Remind Dr. Henna that we're prepared to do everything in our power for the invasion. Tell him that. Tell him Betances convinced the French and Italian supporters to part with their money. Henna will be happy to hear that. And, are you sure you want to leave without eating something?"

"Yes, Lola."

"All right, then. Did you remember to give the doctor the names of our contacts in Mayagüez? Ask Estrada Palma why these names don't appear on the donor list, nor our friends and relatives in Caracas and Santo Domingo. Ask him that."

"Yes, Lola, to all your concerns. I spoke to Henna, informed Estrada Palma about the names and I'm not hungry. Right now, I'm anxious to get to the meeting and into action. Want to make sure Estrada Palma abides by the articles of the party."

He placed the bowler on his head and grabbed his briefcase. Then he gazed at his wife's pressed lips, the strained expression on her face, and spoke gently. "You know, in Estrada Palma's head, Puerto Rico is his least concern. I need to be there to remind him."

"Humph!" Lola's crinkled eyes became brown slits of concentration. "So, you're admitting that while the old man cooks in Cuba, he lets the Puerto Rican issue simmer on the back burner! That's why you, Figueroa and the good Dr. Henna have to light a fire under him. He *needs* to give us the promised funds! When it comes to Puerto Rico, all the members of the Section must push our interests because on that subject Estrada Palma oozes like spilled molasses. By now, I would have moved mountains. If women were allowed to be at that meeting . . . "

"*Ay, Lola!*" Hoping to quell his wife's indignation, Bonocio gave her a perfunctory embrace, but Lola would have none of it.

"*¡Mujer!* Be reasonable. He has to balance the cost of insurrection. The man walks a fine line. Even I'll admit to that."

"You're hopeless, Bonocio!" She rolled her eyes in exasperation.

"*Madre mía,* what would you say if I told you that on the day of the Club Rius Rivera's inauguration, he was the guest of honor, and didn't show up? He gave as excuse that he was tied up with business.

"Bonocio! The man's office and home are a few minutes' walk to Inocencia's house! He could at least have shown his face! You're too kind to think well of that man."

"There may have been a good reason, Lola. He probably forgot to let the club know."

"*¡Hombre!* I'll excuse you this time . . . if you promise to return as soon as the meeting is over. I'm anxious to write to Betances and Doña Marta about the plans for Yauco. Promise?"

His mumbled response was lost in the hurried kiss he planted on the top of Lola's head. Then he was gone.

Lola stared at the closed door, her arms crossed in front of her. *This'll be the Section's thirty-first meeting! How will Dr. Henna promote an invasion plan where all others have failed . . . failed before they even started?*

# 2

# NEW YORK, 1897

A dining table served as Dr. Henna's desk, his hardwood gavel casually resting on its sounding block. The desk overwhelmed the small meeting hall, Chimney Corner Hall, named for its rounded corner fireplace. When the pile of chairs stacked in the corner were spread out, there wasn't enough space for all the seats. Some lucky members secured seats; others straddled rickety chairs, or leaned against the walls or doorframes, hopelessly spilling out into the hallway. Still, the eyes of every person in the room were riveted to the minute details sketched on a hastily drawn chart. In bold x's and check marks, the chart highlighted disembarkation points in strategic locations along the coasts of the homeland. It illustrated the long-awaited invasion of Puerto Rico.

Across from the desk, General Agustín Morales stood as tall as his 5'5" height would allow. Holding one end of the chart up to his shoulder, he projected his gruff voice over the heads of sixty, or more, expatriates. Blacks, whites, mulattos and *indios*, the Puerto Rican men gathered in the room shared deep convictions about liberation. They belonged to different social classes, yet each had sacrificed what he could afford to fill the party's war chest, and now they hoped to reap its promised harvest.

"The plan is simple," bellowed the general clad in impeccable military garb. "And here is why it will be effective."

The other corner of the chart was gripped in the hand of a tall, light-skinned, coffee *hacendado* from Yauco, Mattei Lluberas. An imposing figure, his features beckoned an ancestral Corsican lineage, but bore the intrepid streak of rebellion found among his countrymen.

Mattai Lluberas and General Morales had arrived in the city several days earlier, eager to broker support, acquire funds, munitions and anything else the Puerto Rico Section could muster. While the blustery general presented his case, Mattei Lluberas studiously gauged the pulse of expatriate reaction.

"I will land one hundred and fifty men on the southwest beaches between Cabo Rojo and Ponce, probably in Punta Brava or Guánica," pronounced General Morales. "The remaining group will disembark . . . oh, I'd wager, just about here in the northwest coves of Isabela." He pointed a stubby, nicotine finger to the scraggy coastline, leaving a ghostly stain on the chart where the Atlantic roiled between Arecibo and Aguadilla.

"In Ceiba or Las Piedras, between Humacao and Fajardo in the northeast, we'll set roadblocks." Morales gestured expansively towards the audience, eliciting their buying into the plan.

"Massive disruptions, captured garrisons, pickets and scouting parties. Even now, our *paisanos* are itching to burn the sugar cane fields and dynamite the Spanish strongholds. This'll be the signal to begin the uprising."

"We believe the people will join in by the hundreds," said Mattei Lluberas less aggressively than the general. "Telegraph wires to the outside world will be cut off. Road conditions are poor, so it should take at least four to seven hours before Spanish reinforcements can be activated."

"*Compatriotas*," barked the general, "garrison troops *only* number between 4,000 and 4,500. We can take them! We'll mimic the *guerrillistas* in Cuba . . . use guerrilla tactics."

Morales puffed up his chest impressed with his own tallies. "Opportunity, my friends! It shines on our efforts. Let's not squander the moment."

On that call, the general ended his discourse with a flourish. He reached for one of the three glasses of water on the president's desk, satisfied that he had made a convincing argument.

"We all support independence," stated Dr. Henna categorically. "Is the exile community prepared to fund an invasion?"

"Yes, Dr. Henna, we surely hope they will," jumped in General Morales. "The exile community can fund our plan with the money from the sale of bonds. We need weapons, recruits and currency to oil certain palms when obstacles present themselves. As time is of the essence, we ask that financial aid from New York begin immediately."

Henna took in a deep breath and scanned the room, then revealed his trump card. "We're in a good position to launch an invasion. Estrada Palma, who, as you know heads the Cuban Revolutionary Party, gave his word that funds and munitions will be available. When do you expect to strike the initial blow?"

"Dr. Henna, members of the Puerto Rico Section," responded an exuberant Mattei Lluberas, "we need several months to round up and train recruits in the Yauco countryside. A cache of 30,000 machetes awaits our return. Two experienced Cuban liberators are already training recruits.

"The independence of Puerto Rico *will* see the light of day."

# 3

## YAUCO, 1897

At the approximate moment the exiles were meeting in New York City, Carlito Cruz, a brown-skinned peasant boy with lanky hair, scrambled along an unpaved road in the lush, southwestern mountains of Puerto Rico. His heart raced fiercely in his skinny chest as he climbed the rough terrain, yet he dared not slow his pace. Small rocks and debris punctured the calloused soles of his feet. They caught between his skin and the loosely tied, makeshift sandals he wore. Suddenly, he winced in agony. His bloody soles felt on fire and became slippery against the sandals. But he willed himself to ignore the pain, to look for the white tower that identified the hacienda of Don Guillermo Velazco, the point of his destination. *¡Ay, virgencita! Let me make it to Don Fidel, before I collapse,* he prayed, and wiped away stinging drops of sweat from his eyes.

As the tower came into view, he forced his weary legs to push open a wooden gate at the western border of the Velazco hacienda. Only then, did the boy allow himself to slow down. He gulped mouthfuls of air into his constricted throat, grateful he had arrived. Closing dry, irritated eyes, Carlito found upon opening them that he faced a rifle barrel.

"*¿Qué haces aquí, chamaquito?* Hey kid, what are you doing here?" barked the surly figure holding the weapon.

"Señor, *ay*, señor, *por favor*, I *must* speak to Don Fidel. Please, señor . . . I bring news!"

"You bring news, huh, or is it matters that don't concern you that you're here to fish out?"

Ignoring the salt-streaked tracks that ran down Carlito's cheeks, the guard prepared to hurl him out of the gate. But the boy dug his lacerated feet into the dirt and grabbed onto the guard's arm.

"Listen to me, you big bully! Let me go! I must warn Don Fidel . . . please!"

"Let go, you upstart," yelped the guard as he grabbed a tuft of the boy's straggly hair and dragged him towards an open field.

There stood Don Fidel Vélez, leader of the Sabana Grande insurrectionists, surrounded by some eighty men wielding machetes.

"What is this news you bring, boy," the wiry Fidel Vélez asked.

"Well, boy? You can tell me your news. But first, take a deep breath. There's no need to rush. I'm right here, ready to hear what you've come to say."

"Señor, I stood by a wagon still as a mouse because I was not supposed to be there, so close to the opened window. That's when I heard two soldiers mention your name ... and that of Don Mattei Lluberas. I heard the tall one tell the fat one, '*Mira, hombre*, there's gonna be an uprising,' and then he said, 'the devils'll pay for it with their lives.' I heard him say the soldiers from Mayagüez will shoot the first volley within a fortnight."

"The devils will pay with their lives? Is that what you heard?"

"Sí, señor."

"You did good, boy."

Fidel Vélez placed his rough hand on the boy's slip of a shoulder. *But the surprise will come from us. We'll need more than machetes for this task.*

Once he saw to it that the boy had recovered sufficiently from his ordeal of climbing up the mountain, he sent him to the kitchen of the hacienda for food and water.

"*Oye, chamaco,* ask María to look after those feet."

Restlessly, Don Fidel paced, tugging on one corner of his bushy, unkempt mustache as he tried to decide the best course of action. Aware they were all marked men, he figured they didn't have the luxury of time and had to act without delay.

He consulted the camp trainers, the Budet Rivera brothers; the *hacendado,* Guillermo Velazco, and José Maldonado Román, the Águila Blanca who caused havoc for the military with his quick and crafty exploits against the authorities. Fidel conferred with the men wielding the machetes whose lives would be on the line. He spoke to trusted workers on the hacienda. Finally, he gathered all of the insurrectionists on the veranda to relate his proposed plan of action.

Vélez began by evoking memories of the Lares revolt back in 1868.

"The similarities between the situation faced by the Lares insurrectionists and our own is uncanny. Once their plans were discovered, they too were forced to strike a blow for freedom before its time. The difference, *compatriotas,* will be in the outcome. We *will* persevere."

Ending his speech, Vélez searched the faces of each one of his men. "You are free to leave or to stay the course, for we're surely headed into destiny." Then, holding the one starred flag in his uplifted hand, Vélez declared, "We can't wait for word from Mattei Lluberas or General Morales. This very night the garrison will be stripped of its rifles. At dawn, it is Yauco that strikes the gong for liberation, and I will be humbled to carry this flag into battle."

Before sunrise on the following morning, Fidel Vélez led a band of some one hundred followers wielding machetes, pistols and an assortment of farm tools to the sleepy center of town. Their objective was to overtake the poorly guarded garrison and commandeer the cache of rifles. They could not have known that during the night the governor had secretly reinforced the post. Destiny saw the ragtag insurgents, marching under the one star flag, scattered by the first volley of gunfire.

Before noon, the insurrection had been snuffed out.

# 4

## NEW YORK, 1897

Inocencia's restless mind was a whirlwind. *We lost Yauco.*
*All right! We don't give up. Work without stop, roll more bandag-*
*es, sell more raffles. Ay! All those performances we've mounted!*

She'd hurried out the door without taking an umbrella.
Now, the sky threatened and she regretted it as she rushed
along W. 116th Street, anxious to reach Lola's house.

The future of liberation seemed as foreboding as the
clouds hovering above. Inocencia ran up the brownstone
steps at No. 138 and pressed her index finger insistently
against the doorbell. *Hurry up, Rosa. It's Thursday. I know you*
*work on Thursdays. Why isn't anyone answering the door?*

She had dressed hurriedly that morning, grabbing a
frayed, everyday jacket instead of one better-suited for visiting. Standing all alone on the front landing, she felt conspic-
uous and peeked through the beveled-glass panels on each
side of Lola's front door for signs of life. Passing strollers
gave her curious looks. *Huh! Do these gawkers think I'm try-*
*ing to break in, that I don't belong here?*

*Ay, I almost forgot the bell at the servants' quarters on street*
*level!* Just as Inocencia made a half turn to dash down the
steps, the front door flew open, and a boarder walked out of
the building.

"Good day," he said tipping his hat to Inocencia, who was about to barrel right through him.

"And to you," she barely whispered, immediately grabbing hold of the door before it closed to let herself into the vestibule. Running up the one flight of stairs, she found Lola standing on the landing.

"Why didn't you answer the bell?" she asked, trying to catch her breath.

"Inocencia, what are you doing here? Weren't we supposed to meet at your house in the afternoon? Did I confuse the time and place again? Come in. Goodness, it looks like you were running. Were you?"

"Ay, Lola, I was," she answered breathlessly as she entered the parlor and pulled out a newspaper from her bag. "But only up the stairs. I need you to look at this article. I'm not sure I understand all the English," Inocencia said as Lola quickly scanned the article. "Do you think this is true? If this really is true, I think we should examine how we're spending our energies. Ay, Lola, all our efforts . . . and nothing seems to succeed."

The *Sun* article was dated September 16, 1897:

*Porto Rico's Sorry State*
*Suffering from Misrule, with Consequent*
*Business and Agricultural Depression*

> Under the date of September 7 a gentleman living in Porto Rico writes to one of his friends in this city: The Government fears that a serious uprising may occur at any moment, and all sorts of precautions are taken to prevent it. Forts are building all along the ridge of mountains across the Island. The forts in course of construction are: One midway between Aibonito and Cayey, another between Cayey and Caguas, another between Adjuntas and Lares, another between Comerío and Bayamón and one more at Luquillo.

"Goodness, Inocencia! What in heavens name is going on in Puerto Rico?" Lola said and continued to read through the article.

> *The country is in a state of alarm. There seems to be no end to the famous proceedings over the Yauco uprising. New arrests in connection with the affair are made almost every day. The jails all over the island are crowded with political prisoners. I know that some sixty persons, including several merchants and farmers, have lately been imprisoned at Camuy, Vega Baja, Sabana Grande and Yauco. There are no indications that the situation is going to improve. Many persons have left the island and others are preparing to leave for fear of incarceration.*
>
> *I do not know whether a revolution is actually preparing or not: but I may say that if this condition of affairs should continue the people here will be driven to revolt. Prisoners are subjected to torture in order to extort from them confessions of their participation in alleged conspiracies. We are now witnessing a revival of Torquemada's methods with all the improvements that the Spaniards' peculiar ingenuity has of late added to the primitive horrors of their infamous inquisition. The practice is now in vogue to feed prisoners on salt codfish with no water to drink until they have been forced to declare whatever their hangman chooses.*

"Inocencia, I am so tired of bad news." Lola lowered the article and rolled her eyes forlornly. " . . . Tired of reading about failed uprisings, tired of losing volunteers, losing crates of supplies to the enemy on the high seas.

"I'm angry about Estrada Palma taking away the funds promised to the Puerto Rico Section. And now this? This is *so* disturbing, I don't know where to turn."

"I know one thing, Lola: we're *not* giving up. We've come too far for that. But here's my thought. What can we, the women, do to attract outside support? I mean beyond our clubs. I mean . . . something big!"

"*Ay, m'ija,* for the first time you're making me feel my age. I think we've done everything, haven't we?"

Lola shoved the newspaper under her arm and pressed both hands together, as if in prayer, then held them up against her lips. She looked at Inocencia, a bittersweet grimace on her moon-shaped face "First, Inocencia," she said, excitement coming back into her voice. "Let's find out more about what's behind this article. Why was it published? To warn commercial investors? Listen to this part."

Lola returned to the article and read aloud:

> . . . *Would that we could throw our yoke off and live the life of independence under the protection of the United States! What a great country Puerto Rico would be then. We are all here either for annexation or independence under an American protectorate . . . "*

"Whoever this anonymous gentleman is," said Lola, "he wants the United States to get involved. And this newspaper isn't the only one fanning the winds of war. It isn't the first to try to influence the American people in that direction. Is this story legitimate? I don't know. That reference to Torquemada is rather overblown, I'd think."

"That makes some sense," Inocencia responded "But, what bothers me is that this piece is so, so sensational."

"Look, if it's true, and I'm sure there's some truth here, then this spells disaster for our movement."

"But, Lola. What if, as you say, it's to get attention . . . just a ploy to sell newspapers. Will it simply agitate people into frenzy? Into war? It did that to me. Is that good for our side?"

She moved towards the window and gazed up at the threatening clouds, almost certain that she'd get caught in the rain.

"Looks like bad weather is moving in, Doña Lola. Maybe that's why I've been feeling so unsettled. I should be thankful. We've been doing *great* work. If we're able to contribute the way we do to the cause, we'll just continue to do so."

"I agree, but maybe we could do better. Shall I ask Rosa to make us some coffee?" Lola folded the paper so that Bonocio could read it on his return.

"I should be heading home." She remembered it was Sotero's day to take Mario to the Menagerie in Central Park. "Oh, Lola! On second thought, I deserve a day out. I'm sure Sotero is clever enough to find something to do with Mario. I'd love to have a cup of coffee with you."

Just then, a loud clap of thunder exploded outside, startling the friends.

"*Ay, madre,*" Lola gasped, rushing to close the windows against the downpour. Afterwards, the women sat in the kitchen, listening to the rain banging against the window panes. Sipping cups of creamy, sweet Caribbean coffee, the friends bonded in the warmth of each other's company. Silently, each woman pondered similar thoughts.

*If only there was someone, or something, that could bring the support we need; then our liberation could finally become a reality.*

# 5
# NEW YORK, 1897

For as far as the eye could see on a crisp October day, all sorts of people lined the streets of the city. Shopkeepers, bankers, lawyers, chimney sweeps, lodgers, housekeepers, factory workers, politicians and club women waved American flags along the route from the Hotel Waldorf on Fifth Avenue to Madison Avenue, hoping to catch a glimpse of Evangelina Cisneros. The Cuban rebel, made famous by New York's sensationalist newspapers, rode by in an elegant, open carriage drawn by four pitch black horses.

The multitudes crowded the sidewalk and spilled into Thirty-third Street, blocking traffic all the way to the thoroughfares of Madison Square Park and the Garden. They trampled the grass in the park, then climbed onto benches to peer over the crowd. From Twenty-sixth Street, the crush of revelers swarmed across to Delmonico's. There, an honor guard of rifle- and machete-toting Cuban fighters surrounded the carriage. Behind them, New York Naval Cadets formed a barrier so that the women's committee, which included Mrs. Alvarez of the Club Mercedes Varona, could escort her into the restaurant.

The farthest thing on Evangelina Cisneros' mind as her carriage made its way through throngs of well-wishers was that she could be the answer to the expatriates' prayers. The plight of the eighteen-year-old stowaway was considered an example of the iniquity of Spanish rule, and Evangelina, herself, personalized the need for U.S. intervention in Cuba's war for independence.

Everyone knew Evangelina's story. New Yorkers could recite the rebel's ordeal by heart, could tell how the "Flower of Cuba" had been captured by the Spaniards, accused of conspiracy and imprisoned for over a year. For weeks, *The New York Journal* had orchestrated her escape, its bold headlines raising alarm about the rape of pure Cuban women and other villainous actions by the Spaniards. Evangelina's story pulled on the nation's heartstrings. Becoming everyone's darling daughter or treasured sister, she swayed Americans to the Cuban cause.

🌟 🌟 🌟

The entire Figueroa household had turned out for the public welcoming. Kirina and Doly joined Inocencia's family to share the historic moment.

"Here!" Sotero shouted to the women. "Try to find a space at the Twenty-fourth Street stand, where we can see and hear the speakers at Madison Square Garden."

Sotero took the bag Inocencia was carrying so that she could shepherd young Mario towards the speakers' stand.

From the stand closest to the Worth Monument, the Seventh Regiment Band began to play, filling the festive atmosphere with popular and military pieces. Young Mario was in his glory! Wearing his favorite sailor suit with full aplomb, despite the outer coat that hid it from view, he strutted to the fanfare of a John Philip Sousa military march as he waved the flags of Cuba and Puerto Rico in his small, chubby hands.

"¡*Muchachito!*" Sotero yelled, yanking his son roughly by the arm. The child had almost been swallowed up in a crowd of revelers.

"Mario! You're forbidden to stray, do you hear? It's dangerous for you to prance about on your own. Do you want to get lost? Or wind up in an orphanage . . . or in jail?"

Inocencia cringed when he spoke to the boy like that. She leaned over to the frightened child who she saw was on the verge of tears. "Mario," she crooned softly, "listen to me, *corazón*. Come here. Do you see this stone monstrosity? Look at it very, very closely. It is very tall, isn't it."

"Um hum." The child choked back his tears.

"Can you memorize what it looks like? If you lose sight of me or Papá, stand by the monstrosity and *we will find you!* Is that an acceptable solution, Papá?"

She gazed up at Sotero, her expression pleading for his approval. Sotero scanned the square, making sure there were no other similar monuments. He crouched beside the statue to read its inscription.

"Well, wouldn't you know it. This General Worth fought in the war between Mexico and the United States. Highly decorated. Promoted to major-general because he helped rob a third of the Mexican nation to expand American borders." Shaking his head in mock disbelief, Sotero issued a wry smile towards his wife. "Of course, it doesn't mention that here. Seems you can't get away from annexationists, no matter where you go, doesn't it? I guess we'll have to trust the general to protect our child. It's a good plan, Inocencia. Tell the boy. Let's just hope we don't have to use it."

At approximately eight o'clock, bright searchlights began to scan the crowds from all directions. Fireworks lit up the sky. A startled Mario scooted towards his mother and clutched the edge of her cape. Pink mouth agape, a mixture of rapture and fear played on his boyish features.

Sotero and Inocencia grinned at one another. They laughed at their young son's amazement and gave in to the thrills triggered by the succession of explosive pyrotechnics.

"Ohhhh . . . ahhhh," echoed through the crowd with each explosion. Before either Sotero or Inocencia realized it, the three stood holding hands, caught in the heart of the enchanted moment.

"We should take the boy to the new Steeplechase Park in Coney Island, Inocencia!" shouted Sotero over the noise.

Aglow from a starburst's reflection, Inocencia turned to him and thought, *Do you remember, Sotero, the last time we were happy under a canopy of heavenly constellations?* Silently, she added this moment to a list of happy occasions. She held Sotero's hand tightly, not wanting to let him go. *But nothing lasts forever.*

As Evangelina Cisneros drew near, Sotero and Inocencia began to search the faces of the throng, craning their necks to catch their first glimpse of the rebel.

"Here, Sotero, please hold the banner for me while I adjust the binoculars." Inocencia handed him a parcel stuffed with the club banner of Hermanas de Rius Rivera. She intended to hoist the banner when Evangelina appeared as a sign that she had Puerto Rican support.

The speeches began with Senator Thurston of Nebraska. By the time Dr. Henry Lincoln Zayas, president of the Club Oscar Primelles, began to speak, a roar swelled from the crowd. Like a tidal surge, it rippled from Twenty-sixth Street all the way to the park. An undercurrent of murmurs floated in waves, from group to group, alerting the multitude that the girl was in their midst. As the cheering reached its pinnacle, the crowds parted not far from where Sotero and Inocencia stood, and the rebel appeared escorted by Karl Decker, the man who had rescued her.

Holding her furs up close to her neck, Evangelina walked with the confidence of one who practiced humility. In truth, she was not humble, but honest. The girl exuded surprising dignity for one so young. As she stepped up to the stand, the snowy sparkle of her white satin dress drew the crowd's attention like a beacon flashing across the night sky.

Inocencia held the binoculars to her eyes and saw a beautiful young woman with skin so white she looked like a frozen fairytale princess. She studied every inch of the rebel's appearance, noting her abundant head of black hair, ringlets framing her delicate features. She focused on Evangelina's eyes, large and luminous, like a child caught between fear and curiosity. A pinkish glow was barely detectable on her lips and cheeks. Then, just as the rebel began to say *¡qué viva Cuba libre!*, Inocencia gasped and dropped the binoculars.

"The princess!" Inocencia swirled around and grabbed Sotero's arm. "Look at her! She looks like the princess!"

Sotero stared through the recovered binoculars. "Yes! You are right, Inocencia. She looks enough like the princess to be her twin. The same slender frame, black hair and large eyes that command attention. But as I recall from our conversation with the princess, Victoria Ka'iulani is taller, a bit darker in complexion."

"But Sotero. What are the odds that two young women who could pass for twins, from different nations, different parts of the world, would both find themselves in one place fighting for the liberation of their people?"

# 6

# NEW YORK, 1897

"Princess Victoria Ka'iulani Kleghorn is heir to the throne of the Hawaiian Kingdom," Sotero had explained two weeks earlier, prodding Inocencia to hurry along. They were going to be late for Dr. Henna's reception in honor of the princess.

"I'm moving as fast as I can. How is one expected to dress to meet a princess? Am I supposed to bow when we're introduced?"

Inocencia fumbled with her hair once more. Then she grabbed the black silk cape and elbow-length white gloves from the bed. As she walked out of the bedroom, she snuck a peek in the mirror and frowned. "Humph! I'm as ready as I'll ever be. At least Lola will be there. She'll help me tame this stubborn hair."

The Figueroas mounted the waiting hansom cab, badgering the driver to take the shortest route across town. When they arrived at Dr. Henna's, they were informed that the princess had been delayed. Inocencia handed the butler her cape and smoothed her hair, while Sotero removed his hat, stuffing it with his silk scarf. Handing it to the butler, he murmured, "Thank you, James," and the couple made their way into the drawing room. They joined Lola and Bonocio in

the Hennas' glass-enclosed sun parlor adjacent to the drawing room.

"This room is beautiful," Inocencia whispered to Lola. "I
haven't visited too many homes as splendid as this." She
glanced around, noting the doctor's art collection and prehis-
toric sculptures. When she came to the musical instruments,
she flashed Lola a quizzical smile.

"You'll be even more impressed to hear the magnificent
sounds from that piano, if the good doctor decides to play
for us. He's very talented, once considered making his career
in music.

"And look here, Inocencia." Lola pointed to two
guitars—a *tiple* and a *cuatro*—mounted on special stands.
"These can only be from Puerto Rico."

Just then Ada Henna approached the group and offered
polite excuses in a soft, silvery voice.

"Well, here you are! I didn't have a chance to welcome
you properly," she said, and whisked the Figueroas away
with the promise that she'd return them momentarily.

"Madame Figueroa," Ada said, "Madame Tió has been
telling me all about you. I've met your husband before. Now
I've the pleasure of welcoming you to my home."

Inocencia was surprised to be singled out. *What a lovely
woman. I didn't imagine the doctor's wife to be so charming.*

Linking arms with both Sotero and Inocencia, Ada
Henna guided the pair towards her husband, who stood
beside a lavish buffet table. "Our guest of honor is delayed,
you know. So don't be surprised if my dear husband talks
your ear off before she arrives."

"Put simply," explained Dr. Henna, joining the three at
the table, "Princess Ka'iulani is in New York to meet with
members of the Hawaiian Political Association and the Patriotic League. They're petitioning against annexing the kingdom to the United States. It was her idea to meet with us.

She understands the similarities between our struggle in Puerto Rico and what's already happened in her kingdom."

"Have you met the princess before, Dr. Henna?" asked Inocencia.

"I have. About four years ago. Had occasion to speak with her. Then, she was on her way to Washington to denounce the overthrow of the queen, her aunt Liliuokalani, by American sugar planters. The princess still fights annexation. At this point, it looks like the damage is done."

"Oh, Julio! Let the Figueroas circulate, please. You've managed to monopolize the conversation again!" Ada Henna scowled playfully at her husband.

Suddenly, all eyes turned towards the doors. Princess Ka'iulani had entered the drawing room.

From the moment she arrived, Inocencia could not take her eyes off Victoria Ka'iulani. She was tall and carried her height like a queen. Organdy sleeves on an off-the-shoulder white silk gown accentuated her dusky complexion, making her face lively and inquisitive.

The princess chose to address the guests in Spanish, one of the many languages she spoke. She'd been educated in England to become a queen—an articulate, international leader. Completely bowled over with the princess's accomplishments, Inocencia stood by Sotero's side in awe of the woman.

"Honored guests," said the princess, "I asked to meet with you because your movement sets an example for my people. I believe where injustice and exploitation exists, revolution becomes a duty.

"When I discovered my aunt was deposed, my kingdom annexed to the United States, I protested. In Boston, New York and in Washington, I made speeches, negotiated with heads of organizations—I even met with President Cleveland—all to no avail. By 1894, a new Republic of Hawaii had been declared, under new laws and sovereignty."

The princess sat down in a straight back chair and folded her hands on her lap. She continued, "If our people had been allowed to vote, I don't believe any of them would have wanted annexation. My own objections were met with scorn, derision, as if the color of my skin denied me intelligence or the right to speak."

Fascinated by the princess' story, Inocencia felt chills along her spine. During the entire reception, she watched the princess moving among the guests with great poise. Ka'iulani spoke quietly to one person, then another, until suddenly she stood before Inocencia. Stunned by the princess' attention, Inocencia did not understand her questions, at first.

"I said, Mrs. Figueroa, that I'm curious about your clubs. You've headed several, I'm told."

Once Inocencia got over her nervousness, she told the princess her story. She chatted incessantly and laughed at the right places, as if she'd known Ka'iulani all her life. She looked directly into the princess' eyes, not feeling the need to treat her any differently than she'd treat Lola.

"And that's why I think liberation comes in many guises," said Inocencia. "There's racial and class liberation, of course, but also the liberation of women to do something meaningful with their lives, to leave a legacy.

"Princess Ka'iulani," she continued, "the groups I've been fortunate to create . . . because, mind you, I'm not alone in this work . . . " Inocencia glanced over at Doña Lola, indicating with a sweep of her arm that Lola was the true champion of activism. "So many women give of their time and energy to make our groups a success. *Our* clubs were formed to raise money, help the widows, the children, the elderly, all of whom have suffered because of war."

"Mrs. Figueroa. In my kingdom, I will be an ordinary person, but not so ordinary that I can't do some things I want to do. If I decide to create perhaps a group like the American Red Cross for my people, or groups to advocate for our needs, I think I will succeed."

"You know, we women are not always in control of our own lives. So it makes it very difficult for us to do the work we do. But when we are committed to an ideal, *then*, Princess, we can move mountains!"

"Thank you for telling me your story." With that, the princess turned to others in conversation.

Inocencia's cheeks were tingling as if they were on fire. She was breathless and elated at the same time. She pretended an interest in the surrounding conversations about the Philippines, monarchies and colonies, but she was thinking all the while, *Imagine, me giving advice to a princess!*

When she had gathered her wits to look again at the princess, she found Ka'iulani smiling in her direction.

*Princess Ka'iulani! I hope you'll be able to leave the past behind and have a happy life. You deserve it.*

With that thought, Inocencia lifted her chin and smiled right back at her.

# 7

# BROOKLYN, 1898

On the evening of February 15, 1898, the Secretary of the Navy in Washington, D.C. had barely entered the comfort of a restful night's sleep when he was awakened by loud pounding on the door. How long the knocking had been in progress, he couldn't say as he'd incorporated the mayhem into his dreams. He shook his groggy head and pulled on the dark blue robe that lay at the foot of the bed. Barefooted, the secretary opened the door. To his surprise, the military guard on duty handed him a telegram.

"Call the White House! Wake the president without delay," the secretary shouted to the guard as he began to make sense of the alarming content of the telegram. No sooner had President McKinley pressed the receiver to his ear, when the secretary blurted out:

"MAINE BLOWN UP IN HAVANA HARBOR AT NINE-FORTY TONIGHT.
MANY WOUNDED AND DOUBTLESS MORE KILLED OR DROWNED."

The battleship USS *Maine* had been constructed at the Brooklyn Navy Yard, the pride of Irish, German and Italian immigrant laborers. The news of her destruction spread throughout the poverty-ridden neighborhoods of Williamsburg, Clinton Hill, Fort Greene and Vinegar Hill, devastating the worker families in their grimy tenements. They felt the loss of the two hundred and sixty-six casualties, twenty-two African American firemen and coal passers among them, as painfully as if they were grieving for kin, struck down in the prime of their lives.

In the Wallabout district, a seafaring family said a prayer at their dinner table for old John Bell, a cabin steward who flaunted his impressive sideburns and pointed goatee. Stooped and white-haired, the genial seaman had survived the Civil War, but not the USS *Maine*.

In Weeksville, the preacher at the Missionary Church eulogized William Lambert, the black fireman who was the star pitcher for the Maine's baseball team. Parishioners hung a black wreath on their door in his honor and to remember the entire team. All but one had died in the explosion.

The ironclad USS *Maine* had seemed invulnerable. The first of the fleet to enter the port of Havana since 1895 when the war began, the ship's mission was to protect American interests, not to destroy Havana's buildings or shatter its windows or lay to rest more than half of its American crew in the ocean's briny grave.

"No Spaniard would be guilty of such a heinous act," declared the Spanish Ambassador, Enrique Dupuy de Lôme to the U.S. press as he ushered his family into the safety of an upscale hotel.

"Spanish cruisers have been actively assisting in the rescue efforts," Dupuy de Lôme yelled, slamming the door behind him.

Outrage seared the hearts of the nation, and the people took up the cry, "Remember the Maine, to Hell with Spain."

# 8

## NEW YORK, 1898

"*¡Demonio!*" Bonocio Tió mumbled under his breath as he peeked through the cab's window. "I can barely make out the walls of the pyramid in this rain."

Wiping the mist off the glass, he looked again for the thick, gray walls of the Egyptian Pyramid, the name he jokingly gave to the Croton Reservoir on Fifth Avenue. Just before he located Dr. Henna's brownstone across from the aqueduct, a fleeting image of Lola, smiling and strolling with him along reservoir's promenades, came to mind.

At No. 8 West 40th Street, he made a fierce sprint for the stairs through gale winds and a heavy downpour, the worst the city had seen that winter. When Dr. Henna heard the bell, he rushed past Mrs. Riley to open the door. Bonocio Tió was the first to arrive.

"Ah, Don Bonocio, thank you for coming," he said, holding the door firmly against the wind. "Come on in, come in out of the storm, old friend."

"Oh, don't close the door yet, Henna. I think I saw Roberto Todd getting out of the cab behind mine."

Droplets of rain glistened on Bonocio's snowy beard. He stomped his feet on the floor mat, then removed his hat and overcoat. On his heels, Roberto Todd made an entrance, and both men handed wet, heavy outerwear to Mrs. Riley, who struggled to hang the coats in the hall closet.

Bonocio looked around for other compatriots. Before long, Manuel and Alejandro Besosa stomped into the foyer, followed by the Steinacher brothers, Gonzalo O'Neill and Sotero Figueroa. All of them were drenched through and through. Some twenty members of the Puerto Rico Section soon filled the room.

The mood was ominous; somber as the low lying clouds that were flooding the streets outside. A sense of foreboding hung heavy, torn as the patriots were between the promise of imminent war and fear of a U.S. invasion. They dreaded being left out in the cold, ignored in matters to which they had devoted so much of their lives and for which many had lived in bitter exile.

"¡Ay, compañeros! Worrying about an American invasion in Puerto Rico won't get us anywhere. We need to plan our next move," warned Sotero, running his hand through his damp hair.

"Oye, Sotero. You heard that speech by that Roosevelt fellow with the high, whiny voice? 'What this country needs,'" Don Bonocio mimicked, "'is a splendid little war to end the panic of 1893.'"

"If the United States declares war over this incident, Don Bonocio," retorted Sotero, "Puerto Rico's struggle for independence may be an unintended casualty."

"Something to be considered, Don Sotero," said Bonocio.

Manuel Besosa rubbed calloused hands together, encouraging circulation back into his frozen fingers. "Paisanos," he exclaimed, "we've just about secured our autonomy from Spain. If the Americans invade, they have to negotiate with our new autonomous government. Right?"

"You may be right, *compañero*," Sotero bristled, "but half a loaf of bread doesn't end starvation. Even with autonomy, Puerto Rico remains tied to Spain."

Before anyone else could voice an opinion, Dr. Henna called the meeting to order. There was no denying that the explosion of the battleship Maine in Havana Harbor and impending American war with Spain weighed heavily on his mind. His usual ruddy face was ashen.

"In brief, my friends, the Section's mission has encountered an unexpected obstruction."

*It sounds as if he is informing the family that the patient is terminal,* thought Sotero.

"I'm sure I speak for us all when I say we're aghast at the explosion of the USS *Maine*. In my mind, there's little doubt the United States will retaliate."

"Henna, we've all read the fever pitch articles the newspapers are using to incite the nation to war. I think retaliation will be inevitable." Bonocio looked around to see how many patriots agreed with his observation.

"Ahem, well, to continue. If Puerto Rico is invaded while still a Spanish possession, it could become a prize of war, booty for the United States. If the autonomy charter for self-rule is recognized by the Americans, then the autonomist government should be the Island's legal representative, in which case Puerto Rico *may* be viewed as free and independent. Notice, I emphasize the may. The situation is so volatile, anything could happen."

"What then becomes our role?" wondered Sotero aloud. "The Section's mission *is* to free Puerto Rico. In both cases, that could be accomplished, but not through our efforts, and probably not in the direction we'd like."

A succession of uhs, ohs and ahems filled the room. Feet shuffled. Gasps, whispers and rigid shoulders prevailed as heads turned this way and that. Members crossed or

uncrossed their legs, and Henna began to absorb his compatriots' overwhelming discomfort. After so many years of sacrificing their lives to the cause of independence, the prize
hung in the balance and could be yanked away from their
grasp in a second.

"Ahem, gentlemen, *por favor* . . . I now call upon Roberto
Todd. His knowledge of the law will serve us well in what I
have to propose. "Don Roberto, would you like to do the
honors?"

At thirty-six years of age, Roberto Todd had shouldered
the mission and administrative duties of the Puerto Rico Section right alongside Henna. In the bargain, the two had
struck a warm friendship, with Don Roberto becoming to
Henna like the son he'd never had. Now, Todd stood before
the members, sleek black hair and neatly trimmed mustache,
ready to take the battle to the next level.

"Don Sotero, you always argue for 'the distinct personality
that is Puerto Rico,' a separate identity from that of Spain.
Well, with that thought in mind, Dr. Henna and I are going to
Washington, D.C. Our plan? Simple enough. We're going to
teach those Americans some lessons about Puerto Rico . . .
make them understand we, Puerto Ricans, have been fighting for liberation. Just like the Cubans. We're going to get
President McKinley and Secretary Roosevelt to agree that if
they invade the Island, they must allow the people to vote on
the kind of government they want. And here's where we
come in. We'll demand that a committee of the Puerto Rico
Section be in attendance as observers and aid the transfer-
ence of power."

Dr. Henna gestured towards an array of detailed maps,
photographs, tables, charts and reports on the console and
invited the gentlemen to explore the documents he and Don
Roberto had collected for the task.

*God help us all,* Henna sighed, suddenly locking tired eyes with Sotero Figueroa. For a split second, the adversaries stared at one another, not in anger, but in a spirit of reconciliation. They realized that each had earned the respect of the other. With words unspoken, they seemed to say, *Well, old friend, this is where we part company. The future, whatever it will be, is no longer in our hands.*

"Please, don't hesitate to add materials or suggest any ideas you may have for a fruitful encounter with the U.S. officials."

On the 25th day of July, the members of the Puerto Rico Section learned that General Nelson Miles had landed U.S. troops in Puerto Rico. No one from the Puerto Rico Section was onboard the general's ship to either observe or advise.

# 9

## NEW YORK, 1898

"The truth? You want to know how I feel?" Inocencia's face fell into deepest anguish. She stopped in her tracks to compose herself, then faced Doña Lola. "Empty. I feel empty. I've a huge hollow space right here." Letting go of her son's arm, she made a circle with her hand around her midsection.

"And angry . . . and . . . sad, Lola. I'm so sad I could cry and cry and never stop. How can anyone feel anything else?"

"*Ay, m'ija.* I'm sorry. I sympathize, but the decision wasn't ours to make. I don't think they had a choice, once the Americans invaded."

As if to mock Inocencia's sentiments, it was a brilliant August day with not a single cloud in the sky. She held up a yellow, ruffled parasol over her head with one arm, while with the other she latched onto Mario. She was not about to lose the rambunctious five-year-old in Central Park. Lola's green umbrella matched the fabric of her checkered day dress. It dangled by its handle from her elbow. Suitable for strolling the perimeter of the park's sheep meadow on a summer day, in recent weeks she had taken to using it like a cane when she walked long distances.

"I can't imagine what they must have gone through," Inocencia sniffed, " . . . how they must have felt, Henna and the rest, facing the unbearable truth in Chimney Corner Hall. To think, our flag was *born* there. They'd seen so many

217

victories in that place . . . so many promises." Her eyes were swimming with tears, but she managed to keep them from spilling down her cheeks.

"All thirty-eight patriots voted to dissolve the Section."

"I know. When Sotero came home that afternoon, he walked in looking like a tired, old man. I actually thought he'd had an accident."

As the women drew near the meadow, Mario suddenly pulled himself away from his mother's grip and ran towards a flock of gray and white sheep. Their curly fleece was just beginning to come in, but Lola held a handkerchief to her nose anyway so as not to smell their gamy, wet wool.

"Mamá, look! Big ones and little ones! Come see," Mario shouted as he ran across the road after the animals.

"Wait for me, Mario. Be careful. Don't pet the sheep . . . "

"Look! Teeny weeny ones," he yelled, squealing with laughter as one frisky lamb tried to nibble at his sleeve.

"You're going to get bitten, Mario!"

"He's a boy, Inocencia." Lola studied her friend in pretend exasperation. "Let him be. Boys are supposed to get into trouble."

"So, you're saying I should blame you if he gets bitten?"

"Blame me, but *let* the child have some fun!"

Just as the two friends approached the sheep, the shepherd crouched down beside Mario and guided the child's hand, instructing him on petting the lambs.

Mario thus occupied, the friends continued strolling along at a leisurely pace for a while before Inocencia turned a quizzical gaze towards Lola.

"What about us?" she asked. "What happens to us, to our *compañeras* who've given so much to the clubs? It's like, from one day to the next, our lives have been snatched away from us. Like it was all a dream."

Lola couldn't bring herself to respond. With one hand on her makeshift cane, she kept her eyes fixed on the path before her, lost in her own thoughts. She thought about her thirty years of struggle, countless letters she'd written every day, the fundraisers, piano concerts, poetry readings, meetings. . . . She remembered the feeling of exile. Her entire life *was* the movement. *How do you suddenly let go of something that's dominated every waking hour of your entire life?*

"*Ay,* I don't know, Inocencia. I suppose we should call the last meeting of all our clubs and dissolve them, like the men did with the Puerto Rico Section."

"That's one set of minutes I'll regret pasting into the Mercedes Varona scrapbook," Inocencia lamented. She bent down and pulled up two daisies from a vast expanse of wild flowers. She held one up to her nose and handed the other to Lola.

"*¡Ay, madre!* Inocencia, listen. The scrapbook is *very* important. Put it away with any notes you have about the clubs. Include newspaper clippings, photos, even letters if you have them."

"What good will that do? Nobody wants that old stuff." She began peeling the petals off the daisy one by one as if she were shredding pages into a dustbin.

"It's for Mario, my dear. And for my Laura's children, and all of our children. It's for them to see what we believed in and how we honored our commitments. That's what Dr. Henna vowed to do with the minutes and letters of the Puerto Rico Section. He has bundled everything in lock boxes. He'll keep them in his home until they can be published."

"You mean, take these papers with us if we have to leave?"

"*¡Seguro que sí, mujer!* This is our legacy. Put everything in that box where you keep Martí's cup and saucer."

"Hah," Inocencia laughed, "I should never have told you about that box."

"But you did. And now I ask you, do you think you'll ever return to Puerto Rico?"

They'd been so committed to the idea of liberation that they hadn't had time to think about anything else. What would a future without liberation look like? Was it even something the friends could envision?

"Oh, Lola, you know I don't like New York, but Mario was born here. He says some words in English now and again . . . my girls are buried here! I have to confess, though," Inocencia continued, "I like the freedom I have here. It's different from Ponce. You know, I like the sense that I can do or be anything I want to be here. I can even form political clubs, if I want to."

A wistful smile crossed her lips. Memories of the day she founded the Club Mercedes Varona flitted into her mind. *How frightened I was that I'd fail.*

"And what should I do with the money we raised for Club Hermanas de Rius Rivera? It's quite a bit, you know."

"How much did we raise?"

"About $200.00! I'm so proud of what our club accomplished, I wish I could shout it out for everyone to hear."

"*¡Qué bien!* Well, I suppose that money goes to Dr. Henna. Didn't Sotero tell you? When the Section resolved to create a League of Puerto Rican Patriots, they decided all monies left over should go to fund it.

"You know, the Patriots want to pressure Congress into letting the Puerto Rican people vote on their own status, and also to educate our people about their rights under American law."

"That's a ray of hope, Lola. The club women should be pleased to hear about that."

"Let's start heading back."

Lola and Inocencia called to Mario and soon each one was holding one of the boy's hands as they strolled away.

# 10

## NEW YORK, 1898

"Lola!" Bonocio said, sounding alarmed. "I just received a telegram from our contacts in San Juan: Listen to this. General Brooke has seized Guayama. He is advancing into Cayey."

"Oh, my goodness! So, the eastern coast is in American hands already?"

"And with troops along the western coast, they'll soon take the entire Island."

"At last! We're free of Spain," declared Lola, "but now our work is cut out for us. Somehow we have to free the Island from an American military occupation as soon as can be. We need our absolute freedom to build the country."

"It's not so simple, Lola. I'm afraid you're much too trusting. Do you seriously think, as General Miles says, that the purpose of the invasion is to bring Puerto Rico a 'banner of freedom'? Of course, not! Already there is talk of naval bases, of building canals across Panama to move cargo from the Atlantic to the Pacific and even of building an American empire.

"We just got rid of the Spanish empire, now an American one?!

"Ay, Bonocio, our compatriots need to move fast, do everything we can to avoid a forced annexation to the United States! As long as a treaty hasn't been signed, as long as Puerto

221

Ricans want full independence, we need to work toward that goal."

"It worries me to know this, Lola, but I have it on good authority, from Roberto Todd. The first thing Mr. *Rough Rider* Roosevelt asked Todd and Henna when they met was if there was a harbor deep enough in Puerto Rico to command naval operations in the region."

"That doesn't prove *anything*, Bonocio . . . except that large battleships can dock in San Juan harbor."

"There's more. A week or so later, Don Roberto and Mr. Roosevelt spoke in private. It is hard to believe, but Undersecretary Roosevelt said the U.S. government didn't have information on Puerto Rico, not a single bit, until some of our people made an appointment to see him. Evidently, these so-called representatives of our people handed them the keys to the kingdom, in minute detail. Everything Washington D.C. needed to seize our homeland was laid at their feet."

Lola was dumbfounded. She felt as if the ground had shifted under her. "That wasn't supposed to happen," she said. "I still have hope . . . Remember, Bonocio, we're dealing with a powerful, democratic nation that understands and defends the sanctity of liberty and self-rule. Didn't the United States fight a revolution for its own independence from the British?"

Bonocio responded softly, "I'm afraid Puerto Rico, as the key to the Caribbean, is too good a prize to give up!"

Hearing the logic in her husband's dire conclusions, Lola closed her eyes in resignation.

"*Ay,* Bonocio, my love," Lola rasped, as if her words were coming from the depths of her soul, "If there is to be a military government, or annexation to the United States, we *cannot* return to Puerto Rico."

# 11

## NEW YORK, 1899

At the point in the dream when everyone she'd ever loved had abandoned her, Inocencia screamed. She screamed and screamed until her throat burned raw. No one cared enough to help her. An unforgiving icy blast assaulted her bare legs. She began to shiver, until suddenly, her eyes flew open. Entangled in layers of sheets, her heart pounded furiously in her chest. Overwhelming despair filled her inner emptiness, and she bolted from the bed and ran down the stairs two steps at a time, like a wild woman, to find her son.

The kitchen was invitingly warm. The aroma of fried dough and freshly baked breads was everywhere. Each burner on the wood-burning stove was in use. At the enamel top table, Mario and Titi Doly kneaded dough. The shelf space in the cold pantry's closet held dishes and platters of prepared food, and the sink was filled to capacity. Pine shelves along a kitchen wall held the clean dishes and cups. These would be used to serve the guests that evening.

Kirina opened the cast iron door of the oven using two thick pot holders to check its contents. The smell of roasted chicken permeated the cozy room.

From the kitchen door, Inocencia spied the black coffee pot on the top of the stove and hoped its contents might still be drinkable.

"Well, sleepyhead, you finally decided to join us," said Kirina, smiling at her sister. The sisters had arrived early that morning to help Anita prepare.

"I can't imagine what happened to me. I never sleep past daybreak, especially with all the things we have to do before evening."

Wrapped in a woolen shawl she'd managed to grab in the final moment of her flight down the stairs, Inocencia drained the last drop of coffee from her cup. She placed the cup on the pile of china in the sink and sidled over to Mario, who sat on a tall stool at the table. Leaning over the child, she hugged him tightly with both arms, aching to feel the warmth of his small body against her own. Before he could object, she planted a long hard kiss on his curly head. He wiggled out of her embrace, but not before Inocencia inhaled the sweet scent of raisins and honey in her boy's hair.

"I know. You're five, too big for kisses," she said, rumpling his hair.

"Look, Mamá, I'm helping Titi Doly make the *empanadillas*. See? I put meat in the *masa*, and see? All done." He clapped specks of flour into the air while Doly added his offering to the iron frying pan.

"You look awful," Kirina scolded, putting her arm around her sister's shoulder. "I think you're not fully awake. Everything is under control here, so why don't you go upstairs and freshen up? Sotero offered to pick up some of the special foods we ordered from the Bodega Española."

"Oh, did I tell you Doña Gertrudis sent a note? The club women are preparing all sorts of delicious dishes."

Inocencia tried to show Kirina her appreciation, but her face crumbled into tears. "Oh, I'm so sorry. Ay, Kirina. I've had the most frightful nightmare. It felt like my whole world was vanishing right in front of my eyes! I can't remember exactly . . . but there was this sense of dread, and I was left all alone . . . I can't explain it," she said catching hold of her sister's hand.

"There now. I'll go upstairs with you if you wish." Wondering what was really going on with Inocencia, Kirina could do nothing else but stay by her side.

It was not an everyday matter for the Figueroas to be hosting a formal evening in their very informal home, but nothing had been the same since the war ended.

That evening, as Inocencia adjusted Sotero's white bow tie, she said, "There! You look splendid in your evening finery. I'd even say statesmanlike with those maturing silver speckles running through your mustache. Now you need some more grey hairs on your head."

"Inocencia, the guests are beginning to arrive. One of us has to be at the door to greet them."

Sotero's exasperated tone of voice brought up the dreadful dream. *That wedge between us, so strong. Were we ever meant to be together? But if we are not together, will I lose my son? A father has legal rights over the family, everyone knows that!*

Obsessing on her fears, Inocencia struggled to work a tortoise shell comb into the French twist Doly had arranged for her. She dabbed pomade along her center part and added a touch of pink rouge to her lips. When she stepped over to the mirror, she was satisfied with her image, pleased to see the green silk dress she wore hid the slumps of aging. The skirt fell to the tips of her shoes, like an inverted champagne glass. Pursing her lips, Inocencia noticed the gowns' low cut neckline. *Oh, no. This is much too revealing.* She lifted the fabric higher over her bosom, then decided to let it fall as it was. She was a woman now, more confident in herself than she'd ever been.

As she unfurled the black ostrich plumed fan she'd inherited from Doña Emilia, she turned towards her husband. "Sotero, look at us. We do make a handsome couple, don't you think?"

He paused in the final stages of dressing to observe his wife, curious that she should ask such a thing. *She looks sad, so serious,* he thought. Thin creases he'd never noticed before ran along the sides of her mouth. *Ten years! We've been together ten years. It seems a lifetime.*

"Yes, my dear. We certainly do."

The party was in honor of Don Eugenio María de Hostos, but the evening soon became more than that. The finality of the Paris Treaty between the United States and Spain could not be erased from people's minds with festivities and fine clothing. Barely dry on the official parchment, the words that liberated Cuba, gave Puerto Rico to the United States as a prize of war. Dark clouds hovered over the start of 1899.

Standing at the door, Inocencia became a charming hostess, embracing her friends with an overabundance of enthusiasm.

"I'm so glad you're early," she whispered to Lola, handing Anita the cloaks and shawls. "Maybe we'll have a chance to talk, just the two of us?"

"Of course, my dear." Lola registered the anxiety in Inocencia's eyes. "Can it wait a bit? I was told Don Eugenio was looking for me."

Heads bowed in conversation, Bonocio and Don Eugenio awaited Lola in the parlor. When she joined them, Eugenio did not say a word. He merely handed Lola a copy of the treaty so that she could read it for herself. "The verdict is in," he said softly, and left the despondent couple to commiserate in private.

Throughout Sotero and Inocencia's formal rooms, the guests recalled parties from their youth; others lamented the lost opportunity for independence. They drank wine and champagne and helped themselves to the festive table laden with food. The rustle of ladies' gowns as they flitted from one room to another added a soothing background swish. Emilio Agramonte and Gonzálo Núñez played their guitars. Lola agreed to recite a poem. Even Patria offered to recite one of her own.

Setting aside his serious nature, Estrada Palma held court in the foyer like a conquering hero. He was destined to become Cuba's first president. Glowing in the aftermath of victory, Estrada Palma declared to everyone within hearing distance, "¡Compañeros! Join us in a toast. We have a new nation to build."

Clinking glasses of champagne, Estrada Palma spoke of a constitution to write, representatives to elect and laws to pass. Everyone, it seemed, had a personal stake in Cuba's future.

A very different scenario played itself out in the formal parlor, where in hushed, somber tones Don Eugenio María de Hostos spoke with his old friend, Dr. Henna.

"Tomorrow morning, I'll have a messenger deliver a copy of our League of Patriots document. We'll personally present it to President McKinley in Washington," he said.

"Oh, Don Eugenio!" Hostos turned to face the Cuban Consuelo Serra. "I am so pleased that your League will propose giving the people of Puerto Rico a vote on the form of government they wish to have."

"Thank you, Señorita Consuelo."

"I teach American history, you see, and I completely believe this nation's democratic values will prevail in your homeland."

In stark contrast to the school teacher's sentiments, Sotero was confiding to Don Bonocio, "The treaty doesn't bode well for building a free nation in Puerto Rico. It seems to me, we're back where we started, maybe in a greater struggle than before . . . and I'm no longer a young man." Raising one dark eyebrow to make his point, Sotero offered a cock-eyed smile, hoping someone might refute his comment about age.

"But, I assure you," he continued, "my blood still boils in anger. I'll never surrender my commitment to independence! Never!"

"I'm on your side, Don Sotero," Lola agreed.

"*Hombre*, I'm also on your side," added Bonocio, "but I'm old and tired. It's been a long haul, taken a toll on all of us. Lola and I have decided . . . we're going back to Cuba, not because we're surrendering. We can add our convictions to the making of a *Cuba libre*, a free Cuba. That may help our poor Puerto Rico . . . at least until the situation changes. And our daughter Patria needs to resume her life, return to teach at the university."

"Don Bonocio. The truth is until tonight, I wasn't sure what I was going to do. You, Estrada Palma, and the others, well, it seems to me there's work I can do in Cuba, as well," offered Sotero. "I can bring Martí's vision to fruition. 'To gain the independence of Cuba and promote that of Puerto Rico.' Remember? That was our pledge," added Sotero. "Half of that pledge is a reality. The second half awaits our commitment. Cuba is probably the best place for me, as well."

Instantly, Inocencia rose from her chair, casting a worried look at Lola. It was the first mention of going to Cuba she'd heard. She made her way to the women of Club Mercedes

Varona in the adjoining room. Lola followed quickly in Inocencia's wake. Grabbing hold of her arm, she pulled Inocencia into the kitchen.

"Stop! Tell me what's wrong?" Lola held onto her friend's arm as if to anchor her in place.

"Lola! He's going to Cuba! What about me? And Mario? Are we going to Cuba, too? Did Sotero mean us as well?"

"Hush! Have you talked to your husband? Think! It seems I'm always asking you to think! Your family is better off together! Talk to him. Now, just take a deep breath, and let's return to the guests."

"But Lola. What if I . . . What if I've made a life here?"

For a long, compassionate moment, Lola remembered the girl who'd defied her father. Remembered the day she'd sat in her garden so sure of herself; so certain of her lofty ambitions. *I have a lot of work to do, don't I, Doña Lola,* she'd said.

"Will you be able to support yourself and your child on your own? Think, Inocencia! You don't know what opportunities there might be for you in Cuba."

They held onto each other's hands for what seemed like forever, until finally, Inocencia lowered her eyes and nodded.

As the midnight hour approached, family members began to group together to be near one another at the stroke of the New Year. It was a sobering moment—the time to remember all that had transpired and mourn those who no longer were present. To embrace, lament, ask forgiveness, to hold onto one another as they entered the New Year.

Sotero found Inocencia. Taking hold of her hand, he rushed her into the kitchen and out to the back porch.

"Before the madness begins, I need to share my decision with you."

Inocencia took a deep breath. She focused intensely on the words coming out of Sotero's mouth. Her stomach was quivering. The cold air caused goosebumps to rise on her bare arms and neck. Still, she stared at Sotero, straining to catch his words, not wanting to misunderstand his intentions.

When she searched his facial features for what he was saying, and not saying, she recognized the old, familiar expressions, the passion for justice, for righteousness and readiness for battle. They burned like embers in Sotero's dark eyes.

"I've given thought to this . . . to thinking about our life together. I'm convinced the wisest thing to do is to ship the printing press to Cuba. You do understand . . . revolutionaries like us are needed there now, more than ever . . . to make sure Martí's vision becomes reality!"

"Ay, Sotero! But, what about me?"

"Inocencia! I can't believe you would ask such a question. You're my wife. I'm not about to leave you and our child behind. If I'm to fight again for Martí's revolution, I want you beside me . . . you and your clubs!"

She flung her arms around her husband's neck, burying her face in his shoulder, and began to weep. She mourned the loss of innocence. She wept for their infant daughters, for the defeat of their homeland, for their misunderstandings. She wept because she and Sotero might have a second chance to build a dream together.

In the distance, church bells pealed a welcome to the New Year.

※ ※ ※

Lola was startled. She hadn't expected to hear church bells.

"Ay, Bonocio listen, the bells toll for the death of our struggle," she whimpered, gripping his hand in hers.

He didn't have to put his feelings into words. The grief on Lola's clouded face said it all. *They toll for Lares,* she thought, *for Betances and Martí, for my islita azul, for our dream of liberation.*

The year 1899 was less than a minute old, when Gonzálo Núñez began to strum familiar notes on his guitar. Gently removing interlaced fingers from Bonocio's, Lola rose from her seat and stood near the fireplace. The gaslight from the overhead chandelier cast a warm glow on her graying head.

She raised her chin defiantly, then closed her eyes and, in a soft plaintive, voice began to sing,

| | |
|---|---|
| *¡Despierta Borinqueño,* | Awaken Borinqueño, |
| *que han dado la señal:* | they've given the signal: |
| *¡Despierta de ese sueño* | Awaken from that dream |
| *que es hora de luchar!* | it is time to fight! |

# Afterword
## HAVANA 1923

Inocencia Martínez had fallen in love with the used 1917 Model T. The alarming signs of wear and tear that scared off more experienced buyers only managed to endear the old vehicle to its new owner.

She lightly caressed the headlight on the right side and discovered it was off center. Some areas on the front and back fenders were scoffed, and she tried to imagine the original glossy black that had once covered them. Opening the car door, she climbed up into the driver's seat. Leather seat cushions that had been the height of fashion bore signs of spilled liquids, cigar burns and overall neglect. And when Inocencia attempted to turn the crank on the rusted crank shaft, she was convinced she had broken her arm.

Within the first half hour of ownership, Inocencia had grabbed an oil-stained cloth wedged under the driver's seat and begun to polish the fenders. Now and then she'd spit into the cloth, applying such vigor that the flabby flesh on her upper arms flapped with each scrubbing. She attacked the doors, tires, glass and trunk next, thinking all the while of the places she would visit.

For one day, she would forget about running the boarding house. *If anyone has a problem or complaint, it'll wait.* She searched for a handkerchief in her bag to wipe her dirty hands and saw the invitations she was supposed to mail for Cuba's National Congress of Women. They lay in a neat bundle in the oversized satchel. Pushing them aside, Inocencia sighed in exasperation. She hadn't wanted any obligations today. But as her grimy fingertips rustled in the bag, she felt an envelope. It was a petition requesting of the government a veteran's pension because she'd served the Cuban Revolutionary Party.

"Shoot," she whispered annoyed. *Well, all of that can wait. Today is my day to enjoy any way I wish!* Shoving her bag onto the passenger seat, Inocencia climbed behind the wheel of her new car.

*Mario'll be so proud,* she thought, *to see his mamá driving her own car! I should drive to his office. Surprise him!* She moved her hands around the steering wheel, pretending to drive in the city's commercial district. *Wait! That's a crazy idea. The tires could get stuck in a rut between the cobblestones, or I might hit a milkman riding on a donkey. Oh, that would never do.*

She grinned at the absurd image and positioned the timing and throttle levers. She then released the hand brake. Quickly, she huffed her way down to turn the crankshaft on the front of the car.

"Now, my chickadee," she chirped lovingly to the car, "you must start without giving mamá any trouble."

At first, nothing happened. Inocencia's ruby red lips pressed together. Her eyes hardened into slits of speckled green. She glared at the car, daring it to disobey. With a second, vigorous half crank, she heard the engine sputter. Climbing quickly on board, she released a small amount of gas from a third lever on the steering wheel. The car sputtered again. Suddenly, it lurched forward, the tires squealing eerily into a roll. Drenched in perspiration, Inocencia let out a sigh of relief and began an adventure destined to go wherever the road might lead.

She chugged along a paved avenue doused by waves from the intrepid sea that refused restraint behind the ocean wall. The road was El Malecón. It stretched for miles, but Inocencia knew that once away from the city's traffic, the road became less traveled. Ocean breezes ruffled her short, russet curls. A feisty wind nuzzled her face with a misty coolness, and she licked the salted moisture on her upper lip. Reaching for the gas lever, she gave it a short squeeze and felt she could drive forever.

Inocencia followed the coast lined with royal palms until she came to a main road of massive residences. It was La Línea. Weaving in and out of unfamiliar side roads, she cruised along streets of imposing Italian renaissance mansions. She gazed at the tinted glass windows of majestic homes on manicured lawns.

She'd reached the famous neighborhood of El Vedado. Cruising along, Inocencia gawked brazenly at the worldly possessions of the super wealthy, passing by one mansion after another, and thinking she'd catch a glimpse of real flesh and blood rich people. Suddenly . . . could it be? She gripped the wheel, a strain of long forgotten memories clouding her face.

It was Lola!

The old woman wore a large straw hat to ward off the sun, but Inocencia could tell it was her. She knew *everything* about Lola: her walk, her stance, the way she tilted her head when she spoke, her hand gestures. She wore a light brown smock over her dress, and Inocencia recognized the familiar wire-rimmed glasses. She walked with a cane. Using it like an extension of her arm, she pointed to something on the ground. Inocencia could not tell what it was. The woman spoke spiritedly to a younger woman and a man accompanying her. Instantly, the memory of her voice replayed itself in

Inocencia's mind, although she couldn't hear a word the old woman was saying over the noise of the car's engine.

Her heart was pounding wildly in her chest. Still, Inocencia could not break her stare from the group in the garden. The family never even noticed her, or the Model T chugging gracelessly along Calle Cuatro. Left unnoticed, Inocencia sensed a wrenching loss, a pang of rejection, as if the years she and Lola had been friends, had devoted to the cause, never happened. *Ay, Lola! How did we allow the time to slip away from us?* Instantly, Inocencia decided what she was going to do.

The house in El Vedado was in total disarray. Boxes, crates, suitcases and bags overflowing with umbrellas, hats and shawls were strewn throughout the front rooms. Workmen came and went, leaving dirty footprints in their wake as they carried boxes to a waiting pickup truck. The furniture in the formal rooms was covered in white sheets and the Venetian chandelier in the dining room was trussed up in voluminous silk wrapping.

"Mamá! Where are you," called Patria from the foyer. The attractive woman was stylishly dressed in a white traveling suit, thin shoe straps across her instep. She placed a cloche hat with a wide yellow band on a sheet-covered table and pulled on a pair of calfskin gloves.

"*Aquí,* Patria. *Estoy aquí.*" Lola sat in the armchair by the dining room window, the cane within arm's reach against the wall. Her tired weathered face signaled she no longer had the energy for such upheavals.

"It's hard for me, Patria, all this packing and moving. I can't find any of my books; my desk is in storage and my papers are scattered. Why did your husband have to renovate the house at this time?"

"Mamá, we told you months ago. The workmen are scheduled to remodel now. And besides, think of what a wonderful time we'll have visiting Laura and the children in Mayagüez, visiting New York. . . . You did agree to give a recital there, remember? And then we'll visit all those wonderful places you and Papá loved so much in Europe."

"But, my darling daughter, your papá will not be with us." She touched the cameo locket she wore around her neck that held a cut of Bonocio's hair.

"No, but he'll always be with us in spirit. Mamá, please. We are running very late. The ship will not wait for us, so please hurry!"

As Patria left the room, a carpenter appeared holding an envelope in his hand.

"Señora, this letter just arrived. The postman handed it to Lola. What shall I do with it?"

"Oh! Well, give it to me. It might be important."

Lola ripped open the envelope, pushed up her glasses to the bridge of her nose and read:

*My dearest Lola,*

*Yesterday, I saw you in the garden of your home in El Vedado. You were with Patria and a young man I assume is your son-in-law. I longed to talk to you, but I didn't want to interrupt. I was driving by in my new used car. When I got my driver's license two years ago, I thought of you. You would have laughed to see there was no title designation for women on the license! Only men. So I am Sr. Inocencia Martínez! So few women drive, let alone own cars, that the bureau hasn't gotten around to adding Sra. yet. But I got even. I gave my age as thirty-nine and no one dared to question me, una vieja of fifty-five years!*

*Mario graduated from university. You'd be proud to know he took degrees in Civil Engineering and Architecture. My boarding house barely provided for us both, but Sotero helped some before we divorced.*

*It has been so long since our revolutionary days in New York. I regret our paths never crossed again. I hope I've lived up to the expectations you had of me. I know you are very busy, but if you would like to attend the First National Congress of Women, in Havana this April, I'll be representing Havana's Women's Club. I'm going to speak on abolishing the double standard and giving women the vote. The honest truth is I would love to see you.*

*From one who never forgot your kindness,*
*Inocencia Martínez*

Blue-veined hands flew up to Lola's face, and her eyelids crunched tightly together. She rose unsteadily from the armchair. The letter fluttered to the floor. Groping for her cane, she began to hobble towards the door.

"Fernando! Patria!" Lola yelled as loud as she could over the noise of the workmen. From the entrance, she saw her daughter and son-in-law getting into the car.

"Wait!" We can't leave yet. We must stop in Havana Centro! *We must!* There is someone I *must* see."

# TIMELINE OF EVENTS
## 1815–1899

### 1815

Spain grants the *Cédula de Gracias* to reform trade and spur economic growth. It encourages Spanish immigration through land grants and low taxes. In later years, Catholic immigrants from France, Great Britain, Germany, Ireland, Corsica and Italy, who profess loyalty to the crown, receive land grants. The U.S. becomes Puerto Rico and Cuba's dominant trade partner.

### 1821–1849

A series of slave uprisings rock Puerto Rico. Abolitionists are exiled and anti-vagrancy laws passed. *La Libreta,* a passbook system that records the work, debt and family history of landless individuals is passed in 1849. It forces workers to remain in one location and work for the local landowners.

### 1859

The abolitionists and supporters of Puerto Rican independence, Dr. Ramón Emeterio Betances and Dr. José Francisco Basora are exiled for establishing a movement to free the slaves.

## 1865

The Sociedad Republicana de Cuba y Puerto Rico is founded in New York City by expatriates to fight for independence from Spain.

## 1867

Dr. Betances founds the Comité Revolucionario de Puerto Rico in New York City. He issues the Ten Commandments of Free Men and encourages an armed insurrection against Spain.

## 1868

Lola Rodríguez de Tió writes the poem, "La Borinqueña." It is set to music and becomes the revolutionary anthem for the liberation movement.

On September 23rd, El Grito de Lares, Puerto Rico's major revolt against Spain, is violently crushed. El Grito de Yara in Cuba succeeds and launches the Ten Years' War.

## 1869

Emilia Casanova de Villaverde creates La Liga de las Hijas de Cuba in New York City, the first women's club to aid the war effort in Cuba.

## 1873

Slavery is abolished in Puerto Rico, as is the infamous passbook system, *La Libreta.*

## 1880s–1920

Tobacco industries expand in U.S. cities, including New York, Philadelphia, Tampa and Key West. A militant and progressive artisan class of self-educated tobacco workers turn their factories into halls of learning through the practice of hiring readers or *lectores.*

## 1887

A dictatorial period ensues in Puerto Rico under Governor Romualdo Palacio known as the terrible year of *los compontes*. Spanish authorities persecuted, incarcerated and exiled Puerto Rican autonomists and liberationists. Dozens of voluntary exiles migrated to South America or to the expatriate enclaves in the United States.

## 1892

The Cuban revolutionary leader, José Martí, founds the Cuban Revolutionary Party in New York City. A number of clubs, including Los Independientes, Club Borinquen, Las Dos Antillas and the Club Mercedes Varona affiliate with the party and pledge their support to Cuban and Puerto Rican liberation.

## 1892

The official newspaper of the Cuban Revolutionary Party, *Patria,* is established in New York. Sotero Figueroa becomes the newspaper's administrative editor.

## 1895

José Martí dies in military action in the battle of Dos Ríos in Cuba. Tomás Estrada Palma becomes the head of the party.

## 1895

The Puerto Rico Section of the Cuban Revolutionary Party is founded in New York City. Dr. Julio José Henna becomes the head of the section.

## 1897

Spain grants Puerto Rico a Charter of Autonomy initiating the establishment of a Puerto Rico autonomist government in the island. The charter does not grant the island its independence, but paves the way for Puerto Rican representation in the Spanish legislature.

## 1898

The battleship, USS *Maine* explodes in Havana Harbor on February 15. The United States declares war on Spain and the Spanish-Cuban-American War begins.

On December 10, 1898, the Treaty of Paris is signed by Spain and the United States. Spain relinquishes control of Cuba and cedes to the United States the islands of Puerto Rico, Guam and the Philippines.

## 1899

A U.S. military government is instituted in Puerto Rico.

# READING GUIDE

1. Why do Don Antonio and Doña Alejandrina object to their daughter, Inocencia's marriage?

2. Full of enthusiasm, Inocencia leaves Puerto Rico in 1889 to begin a new life in New York City. What are her first impressions of the city? In your estimation, does living in the city prepare her for playing a more or less effective leadership role in the coming revolution than if she had remained in Puerto Rico? Can you cite examples from the book that support your conclusions?

3. Inocencia's New York community of Puerto Ricans, Cubans and other Spanish-speaking expatriates is not necessarily seeking a new or better life, although some do benefit from the "bitter fruits of exile," as one character remarks. The rebels are looking to achieve certain goals that cannot be achieved in their colonized homelands. Why do they seek these goals in the United States and how do these goals reflect the American dream?

4. Early in the story we're introduced to Doña Lola Rodríguez de Tió, an educated woman and a poet. Later we meet other accomplished women, like Doña Emilia and Doña Gertrudis, who also represent a diversity of class and racial experience. In what ways is Inocencia influenced by these women? How does she interact with them and they with her?

5. What are the obstacles facing Inocencia as she begins to organize the Club Mercedes Varona?

6. How does Inocencia cope with the personal tragedies in her life? Can you tell from the story if Inocencia becomes a stronger or a weaker person because of her troubles?

7. Doña Lola is exiled to Cuba for her political activities against the colonial government in Puerto Rico. How does she continue to fight for liberation? Is her life in exile better or worse than Inocencia's?

8. When the battle ship USS *Maine* explodes in Havana Harbor, Americans are outraged. Many demand revenge. We are told of the sorrow among the Brooklyn Navy Yard families, particularly those who knew someone on board the ship. What do you think the reaction was in the expatriate community? How did this horrific event impact the liberation movement?

9. When the Puerto Rico Section of the Cuban Revolutionary is dissolved, Doña Lola and Inocencia must decide what to do with their clubs. In the conversation Inocencia mentions the scrapbook. Lola asks her to save it. Why does Lola want to save the scrapbook? Do you think her reasoning is valid?

10. As the New Year of 1899 begins, the guests at Sotero and Inocencia's party are faced with making life-changing decisions. What decision would you have made? Why?

# GLOSSARY OF TERMS AND PHRASES

Aquí, estoy aquí—Here, I'm here.
Ay, gracias a la virgen—Oh, thanks to the virgin referring to the Virgin Mary.
Ay, los pobres—Oh, the poor.
Buenos días or buenas tardes—good day or good afternoon.
Cálmase—calm yourself or calm down.
Chamaco—a kid, a boy.
Campesino—peasant.
Compañera/o—companion or fellow traveler.
Compatriota—fellow countryman.
Conquistador—conqueror.
Cómo molestas—how much you bother me or what a pest you are.
¿Cómo puede ser?—how can it be?
¡Darse prisa! ¡Se acercan soldados!—Hurry up. The soldiers are nearby!
Demonio—a demon or the devil.
Doña and Don—Madame, or Mrs. and Sir, or Mr.
Doyenne—a woman of high regard. A respected leader.
Duérmete, que viene el cuco—Go to sleep before the bogeyman comes.
Estúpido—stupid.
Gracias—thank you.
Guanábana—a tropical fruit. Soursop.
Guardia Civil—civil militia or policemen.
Guerillistas—guerrilla fighters.

Hacienda and hacendado—a large agricultural estate and the owner of such an estate.

Hombre—man.

Horchata de ajonjolí—a sweet drink made from sesame seeds.

Indios—people of Native American descent.

La Borinqueña—the national anthem of Puerto Rico.

Lorgnette—pair of eye glasses held together on one side by a long handle.

Madre de Dios—Mother of God.

Madre mía—my mother.

Mambises—soldiers of the Cuban Army of Liberation.

M'ija or M'ijita—my daughter or diminutive for my daughter.

Muchachos—the men or the guys.

Mujer—woman.

Niña—female child.

Nenita—little girl.

No se moleste—do not trouble yourself.

No seas tonta/o—don't be silly.

Por favor—please.

Qué bien—how well, or that's good.

Quenepas—a tropical fruit sometimes called a Spanish lime.

Reinitas—warblers.

Seguro que sí, mujer—absolutely, woman.

Señora and señorita—a married woman and an unmarried or young woman.

Sinvergüenza—having no shame.

Soirée—a festive evening party or social gathering.

Una vieja—an old lady.

Velo y corona—a bridal veil and crown.

Yuca and Yautía—Caribbean root vegetable known in English as Cassava and Taro.

# SOURCES

Among sources, I would recommend the following: Josefina Toledo's *Lola Rodríguez de Tió* and *Sotero Figueroa, Editor de Patria*; Harold J. Lidin, *History of the Puerto Rican Independence Movement*; K. Lynn Stoner, *From the House to the Streets: The Cuban Woman's Movement for Legal Reform, 1898–1940*; Félix Ojeda Reyes and Paul Estrade, *Pasión por la Libertad. Centro Journal* Vol. X, Nos. 1 & 2 (1998). *Memorias de los trabajos realizados por la Sección Puerto Rico del Partido Revolucionario Cubano, 1895–1898*; Roberto H. Todd's biographical sketch of Dr. Julio J. Henna; and The Puerto Rican Heritage Poster Series and Study Guide, Center for Puerto Rican Studies, Hunter College of the City University of New York.

# AUTHOR'S BIO

Dr. Virginia Sánchez Korrol is a historian and novelist. She wrote *From Colonia to Community: The History of Puerto Ricans in New York City* and *Feminist and Abolitionist: The Story of Emilia Casanova*. With Vicki L. Ruiz, she co-edited *Latinas in the United States: A Historical Encyclopedia*. Her first children's book is *A Surprise for Teresita/Una sorpresa para Teresita*.